THE MAKING OF A SHAMAN

Norman W. Wilson PhD

THE MAKING OF A SHAMAN

Cover Design by

www.srwalkerdesigns.com

DEDICATION

To all those who would be lovers who have yet to learn
what love is.

ACKNOWLEDGEMENTS

First and foremost a huge thank you to Suzanne, my wife, for her patience, understanding, and support. A thank you to the First Nation People of Canada for teaching me so much, especially Elisapie, and to my book cover designer Stephen R. Walker for capturing the essence of my story.

A special thanks to Stuart Holland of Zadkiel Publishing for giving life to my manuscript.

CHAPTER ONE

Shortly after our arrival at the one-room log cabin that would be our home for the summer, I discovered a small rowboat. I wondered who had left it there. It was just the right size for a seven-year-old, and it seemed to be in good shape, so I decided to use it to explore one of the many islands in the Réservoir Baskatong [1]. I rowed over to what I thought was a snow-capped island. I dragged the boat up onto the sandy beach, secured it, and began my exploration.

For a time, I followed natural trails, and sometimes I had to crawl over an outcropping of rocks as I climbed toward the top. Much to my surprise, it was white rock and not snow. As I slowly worked my way over some jagged rocks, I heard a noise. I stopped. I stood very still and listened. Maybe, I thought, it's a bear or a wolf. I looked around for something to use as a weapon. I picked up a few rocks and piled them at my feet, keeping one in each hand. I figured if I spotted whatever it was first; I could throw the stones at it and frighten it away. I heard a noise again and this time it was a decided groan. It must be someone is hurt, I thought. Then I heard a very clear "Oh, yes, yes."

There was no mistaking that sound—a human voice. I eased my way around the cliff and looked down at a small clearing. I saw them. A young naked man was on top of a young naked woman. From here I figured he had to be at least seventeen years old. Spellbound, I stopped to watch. He was doing pushups with his butt. She had her legs wrapped around his middle and her arms around his neck. I squatted and continued to watch. She frantically kissed him all over his face. She grabbed his long black hair and pulled it. He grunted a couple of times and then lay very still. He turned his head, looked up at me. *I am in big trouble*, I thought.

I am sure I heard him say, "Have no fear. All of this you will understand."

A bright blinding flash filled the small clearing. I blinked. They were gone. I scrambled down the side of the rock to where they had been. No sign of them. I looked around the area. No foot prints. The hair on the back of my neck stood up. I sucked in my breath and scrambled back up the outcropping. I half ran and half stumbled as I slid down the other side.

I breathed a sigh when I came to where I had left my boat. It was still here. I untied it, dragged it to the water's edge, jumped in, and used an oar to shove off. I pulled on the oars as fast as I could to get out of there.

As I neared our log cabin, I began to calm down. Not one word would I mention about what I saw. I'd be grounded for sure if I did. I pulled the boat up onto the bank, tied it to a stake, and climbed up the bank to the cabin.

I had to go to the bathroom really bad. We had no inside plumbing or running water. We had a two-hole outhouse. As I relieved myself, I wondered if our poop filtered down into the lake and fed the fish that we ate. Gross, totally gross, I thought as I pulled up my pants, and hurried to the cabin.

My mother was standing on the front stoop when I came around to the front of the cabin.

"Where have you been?" she said.

"Out in the row boat."

"Good lord. Who knows how long it has been there? It could be rotten, and you would have drowned. Don't go off again without telling me, you understand? And did you even have a life jacket on?"

"It was dry inside and had no signs of leaks. I just went over there," I said pointing toward the white stone mountain. "I forgot to take a life jacket out of the trailer."

"Next time tell me when you are going off somewhere and wear your lifejacket if you are on the water. You hear me?"

I nodded my head as I shuffled my feet.

"What's the problem?' my father said as he came to the door.

My mother told him.

"Well, he knows how to swim."

I bet he hoped I drowned, I thought as I scooted past them. I was starving. I opened a box of crackers and a jar of peanut butter. I had woofed down half-dozen crackers before they came in.

"What's the matter with you? Can't you wait for your supper?" my father said.

I looked down at my feet as I swallowed the last piece of cracker.

"It's alright, George. I won't have dinner ready for a while. You have time to test your new outboard motor and boat."

He went outside, went down to the water, got into his new Dundee, and shoved off.

I finished unpacking the stuff I brought with me: three books, three notebooks, two pens, one toy truck, and a telescope. I thought the telescope would be great to play pirates with. I didn't have a sword, but I planned to make one.

I went back outside, taking the telescope with me. I remembered seeing a ladder lying along the backside of the cabin. It was quite heavy, and I had to work to get it upright. When I did, I leaned it against the wall of the cabin, tested a couple of rungs, and carefully climbed up to the roof.

I used my telescope to watch my father giving his boat and motor a test run. It's a good thing he wasn't that far from shore. My telescope wasn't very powerful. I then turned to the other side of the roof to see the wigwams. There were three of them. My mother said the Indians lived in them during the summer. I hoped to see one. The only Indians I ever saw were those in the movies. No Indians seemed to be around. Maybe that young man and woman were from the wigwams, I thought. I heard my mother calling. I climbed down, tipped the ladder over, pushed it back against the base of the cabin, and went to see what she wanted.

Go out to the trailer and get that box marked fragile. Be careful and don't drop it. It's a gift for the Indian women I met while your father and I were here last summer."

"Okay."

I found the box marked fragile. I moved it to the end of the trailer, jumped down, and picked up the box. I took two steps and fell flat on my face. The box hit the ground and tumbled a couple of feet. I sat up, wiped the sand off my face. My hand had blood on it. I cut my chin. I tied my shoe. One or the other was always untied. I picked up the box, praying whatever it was, wasn't broken, and went into the cabin.

"What on earth happened to you?" my mother said.

"I fell."

"You dropped the box. Oh, dear, I hope you didn't break anything."

She opened the box. Inside there was a kerosene lamp. Luck was with me. It wasn't broken. There was also a small can of kerosene. She used the newspaper wrapping to clean the lamp's globe. Satisfied, she put the globe on the lamp and sat it on the kitchen table.

I'll go visit the Indians tomorrow. And you will go with me. Mind your manners and speak only when you are spoken to. No fidgeting."

"Fidgeting? Now what?" my father said as he walked in. "All he ever does is fidget. Drives me nuts. What happened to his face?"

I waited for my mother to tell him I had tripped over my shoelace and dropped the box. She didn't. She said I tripped. I crawled up on my bunk, and opened one of my books and pretended to read. The scarcer I was the better it was. At least, that's the way I felt about it.

Dinner was over by 5:30. It was already dark, and my mother had lit our kerosene lamp. After dinner, I wrote in a notebook. I described the day's events. My parents played gin rummy. Bed time for me was 7:00 o'clock. My parents went to bed shortly after that.

As I lay on my deerskin bunk, I heard a swishing sound. The sound became clearer. Flapping wings. I felt a slight thump next to my head, actually right on my pillow. That damn bird has pooped on my pillow, I thought. I didn't dare move for fear of waking my parents.

"Quiet yourself. I have a message for you," the bird whispered.

"What kind of bird are you? Only parrots talk."

"I am a bat. I am here on your pillow so don't thrash around. Furthermore, I didn't poop

on your pillow. No more questions. Tomorrow, be alert. Check your perspective."

"Check my what?"

"Check what you see, accept what you see and hear as you did today."

Wings whirred and all was quiet, well almost quiet. I heard heavy breathing coming from my parents' bed.

Sleep was fitful as I waited for morning and the promised visit to the Indians.

***

Morning announced herself with a bright beam of light through the lone window in our log cabin. Anxious to find out if what I heard the night before was true or not I sat up in bed and looked at my pillow. No bird poop but there was a single small black feather. I picked it up and put it between two pages in my notebook. I popped out of bed and nearly stepped on a round rubber thing lying not far from my parent's bunk. I pulled my pants on, untangled my shirt, and got that on. I tackled my socks and shoes. *Next time when you go to bed untie your shoes, dummy.* I thought.

I went out to the stoop and looked across the lake. The sunrise was bright red with golden streaks through the red. My mother came from behind the cabin.

"You need to go to the outhouse?" she asked. "I left some paper there for you if you do."

"Isn't it beautiful?" I asked.

"What?"

I pointed toward the sunrise.

"Yes. Now don't be gone long. Breakfast will soon be ready.

After my trip to the outhouse, I went down to the lake, washed my hands and face. The water, like the morning air, was cold.

At the table, my mother announced she had some baking to do, and we wouldn't be going to visit the Indians until after lunch.

"Get your life jacket. You're going with me," my father said. "Give your mother some peace and quiet."

I grabbed my fishing pole and tackle box. Outside, I picked up my life jacket and put that on. I sat on the floor of the boat as my father shoved us off.

About an hour into our fishing, I put my pole aside, moved up to the front of the boat, and just watched the water. The boat stopped. My father had cut the motor, and we were slowly drifting. He had changed from a double hook lure to a single hook and was set to make a cast. When he did the lure struck me in the back of my neck, and as he snapped the pole forward the lure set deep, and I screamed. I was sure had he pulled any harder I would have ended up in the lake and bled to death or drowned. I don't care what people say about kids not knowing stuff but one thing is for sure, they can tell when they are not liked. And my father did not like me.

"Stop screaming and sit still. You are just driving the hook deeper," he said as he pulled out his knife and cut the line.

I thought for a minute he was going to kill me. He cranked up the motor and full throttled us back to camp. As we neared the camp, I began to scream. By the time my father had the boat anchored, I was up the bank screaming even louder.

"What on earth. Oh, my god. George, what happened? Don't just leave that hook in his head."

"I'll remove it as soon as he shuts up. Sit down and don't fidget."

He cut the end of the hook off and pulled the rest out. My mother poured a disinfectant on it and then put a Band-Aid on it.

My father glared at me. "Next time don't change seats."

"Maybe we had better not go visiting," my mother said.

"He's fine. I'm going to take a nap," my father said.

"You want to go? If you do, be sure you have your shoes tied. Bring that bag. It's got the lamp in it," my mother said.

"You want me to bring the water bucket?" I asked.

"No, you can do that tomorrow I'll show you where to go. We have enough water for the rest of the day. Now mind your manners. Only speak when you are spoken to. You understand?"

"Yes. Can we go now?"

I sure didn't want to be left with my father. I was sure he tried to kill me.

I nibbled on ripe huckleberries from the many bushes along the winding path up to the wigwams. The afternoon sun warmed me. My mother, dressed in black slacks and a pink blouse, and what she called sensible walking shoes, hurried me along.

As we got closer to the encampment, the dogs put up a howl. A couple growled and bared their teeth. A man, squatted on the ground in front of one of the wigwams, threw a rock at the dogs. They scattered. My mother nodded to the man and walked on to the middle wigwam. The entrance flap was open, but we didn't enter. A short woman appeared, smiled, and in a halting voice asked us in. Her dress was of deer hide decorated with dozens of colored beads and fringe. Her hair, gray-streaked, was tied in a neat single braid that hung over her left shoulder. A necklace made of blue stones and sea shells hung around her neck.

Inside, there were piles of animal skins on the ground. *Must be their beds*, I thought as I looked around. Along one side several guns were stacked. A large bow and a quiver of arrows hung on a post. A fire pit with a large black iron pot hanging from a tripod contained something that smelled worse than our outhouse. Off to one side, away from the center, sat an old man, with closed eyes, and smoking a long thin-stemmed pipe. The woman pointed to a spot not far from the old man and said, "Sit."

My mother gave the woman the kerosene lamp and can of oil. The woman caressed the lamp, sat it on the ground and then thanked my mother. My mother then handed her a bottle of my father's whiskey. She walked over to the old man sitting in the corner and handed the bottle to him. My mother stared at him as he turned the bottle around in his hands, looked at the top. I didn't remember her ever doing that to someone. *Guess he wants to make sure it hadn't been opened*, I thought. He grunted as he gave the bottle back to the woman. She opened the bottle, brought out three cups, filled each half full and gave one to the man, one to my mother, and kept one for herself. I had never seen my mother drink straight whiskey before. She waited for the man to drink his. He drained the cup with one gulp, tipping it to my mother. The woman tilted her head back and emptied her cup. It really surprised me to see my mother toss her drink down and wipe her lips with the back of her hand.

The Indian woman, I was not allowed to call her squaw, picked up a paddle, probably a canoe paddle and began stirring the contents of the pot. Steam and an awful stink rose up as she stirred. Unceremoniously, she fanned the steam over my way. I coughed, and I inhaled more of

16

that awful smelling stuff. I was sure I would smell like a dead animal the rest of my life.

After a respectful amount of time, we got up to leave. As we walked out of the wigwam, the Indian woman said, "Have the boy come back in two days. I'll have a gift for him."

***

My bed time, seven-thirty, came all too quickly. Because the supply of kerosene for the lamp was limited, my parents retired shortly after that. No noise came from their bed and sleep closed my eyes. I slipped my pants on, grabbed my jacket, and quietly snuck out the door. I walked along the top of the beach toward an outcropping of large boulders. I scrambled up to the top of the largest one. I shivered as a cool night windswept in from the lake. I stood on top of the boulder and looked out at the quartz topped island. A star shot across the sky and I was sure it landed on the island. I saw a flash on the snow-white quartz. Rising up from there was a tall Indian dressed in full regalia. A head piece made of feathers trailed down his back. Spellbound, I watched as he raised his arms up to the sky, spreading them wide, he began to draw a large circle with his right hand. A ring of fire followed the movement of his hand. I nearly fell off the boulder. "Holy shit," I said as the fire circle grew larger enough to reach across the sky and for quite some time, hover over my head. The beat of the tong-tong floated across the water and things got quiet. The fire circle disappeared. I slid down the boulder and scraped my knee. I ran back to our cabin.

I woke up to the smell of bacon frying. Was I really out there last night and did I see what I think I did or was it all a dream? I bent down to pick up my pants and noticed a scrape on my right knee. As I pulled on my pants I felt the bottom of the legs were damp, and my jacket lay in a heap at the end of my cot. It always hung on the peg by the door. A shiver played tag up and down my spine. I shook myself.

As I sat down on my stump stool my father said, "Go and get water after you've eaten. There was barely enough for coffee. Your mother and I are going fishing."

I woofed down two slices of bacon and a hot cake. I picked up the galvanized bucket and ladle and headed for the door.

"Better put your shoes on," my mother said. "The sand spurs can hurt. Let me check your neck."

Instinctively, I rubbed my neck. No bandage. It didn't hurt when I touched where the hole was.

"Goodness, I can hardly see where you got hooked. That healed mighty quick."

I picked up my shoes, went out on the stoop, put them on, and tied the laces as tight as I could. I headed for the deep woods and the spring. I liked the sounds and smells. Once I entered the woods, I slowed my pace, took a deep breath, and slowly exhaled. It was wonderful. I followed the animal trail to the spring. Rotting logs covered with dark green moss populated the area. Even the trees seemed to drip with quiet sweet-smelling moisture.

Next to the spring was a large rock. There seemed to be large rocks everywhere. I sat down to watch the water bugs swim around, doing whatever water bugs do. Images of the naked young man and woman floated by my eyes and brought stirrings of my own. My face flushed. I am not sure which came first, the disappearance of the water bugs or a new stillness in the woods. I sat very still, slipping my hand into my pants pocket to retrieve my jackknife. If it was a bear, I had the metal bucket and dipper to bang. I didn't know what I'd do with the little knife.

Slowly emerging up from the water was the same young man I saw on the island and he was still naked [2].

"Do not be afraid. No harm will come to you. I have another secret to share with you."

18

"A secret," I replied, "what kind of secret? And why don't you have clothes on?

"Ah, yes," he replied. "I am naked so you can see I have no weapons to harm you. In my world, clothes are not necessary. Things are beginning to happen to you and for you. Have no fear. Whatever happens, be like the water, follow a natural path."

"What things?" I whispered.

"I will tell you just one and then I must go. Look for a large bird."

With that, he disappeared.

I bent over the spring, pushed the water bugs aside along with any leaves that were floating around. There was no sign of him.

"Jerk, you didn't ask his name," I muttered.

I scooped up a bucketful of water, picked out a couple of bugs and put them back in the spring, and then headed back to camp. The bucket was heavy and by the time I got back to camp, I had sloshed quite a bit. My parents hadn't come in from fishing. I could see them trolling along the outer side of my island. My mother left me a P and B sandwich and a glass of Kool-Aid. I sat on the bank, eating, and watching the sky for a big bird. None came. *Tomorrow*, I thought, *I will go and get my gift.*

***

The night passed without incident. I slept until my mother called me for breakfast. I felt wonderful. I had a new friend, even though he was naked, and I didn't know his. My father already went out in the boat. I waited until my mother had the dishes washed. Today, instead of using the drinking water, she took the dishes down to the water's edge and washed them there. I helped her bring them back in. Once she had things back where she wanted them, I said,

"Are we going to visit the Indians? Today the old lady said she would have a gift for me."

"Yes. I don't know what to take. I can't take another bottle of your father's whiskey," she replied.

"Take the bread," I said, hoping that was a good suggestion.

"Perfect. I'll wrap in a brown bag and set it in the oven for a few minutes to warm it through. You be sure to say thank you for your gift. The Commissioner of Indian Affairs told your father it is customary for Indians to exchange gifts. What have you got that you can give?"

"I don't know. I don't have anything. Wait, I can give this," I said, pulling out my jackknife.

She smiled at me. "When we go into the store next week, we can get you another one."

"That's a hundred-mile trip and boring. Do I have to go?"

"Well, I don't know about leaving you here alone all those hours. We'll see what your father says."

The walk up to the wigwams seemed to take hours. I wasn't interested in picking any huckleberries. As my mother and I neared the encampment, I once more felt for my jackknife. My uncle, my father's brother, whom I only met once, gave it to me. I remember my father's look of disapproval. Before he could say anything, I had put it in my pocket and ran outdoors. It has been with me ever since.

This time barking dogs did not announce our approach. We waited outside the middle wigwam. We waited for a few minutes before the woman appeared.

"Hallo," she said.

"Hello," my mother replied. "Are you up for a visit today?"

"Yes. Come in."

Once inside, I noted the old man was slouched along one wall. His head bowed; his arms folded, and his pipe held by one hand. Had I not noticed his chest move, I would have thought he was dead. Today, I noticed there were hot coals under the pot, and it did not stink. I didn't wait for her to tell me to sit. Like my previous visit, I squatted in front of the man.

I had no sooner got down on the earthen floor when he stood up and walked in front of me with a small bundle of what looked like grass in his hand. He pushed into the ashes under the pot and held it there until it caught fire. He blew on it until the grass glowed. He walked around me, moving the smoking grass around my body. It had a sweet smell. I thought maybe I still had a bad smell from the stuff in the pot, even if I had taken a bath in the lake.

"Mosquitoes," he said.

"Thank you," I replied, looking up at the man. *He's the one I saw on the top of the white stone mountain*, I thought. *He must be thirty years old.*

His eyes were azure blue. I felt his gaze, and I was sure a smile crossed his lips. The woman broke the silence.

"Come. We go to the water," she said.

Unwinding our legs, my mother and I dutifully followed. The man remained behind. At the water's edge, I saw it—a canoe.

The Indian woman waded into the water and motioned for me to get into the canoe. Once in, I remembered I had seen her on her knees, and I did the same. There was a paddle next to me. She motioned what I was to do. Using the paddle I made a left stroke and then a right one. I was ecstatic. Then the canoe jerked and stopped. I started going backwards. She had a rope tied to the canoe and was pulling me back.

"Good," she said. "The rope was for your safety. You did well. The rope is no longer needed," she said, untying the rope and winding it up.

I jumped out of the canoe, waded ashore, dragging it with me. I was surprised how light it was. She smiled approval. I went over to her and gave her a hug. Embarrassed, I stepped back. She nodded. I handed her my jackknife. She pulled open the blades and ran her finger along each. Satisfied, she folded the blades and put the knife in a pouch she had slung over her shoulder.

"Can I paddle it back to camp?" I asked, looking at my mother and the Indian woman.

"Be careful. You don't have a life jacket with you," my mother replied. "I'll be along shortly.

The canoe made of birch bark had a low seat, so I could actually sit rather than kneel. It was not as long as those used by the Indians, and it was obvious it was made just for me. There was space in the front for a string of caught fish. As I paddled along, not far-off shore, I looked back. The Indian man was standing with my mother watching me.

***

The next morning, my mother had me up before sunrise. She had flapjacks, eggs, and sliced ham ready for breakfast.

"Your father wants to get an early start. He's out checking the car."

I am sure my face dropped because she immediately said, "I asked if you could spend the day with the Indians. They agreed. You behave yourself up there while we are gone."

I gave her a hug. She smiled.

"I told your father," she continued, "that you gave your knife to the Indian woman and I wanted to buy you another one."

Actually, I could hardly control my excitement. They wouldn't be back to the cabin much before dark. My elation was cut by my father coming in from outside.

"Do not go out in that damn canoe while your mother and I are gone. You understand that?"

I nodded my head. It was always your mother and me, never we. My mother had a lunch prepared for me and an afternoon snack, both neatly packed in a small knapsack. I guess she figured I could wait till they got back to have my supper.

I waited until the Buick was out of sight and then with my knapsack, I headed up to the Indians. This time, I held out my hand to the dogs and they gave it a sniff, wagged their tails, and then followed me on to the middle wigwam.

The Indian woman did not come to the entrance to greet me. Wonder if she forgot I was coming to spend the day. As I was about to walk away, the man appeared and said, "Come."

He had a bow and quiver of arrows with him. He was dressed in deer skin. He wore a head band with an eagle burnished into it. His hair was in a single braid and hung over his right shoulder. Undecorated moccasins were on his feet, not like those I saw in a store. He was taller than the other men at the camp; something I had not noticed before. And he probably wasn't as old as I thought.

"Today you will learn how to use a bow. This is not a toy, and you should never aim it at any human. Once you are good enough, we will go into the deep woods to hunt."

He talked just like me. And that surprised me since the women spoke in broken English, as my mother called it. He noticed my surprise and smiled.

"What is your name?" I blurted.

I felt my face turn red.

"I am called Aranck—A-ra-nck," he repeated. "It means stars."

I slowly pronounced his name. He smiled. I liked his smile and his name.

We walked several hundred yards away from the encampment. Aranck selected a tree, drew a circle on it with his knife and then in its center, he placed a small x.

"Watch what I do," Aranck said.

He strung the bow from the bottom to the top, using an animal tendon. He plucked it a couple of times, testing its strength. He bent the bow slightly and removed the string, handing it to me.

Once I mastered stringing the bow, he then showed me how to place an arrow.

"Good," he said. "Now watch how I aim. Is the arrow pointing at the center of the target?"

"No," I replied. My voice must have conveyed some doubt.

"You are sure."

Feeling braver, I said, "Yes."

"Good. Never use the arrow to aim. Use your eye."

With that, he let the arrow fly. I ran to the marked tree. The arrow was dead center.

It took me several practice shots before I hit the tree. Then I hit the target dead center. I repeated that several more times.

"Come. I have something for you," Aranck said.

At the wigwams, he invited me in. The woman was busy, kneading a deer hide. He handed me a bow, and a quiver with seven arrows. There was a small flap on the side of the quiver. I opened it and inside was three extra strings for the bow. He waited for me to string it.

"We now need to initiate the bow. We will go hunting. In the deep woods, you have to be very quiet. Put these on," he said, handing me a pair of moccasins.

He led the way and I watched how he stepped. Every ten minutes or so, he stopped and listened. At no time did we speak. He pointed to the ground, squatted and I did the same. Tracks were of some kind of bird and about four inches apart. Aranck motioned for me to get my bow ready. Once I had an arrow in place, he began to cluck. He did that a couple of times and waited. Then, he clucked again. This time he had an answer. He pointed. Coming into the clearing was a large gobbler.

I readied myself, trying to remember what he had said about sighting. He gave me a little tap with his finger and I let the arrow fly. The turkey fluttered for a brief moment and fell over.

"Good shot, boy," Aranck said, patting me on the shoulder. "Tonight we will have a special ceremony, and eat roast turkey."

He pulled a piece of rawhide from his pocket, tied the bird's feet and then he made a longer loop, tied it off, and had me put it over my head so the turkey was on my back. *I wish I had a camera. No one back home will believe I shot a turkey with bow and arrow*, I thought as we entered the clearing to the wigwams.

It was late afternoon and the bird cleaned, gutted, and trussed was spitted over a bed of hot coals. When the fat melted, it dripped on the fire bed and the flames flared up. One of the women would turn the bird to insure even cooking. Vegetables cooking along the edge of the coals remained a mystery.

The barking of the dogs alerted everyone that a car was approaching. I recognized my parents' Buick. For a minute, I thought my father was going to drive into one of the wigwams. Aranck greeted them warmly. I stayed back, waiting to be recognized. It did not come. My father handed the Indian woman from the middle wigwam two bottles of Canadian. Cups appeared and a round went to everyone. One of the Indian women sliced the turkey and dug vegetables dug out from along the embers. Once everyone had eaten, the cups with Canadian whiskey were gain passed. During this time I said nothing.

Aranck stood up from his cross-legged position and began to speak. I didn't understand the language. Raising his arms skyward, he said, "It is time to begin the "flèche de lumière.

I caught the word lumière which means light. My dozing father came alert after a poke from my mother. Darkness had settled in and the heavens displayed a spectacular aurora borealis. A shooting star graced us as it shot out over the lake. Aranck leaned over to me and whispered.

"Stand and make your bow ready."

I did. My father looked at me, questioning what I was doing.

"Tonight," Aranck said, "we celebrate the arrow of light. The spirits blessed us twice today and now it is time to recognize the one among us for whom this blessing is intended. We thank our young hunter for our dinner of turkey. His arrow flew true and we ask the Great Spirit that his arrows always fly true."

Picking up his bow, he deftly strung an arrow, dipped it into a can of pine pitch, and indicated I should do the same.

My father moved back, uncomfortable with my having a bow and arrow. Once my arrow was dipped, Aranck touched the last of the hot embers and the pitch caught fire. I followed.

"On the count of two, release your arrow over the water," Aranck said.

We fired together and those present clapped and someone began to beat the tong-tong. Aranck raised his hand. The drumming stopped. From out of the air, he plucked a feather from the turkey and gently stuck it in my hair, and then tied a band around my head to hold it in place.

"I present Bird Hunter. Welcome him."

The other Indians stood up, formed a line, and walked over to me, each with a feather from the turkey. As each man and woman gave me a feather, I nodded my head and said thank you. My voice was barely above a whisper.

I waited for my parents to say something. They did not.

My mother stood up, helped my father stand, and pointed me toward the Buick. She drove us back to our log cabin. On the way into the cabin, I asked my mother if she had gotten me a new jackknife.

"You gave yours away. Guess you didn't feel a need to have one," my father mumbled.

I never mentioned a jackknife again.

Nothing more was said and we went to bed. The next day as I was arranging my gifts of feathers, my father walked by to go to the outhouse

"Humph. Hell of a lot of nonsense."

So much for being Bird Hunter, I thought.

The remainder of the summer I spent more and more time with the Indians. Aranck showed me how to shoot a fish with my bow, how to spear a fish, and how to clean them. That was something my father never had an interest in teaching me. The night before we began to pack up to return to the States, I slipped out of our cabin and made my way to the Indian encampment. The bright moon cast strange shadows along the overgrown path. A couple of times I stopped and listened. I was glad I had my bow and arrows with me.

They were gone.

I sat down and cried.

CHAPTER TWO

As we drove along what we called "the cow path" I looked back, taking in the whole area, burning it into my memory. I curled up in a corner of the back seat and went to sleep. I felt a finger placed on my lips and opened my eyes. There he was—Aranck. How can this be? I thought as he removed his finger from my lips. He shook his finger back and forth, and I understood I was not to speak.

He smiled at me, leaned forward, and whispered, "I am with you always. Remember that."

I blinked, and he was gone. I realized my mother was speaking to me.

"You sit up front with your father for a while. I want to take a nap. I didn't sleep at all well last night."

My father eased the car to a stop, and I hopped out and exchanged places with my mother. We continued on this winding dirt road. I figured we had been on it for a good hour or so. I guess my father was anxious to get through with the dirt road because he was pushing the Buick. I lay down in the seat, turned and looked up at him. "There's a car coming around the next cure. It's going to hit us head on," I said.

"What nonsense are you blabbering about now?"

I didn't have time to answer. A pickup hit us head on. My mother fell off the back seat, and I slammed up under the dash. My father lay over the steering wheel. For a minute, I thought he was dead, but he moved, sat up, rubbed his head, and then got out of the car. He did not ask how my mother or I was.

When he was finished talking to the driver of the pickup, my father, leaned his head into the open window and said, "Front fender's shot, headlights smashed, bumper caved in. I don't think we have a punctured radiator so we can go on to town.

"What about the truck and driver?" my mother asked.

"Very little damage to the truck and the driver wasn't hurt."

I wiggled my way back into the front seat, rubbed the back of my neck. My father eased the Buick on by the truck, waved out the window, and drove on, slower now.

When we finally reached the first small town, my father located a garage and had the car checked. He used the telephone to call the Royal Canadian Mounted Police to report the accident. We would have to wait until we got to Montreal to have the car fixed. The police gave the name of a repair shop and a hotel for us to stay at. At a nice hotel called Le Henri, a staff member brought a cot for me to sleep on. Saved paying for an extra room so my father said, anyway.

Before we went to dinner, I got a hot bath. It felt wonderful. It was then my mother discovered the large black and blue patch across my upper shoulders. She was shocked and called my father.

"George, come in here and look at this. I think we should find a doctor."

My father stuck his head into the bathroom, looked at me, and said, "Just get some ice and put on it. That'll take the swelling down."

After a quiet meal in the hotel dining room, we returned to our room. I went to bed. I hadn't eaten much because I felt sick on my stomach. I said nothing about it. The ice pack was forgotten. My parents read for a while and then turned out the light. At some point, before dawn, I felt someone tapping me on my shoulder. I rolled over. It was Aranck. He motioned for me to remain quiet. He blew into my eyes and then said, "Your injuries are no more."

I sat up on the edge of my cot. Leaned down, picked up my flashlight, and went into the bathroom. I shut the door as quietly as I could, flicked on the light, and looked in the framed mirror that hung over the sink. Turning as far as I could, I could see there was no black and blue or swelling. I turned my head back and forth. I had no pain. I smiled at myself in the mirror and gave the image a wink. I flushed the toilet just in case my mother heard me up.

We stayed at the hotel for two days, walked around the streets and ate my first Chinese food. I had never seen a Chinese person before. That was something I could share when I went back to school. I vowed I would never tell about Aranck, about my bow and arrows, or about the turkey I shot. No one would believe me, especially my half-brothers.

We crossed the International Peace Bridge that spanned the Saint Lawrence River. Unlike some other vehicles entering the United States, my father, after saying something to the border guard, waved us on through. I wondered why. I remember him shaking hands with the guard. Nothing special happened until we reached Ithaca. It was late at night and we were driving on a steep and winding road. I was in the back seat, and my mother was up front next to my father. No one was talking, and the radio was not playing.

"Slow down, George. Bad curve ahead," a voice boomed throughout the car.

My father hit the brakes, and the Buick slowed to a crawl. If my father had maintained the speed, he was going; we would have crashed through the guardrails and ended up at the bottom of a steep hill, probably dead or badly hurt.

"Charlotte, how'd you know about that curve?"

"I didn't say anything."

Turning and looking over her shoulder, she asked me, "Do you say anything?"

"No, I didn't' say anything, but I did hear someone say to slow down, " I replied.

"Me too," my mother replied. "Strange."

We arrived home around three in the morning.

Labor Day Weekend was a day away and then school for me.

CHAPTER THREE

In late September, my parents decided to train into New York City. I was excited about the train ride. We had a compartment. As soon as the train was underway, a black man dressed in white and with a brass nameplate on the lapel of his coat came to our compartment and asked if he could bring refreshments. My father ordered a Jack Daniels; my mother ordered a Rob Roy. The waiter looked at me. Neither of my parents said anything, so I said, "I'll have an RC Cola."

As usual, I had a book to read, a note pad, and pen. My parents had books with them. After that we went to a passenger car and took seats. I had one to myself. I opened the train window. It was the kind that slid back. It was a warm day, and the rush of air felt good. The smell from stuff burning along the tracks was choking me, so I closed the window. We exited the train at Grand Central Station. From there we took a taxi to our hotel. After checking in, we hit the streets and went to Macy's. It advertised 'refrigerated air', and it lived up to its ad. It was really cool inside. We stopped at Saks Fifth Avenue where my mother bought a new hat, and my father bought a topcoat. From there, we had lunch at the famous Stork Club. My parents met another couple there. I was too busy looking at the photographs of famous movie stars fastened to the walls to pay attention to what they were talking about. I heard my father mention somebody named Jack Dempsey.

I felt very warm, and I itched. I scratched my arms and legs. My head hurt, and the room began to spin. I fell out of my chair. The man, seated next to me, leaned over and looked down at me.

"Your kid looks really sick, George. He's got some kind of rash all over him."

A doctor was located. We took a taxi to get to his office. The burning along the tracks had been poison ivy, and I got it all over me. The doctor said to bathe me in baking soda. The next day I wasn't any better. A second doctor who said I had inhaled the poison ivy and gave them some pills to give me every four hours. The third day I was really sick. My mother put a whole box of baking soda in the tub of mildly warm and that just irritated me all the more. They decided we should go home. I was naked when my mother wrapped me in a white sheet from head to toe. The taxi driver was a more than a bit wary of us. I remember little of the train ride home.

The family doctor came to the house. He listened to me wheeze. My temperature was hovering at 105 degrees. He gave my mother a bunch of large pills and told her to give me one with a full glass of water every three hours. He said they were sulfa pills. He then told her to pick milkweed pods, squeeze the juice on my skin.

I don't remember much about the next few days. I do remember one incident, and it remained very clear in my mind. I looked out my bedroom window, and as I lay there gazing at nothing, in particular, the sky turned a bright pink. Out of the pink clouds, a giant bird spiraled downward toward my window. Its wings were so large that they covered the window. All I could see was a large head with an open mouth. It was talking to me, but I wasn't sure what it was saying. It had something to do with chosen. "Chosen for what," I said out loud.

My mother walked in, surprised at seeing me sitting up, she said, "Did you say something? How are you feeling?"

"I saw a large bird with huge wings at my window. It flew down out of pink clouds. I think it was trying to tell me something," I said.

"You were hallucinating," she replied as she put her hand on my forehead. "Your fever broke. I'll bring you some chicken soup."

I knew better.

CHAPTER FOUR

Fall slipped into winter, and my general well-being improved. By spring, I was completely well and anxious for school to be over. My ears perked up as my father began to talk about returning to the Baskatong. This time the discussion included having another couple join them. Immediately, I wondered where I would sleep. There were only two beds in the cabin. With the realization that there was no mention of me, panic grabbed me. They wouldn't leave me here by myself for three months, I thought. That fact brought me little comfort. Where would I stay and with whom would I stay? Certainly not with my brothers.

April blossomed into May and June would soon be here. There was no mention of my going to Canada with them. I knew that they wanted to be at the lake by June 1st. The last week of May my mother told me to get ready. I was to select what I wanted to take with me for the three months. I barely held my glee. I just hoped my friend Aranck would be there. When I thought of him, I realized I liked him more than I did my father. It's not that I didn't really like my father; it's just I felt he really didn't like me.

I knew and understood that he preferred my middle bother that was in the US Navy. For that matter, my mother favored my older brother who was in the army. I remember one night, my parents go into an argument, and I heard my father say he hadn't wanted another kid. "Two," he said, "was enough." So I have known for a long time that I really wasn't wanted. "An accident," was how my mother explained it to my aunt Bess.

As it turned out there was another couple going with us. Their names were Bradford, Betty, and Paul Bradford. They drove their own car with a boat on a trailer. We stopped at a restaurant just outside of Syracuse, New York for dinner. I had what they called a basket of chicken and fries. For desert, I had strawberry chiffon pie. By the time we crossed over the bridge into Canada I wasn't feeling very good. I kept quiet about it. My plan for the summer was to be as invisible as possible.

It was late when we pulled into camp. My father poured a drink for my mother and Tom and Betty. They had brought an army cot for me. I went to bed. As I lay on the cot I looked up at the rafters to see if my bow and quiver of arrows were still there. They were. I don't know what time it was, maybe after midnight, I began vomiting. One spasm after another wracked my body.

I was a real mess by the time my parents had the single lamp lit. The vomiting subsided a bit. Diarrhea took its place. Morning's agonizing arrival was not welcome. I began the vomiting routine all over again. Dry heaves this time. I was burning up with a fever.

"The nearest doctor is fifty miles south of here. Guess we had better get him ready," my father said.

"What about the Indians? They have knowledge of such things," my mother said." I'll go up and ask."

A short time later, a new voice entered my consciousness.

"Put towels in boiling water. Wring them out and lay them across his stomach. That will stop the convulsions."

It was Aranck.

"Mix this in water and have him take a sip every few hours. I will stay with him if you have things you need to do."

My mother thanked him.

"It would be good if he were in a sweat lodge. I will prepare one, and you can bring up to my tent. It will drive the poison out of him."

"How soon can you have the sweat lodge ready?" It was my father's voice. The word poison flashed through my mind. Maybe he wants me dead, especially since he didn't want me to begin with.

"Give me a couple of hours. I will come back for the boy. In the meantime, Mrs. Wells change the hot towels once they are cool. Be careful not to burn his flesh."

Aranck came back and told my parents the sweat lodge was ready. They drove us up to the wigwams. There, Aranck had pitched a small tent; a pup tent. A small fire with rocks lying along its outer edges was a couple of feet from the entrance to the tent. Aranck picked me up in his arms and placed me in the tent. He crawled in with me. He removed all of my clothes and neatly folded them and placed them to one side of the animal skins he had placed me on. He went outside. I could hear his baritone voice.

"Hot stones with wet grasses and herbs will create steam inside the tent. I will keep the steam going for three hours. Here is a shovel. When I call you, put a hot stone on the shovel and pass it through that small opening. Have a blanket to wrap him in when I bring him out."

"What grasses?" my mother asked.

"Lemon grass, sage, and Echinacea buds. I will mix that with cedar bark and tobacco."

"Tobacco?"

"Kinnickinnick."

"George, you sure you want to let this Indian have your kid?" Paul Bradford asked.

"Yes," my mother answered. "He is a shaman."

"A what? Betty asked.

"A medicine man."

I lost count of the number of times heated rocks brought into the pup tent. I do remember asking Aranck about his blue eyes.

"They are like yours. Blue eyes see differently. Drink a few drops of this. Roll it around in your mouth, slowly and then swallow it. It will taste bitter-sweet."

"What's it for?"

"It stops the shits. You feel like having some broth?'

"Okay, a little."

Whatever the broth was, it tasted wonderful. I consumed a half a cup. Aranck wouldn't let me have anymore. He said I could have some more with meat in a couple of hours.

The sun shining on my face woke me. I bolted upright. Aranck was sitting next to me, cross legged, and head bent. Slowly, I reached over, picked up my clothes, and put them on. As quiet as my movements were, he woke immediately.

"Ah, so you are better. Good. Come. I will feed you. Your mother is outside in the car."

I tapped on the side front window of the Buick. My mother, startled, immediately opened the door.

"How do you feel?"

"Good," I replied.

"Are you hungry?"

"Aranck is bringing me food."

"Be sure to say thank you. Once you have finished eating you better come back to the cabin. Your father is not sure it's a good idea for you to spend so much time with the Indians."

Shuffling my feet in the sand, I said, "Yes, but I don't see the harm in it. It gives me something to do besides paddle my canoe around the lake. Paul and Betty are no fun. Fact is I don't think they like me much."

Aranck walked back to the cabin with me. He had something wrapped up and carrying it under his arm.

At the log cabin, he presented my parents with two beautifully painted deerskins. Even my father was impressed. One contained a painting of a bull moose and the other of a bear.

***

A couple of days after my bout with food poisoning, I was sitting on the large boulder not far from our cabin. Paul went out to fish by himself. Betty asked my father to take her over to the quartz island. My father had said it was quartz. She wanted to get some photos with a fancy new movie camera and was anxious to try it out. My mother declined to go. She was baking bread and needed to stay in. I realized I was seeing someone waving their arms from a boat. It was Paul. I watched for a couple of minutes. He couldn't get his boat free.

I ran down to the water's edge, shoved my canoe into the water, jumped in, and paddled out to him. He caught his boat's anchor on a stump. In trying to free it up with his oar, it slipped, and he lost it. With some maneuvering, I could see the anchor, took my paddle and gave it a hard shove. It came loose. Paul pulled it up, and started his outboard and took off. He shouted 'thanks' and waved.

I decided to paddle along the back side of the quartz island. As I came around the bend I saw my father's boat pulled up on the shore. I drifted in, pulled up the canoe. I walked a short distance and heard Betty laughing. There they were. My father on top of her, pumping up and down just like the young man and girl I saw there last year. I turned, ran back to the canoe, and got out of there. I would learn it would not be the last time he would be screwing other women. That's what the sixth-grade boys called it. I decided not to mention this to my mother. I would talk to Aranck about it.

I landed my canoe down behind the big boulder, where the Indians had their canoes. I hurried into the high grass, and into the woods just above the wigwams. When I came out into their clearing, I was behind the middle wigwam. I walked around to the front, stood at the open flap, waiting to be recognized. He came to the entrance and motioned for me to come in.

"What troubles you, my young friend?"

"I watched my father screwing Betty."

With that, he looked at me, raised an eyebrow.

"And what do you think of that?"

"I feel it's not right," I replied. "Is it?"

"Sometimes men have to taste the fruit of many trees."

38

"Do you do that?" I felt my face color.

"No. I am womanless. My spirit mate died several years ago. When a man takes a woman as his wife, he keeps that one. To continue to sample others is wrong. Have you told your mother?"

"No. I don't think I should."

"A wise decision. She will learn of this on her own."

"I have another question. Will I sample many women?"

A broad smile spread itself across Aranck's face.

"A few, but there will be one woman for you. You will know her when the time comes."

I returned to the cabin. There, I found out that Paul and Betty would be leaving in the morning. Their ten-day stay was over. I was glad. Most of the summer was ahead of me, which meant I would have more time with my friend, Aranck.

Yes, I called him that. Fact is, he is the only friend I really have. The kids at school were not my real friends. We didn't share things. That's what friends do; share things. Maybe that's what my father was doing, sharing with a friend.

"Some things are not to be shared."

The voice came out of nowhere. I was out on the rock, my favorite place to just sit. I looked around, no one in sight. Then I heard it again.

"Did you hear me? If you did, just say yes to yourself."

It was Aranck.

"Yes," I half whispered.

"Good. We can talk like this whenever you want."

I was totally beside myself. "How can this be?"

"All will be explained. Listen carefully. If you do not want me to read your thoughts and to talk to you, just say 'no' to yourself. When you are ready to receive my words that come through the air, say 'yes'. That way, I will not pry into your private thoughts."

CHAPTER FIVE

This was the summer I would turn twelve and my fifth on the Baskatong.

My mother had what they called a hysterectomy that April. She had been in the hospital for a month and there was some question about our going to the Baskatong. When the end of May came, packing began for our trip. I took only two books with me. I did increase my notepads to six and added another pen. We left shortly after midnight. This time we made no stops, except to pee along the road. We had sandwiches and coffee in the car. For some reason, my father seemed in a big hurry to get to the lake. He drove all night. We arrived around ten the next morning. My father took a nap.

The first thing I did was to check to see if the Indians were there. They were. I tried sending a message to Aranck. No reply. That made me nervous. I hadn't heard from him for over a month. I was anxious to go up to the wigwams. But I had to help my mother bring in some of the stuff from the car.

When my father got up, he unhitched the boat, filled the outboard, and went fishing. My mother and I finished unpacking. As soon as we finished, I raced to the Indian campground. I waited at the middle wigwam. The woman came to the entrance.

"He is not here."

"Where—where is he?"

"In the deep woods. He'll be back in a few days."

Disappointed, I returned to the cabin. As I walked to my favorite rock; I noticed there were no ice flows this year. I noted other subtle changes in the area. I climbed up on the rock. The changes in me were not so subtle. At the top, I stripped off my clothes and sat down, letting the sun warm me. I liked the way I was looking. I was now over five feet tall and had begun to pack on some muscles. Other parts had grown in size. It helped that I was doing a lot of pushups. I wanted weights but my father thought I was too young for that.

Speaking of him, I caught him with another woman. It was a local minister's wife this time. I had taken up playing tennis and one of the local churches had a tennis court. One day when I went to play, I spotted his car parked in the next block. I had to use the bathroom so I went into the church's recreation hall. That's where I saw them. I'd never really seen my father's dick before. It was big and the minister's wife was swallowing it as he shoved it back and forth in her mouth. I got out of there fast, jumped on my bike, and sped away. I was sure he was going to hell for doing it in a church building. I nearly ran down my tennis partner. She wanted to know what the hurry was. I yelled, "Got the shits."

Waiting for Aranck were the longest wait of my life. Because I was spending so much time on the rock, naked, sunning myself, and writing in my journals, my skin took on a dark coppery tone.

"Honestly," my mother said to my father, "If that boy gets any darker people will think he's an Indian."

"He spends all his time on that rock, doing pushups. All he thinks about is how he looks."

"Don't tell me you have forgotten how you were when we first got married," she said.

"Humph."

"He's coming into the seed. Better have a talk with him."

They always did that. Talk as if I were not there. I knew what they meant. We had that in our health class. Boys separated from the girls during those presentations. The basketball coach showed us a film. One day, in the locker room, the coach told us about rubbers and how to use them. We had to promise not to tell anyone. We promised. I wonder if my father used rubbers while he was having sex with those other women.

The next morning Aranck arrived at our cabin door. He waited until my mother opened it.

He had a birch bark basket filled with green stuff. He explained what each was: wild carrots, leaks, several tubers that were like potatoes, and lemon sweet grass.

"Lay these alongside a fish and bake," he said.

"Thank you. George is out back. He'll be here shortly if you want to see him," my mother said. "Please come in."

I will wait here. Thank you."

I rushed out the door, past my mother, nearly knocking her over.

"Aranck," I called. "I have missed you."

"And I you, Bird Hunter."

My father came around from the outhouse.

"Hello, George. Nice to see you back again."

"Thank you, Aranck. The year has been good to you."

"I came to ask your permission to take the boy into deep woods with me. I am going on a hunt for medicine and it would be a good learning experience for him."

"Well, I don't know."

"It would give you and your wife some private time together," Aranck said as he winked at my father.

"How long will you be gone?" my mother asked.

"Two weeks."

"That's quite a long time."

I kept very quiet during this discussion. I felt if I showed too much enthusiasm they would not let me go.

"Can you give me some general location where you are going? You know, in case there's an emergency we can find you," my father said.

"I will draw you a map. Always follow the sun. It is settled, then. If so we will leave early in the morning."

Aranck pulled a sack from around his shoulder, handed it to me. I looked at him. Not sure what I should do, I just stood there.

"Open it. Clothes for you. Indian clothes to keep you from getting scratched up and bitten by bugs."

I pulled out a shirt, pants, and moccasins, and another leather bag. The bags, he said, are to carry plants used for medicine. He had me try the pants. I stepped back into the cabin to do that. I suddenly felt shy undressing in front of the three of them. The pants had a drawstring and they were a perfect fit. The shirt and moccasins fit well. When I stepped back out onto the stoop, my mother said, "Goodness, you sure do look like an Indian. I'd think you were one except for your blue eyes."

"Aranck has blue eyes," I said.

"So he does. Well, George, what do you think? Should he go or not?"

"I guess there's no harm. You behave yourself and don't cause trouble," George said.

I grabbed my bow, quiver of arrows and left with Aranck. Up the path a ways, I turned and waved at my mother still standing on the stoop. My father was not there.

***

"There is some preparation we must do before we leave. First, will be a smudging ceremony. I will use a small bundle of sage, cedar, and copal."

"What's that for?"

"To ward off evil spirits, to protect us, to cleanse our souls. After that, we will strip down and put this on all over our bodies. This will keep the mosquitoes and other insects from biting us."

He handed me a jar of brown stuff and proceeded to strip down. He was a tall man; broad shouldered and began to spread the salve all over him, including his privates. I turned away.

"No need to ever be ashamed of your body or your sex tool. What matters is how you use it."

I slapped the salve all over me including my balls and even the bottoms of my feet. Got my clothes back on and sat down. I noticed there were no women in the wigwam. When I had stopped here two weeks ago I saw only one woman; the same that I had met before.

"Aranck, can I ask a question?"

"Of course you may. You do not have to ask permission. Bird Hunter, what do you want to know?"

"Where are the Indian women? There have always been two in this wigwam."

"Both are my sisters and both widows. The oldest died this past winter. The other one has gone to visit another wigwam four days from here. She will be here when we return.

We spent the rest of the day sharpening knives, checking bone fishhooks, and arrow heads. Aranck showed me how to cut rawhide into narrow strips, roll them and tie them off. I had time to get in a few practice shots with the bow. I hadn't lost my eye for sighting. I hit the mark Aranck made every shot.

"Good. Very good. It's time to start a fire and prepare our evening meal. I will show you how to build a fire without matches or a lighter."

I did what he said, spinning a small stick into another stick. Smoke came up from the bottom piece. He told me to gently blow on the bottom piece. I did and it burst into flames. Add some small twigs and a bit of dry grass. The flames grew and I added a larger piece of wood. I was so intense on getting a good fire going I barely noticed he was staring at me.

"You sure you are not an Indian?" He had a full grin on his face that showed a perfect set of white teeth.

"Wish I were," I said.

"Never wish for something you are not."

"What should I wish for?"

"Understanding and compassion would be a good beginning."

44

"Where do you go when winter comes? You don't stay here do you?"

"I go back to school just like you do."

"Now I know you are teasing me."

"No, I am not. I teach."

"Oh, man. I should have guessed. So what do you teach?"

I teach courses in world religions, mythology, and philosophy."

"I never heard of those being taught in public schools. In what kind of school do you teach?"

"Better put this fish on the coals. Stinging nettles covers the fish. I didn't give any of those to your mother."

"Why stinging nettles? They make you itch and burn."

"You sure are full of questions. Let me answer your previous question first. I teach at a college and come here to be with my sisters and my people. Stinging nettles make the fish taste good and also help you healthy. Here, drink this. Drink it slowly."

"Umm. It tastes good. What is it?"

"It's a mixture of honey, birch bark juice, water, and a couple of other plants from our mother's gardens. It will help keep you safe from evil spirits."

We ate in silence. The fish was the best I had ever eaten. We made sure the fire was out and sat around looking at the stars. The Northern Lights danced across the sky, reflected on the white quartz mountain on what I now called my island. I could barely keep my eyes open. I had finished the drink Aranck gave me and went into the wigwam and lay down on a deerskin he placed there for me.

I don't have a watch, so I am not sure what time it was when I first heard the beat of the tong tongs. The beat was slow and easy, gradually increasing its tempo. My head was spinning, and I felt sick to my stock. The ground shook beneath me. A rumbling drowned out the tong tongs and with a gigantic crash, the earth opened, and I fell through a huge gaping hole. Pebbles, stones, and rocks pelted me. I pulled the deerskin around my head to protect myself the best I could. I remember from geography class that the earth can open and close again. I was sure I was about to be crushed. From the depths, I heard a voice. It grew louder and louder. I thought my ears were going to bust.

"Get out! You don't belong here."

There was a huge swoosh. I was moving so fast it was hard for me to breathe. Someone or something was chocking me. I realized I was pulling the deerskin tight around my neck. I let it go, and I watched it slowly float off into space. It was then that I noticed the stars, wondrously beautiful. I watched the Northern Lights, and they looked different as I looked down at them. Strange ghost-like shapes floated by me. One came up close to me, tipped its head, and disappeared.

Immediately, a beautiful translucent figure appeared. Its radiated light made me feel peaceful. It smiled, and I smiled back. I felt it take my hand, gently urging me to follow. I saw the same naked young man from the island and the deep woods.

"Oh!" I said as I realized who it was.

"It's me," I whispered.

A loud whistle redirected my attention. A bald eagle was circling just above me. It swooped low, landed next to me. It looked me up and down and then; I swear; it nodded its head up and down in approval. It turned, flapped its wings, and took off. I sat up.

An Indian, in a cross-legged position, sat next to me. He had a painted face: once side black, the other white. Under the eye of the white side was a red line, and the black side's eye had a yellow line under it. A necklace of teeth hung around his neck and came to a rest on his bare chest. His hair, unbraided, hung long over his shoulders. Drawn to his eyes, I noticed how dark and blank they were. There was no movement or life in them.

"Who—who are you? What do you want?"

He didn't reply. Instead, he reached for my hand, held it firmly in his, and using a pointed knife, cut an X in my hand. I wanted to scream, but for some reason did not. He held me tight. Blood flowed up and over the edge of my hand, dripping into a fire. The flames flared up and then quieted. He let go of my hand.

I felt someone gently shaking me. It was Aranck.

"Time to eat and we are off," he said, handing me a slice of smoked fish.

"Thanks. I'll be right back," I said.

"No outhouse here. Dig a hole in the sand, here's paper. Cover it when you are done. See those fern plants. Wipe your hands with those."

His word 'hands' brought back a memory. I looked at my right hand. There was a small X in the center of my palm. How can that be? I thought as I dropped my pants. I finished my business, washed my hands with fern fronds.

"Aranck, did you cut my hand?" I said, showing him the cut.

"Of course not. Why did you ask me such a thing?"

"Because in my dream, I saw an Indian dressed in paint. I---."

"Tell me about your dream. Tell me all you remember."

I bent over to pick up my stuff. "Whoa," I said.

"What?" Aranck said.

"I feel dizzy and sick to my stomach."

"Wait here. I will be right back."

He was gone but a few minutes. "Here, chew this, slowly, and swallow the juices. It will make your stomach feel much better."

"It smells like peppermint," I said.

"It is. You have a good nose. We can wait a bit until you feel better."

"No, I want to get going. My mother may change her mind and come up here to take me back. I promise not to be any trouble."

"We will wait until the peppermint begins to take effect. Then we will walk slowly. Along the way, tell me about your dream."

Within a half hour I convinced Aranck I was much better. The sun was climbing, and I was getting nervous that my mother might really change her mind.

When I finished telling him about my dream, he stopped walking and took a long look at me. A smile brightened his face.

"I think you need an Indian name, something besides Bird Hunter. How does Cheveyo sound to you?" He rolled the word with his tongue, "Suh-Vay-Oh."

I said it, and then asked, "what does it mean?"

"It is from the Hopi people and it means Spirit Warrior."

Of course the word 'warrior' immediately clicked with me. "Cheveyo," I said.

"Yes, I like it. Why did you select that name?"

"Good question, Cheveyo. I think it is a good name for you since a warrior visited you during your dream time. He cut the X in your hand, and because you did not cry out or scream Cheveyo fits."

I felt wonderful. *I am wonderful*, I thought, *at least for a while.*

CHAPTER SIX

The first week went by very quickly. During that time, Aranck taught me to look for animal signs, broken branches, nibbled bushes, foot prints, poop, and the smell of pee. Squirrels gave me a problem until he told me to look for nut shells at the bottom of trees. We ate dried venison, fish, and fresh berries we picked along the way. Nights were another adventure.

Once our fire died down, night flies came out—Lightning Bugs. Several landed on my outstretched hand. I accidently squashed one and it left its glow on my skin. An owl hooted in a nearby tree. The night dressed in a gown of sparkling jewels was so clear I was sure I could see forever. Gradually, I identified the major constellations, and as I did, Aranck told me the story behind them. It surprised me that I wasn't scared sleeping out in the deep woods. I had the new hunting knife from Aranck fastened to my belt. When I opened the bag containing my "Indian clothes" I concealed the knife from my parents because I was sure my father would be ticked off.

Breaking the silence, Aranck said, "Tomorrow we begin lessons in plant identification, especially those that are edible."

"How did you learn all of this stuff?" I asked.

"From my father, Mundoo, and he, from his father before him. Because there have been a number of men called Mundoo throughout the history of my gang, I decided to change my name to Aranck."

"Why? Didn't you like your other name?"

Aranck laughed. I heard him get up and move into nearby bushes. He continued talking as if he were still at the camp site.

"I like it fine. I just don't want people to think I have been living for hundreds of years. You probably think that, don't you?"

"No," I replied. Actually, I did feel he must have lived hundreds of years to know all the stuff he does.

"Better go to sleep know. Be sure to cover up. Tonight will be chilly."

"Night," I said, "And thanks for the lessons."

And for being my friend, I thought.

The night passed without incident. I woke up with a real boner. I could hardly get my pants down to piss. I figured with a name like Cheveyo I shouldn't say pee. I made up my mind to talk to Aranck. It was a struggle to get my pants back up.

When I came back to the campsite, Aranck had our morning tea ready. He had made a flatbread, and its smell tantalized my already growing appetite. We finished eating, and I made sure our small fire was completely out. I dug a small hole, shoved the burning embers into it, covered it with dirt, and packed it down.

"So, Cheveyo, you want to talk about sex, particularly having sex with a woman."

It wasn't a question; it was more of a factual statement. Embarrassed, I looked down at my feet.

"It's natural. No need to ever feel embarrassed by what is natural any more than when you have to take a shit. It's a part of life. Back in the States, do you have someone in mind that you would like to have sex with?"

I hesitated and then decided to spill it all out. I sat down, cross-legged.

"Well, there is this girl, named Geraldine, I like. I think she's pretty. I thought for a while, she liked me, but then she started hanging around some of the older guys. It was then I heard some of them talking about screwing her. When I said I didn't believe them, one of the bigger guys told me to go up on the hill behind the school. He'd prove it, he said."

"And did you go up on the hill?"

"Yeah. I saw them doing it."

"And what did you do?"

"I ran from there, went home, and cried, "I said, getting up.

"Do you know why you cried?"

"Yeah." I paused. "Because I wanted to screw her and somebody else was doing it."

Aranck got up, began to pack up our gear. He walked around to me; put his hand on my shoulder.

"Your time will come. Trust me in this. Be patient, my friend."

His calling me friend made me feel better. At least, he did not call me his young friend. And since he said my time would come, I accepted that for now, anyway.

***

I was glad I brought my notebook and a pen with me. There were so many plants and flowers, shrubs, trees, and fruit bearing bushes, I would never remember all of them. He had me smell and taste each plant and I wrote that in my notebook. While we were busy gathering plants, I realized I had my thirteenth birthday. I knew what day we left for the woods and counted the number of nights that had passed. *Strange*, I thought, *I haven't thought about my parents since I left. Wonder if they remembered my birthday.*

I learned about arrowhead, wild lettuce, wood sorrel, sumac, milkweed, Queen Ann's Lace, golden rod, mullein, and Wapato. By the day's end, I was really tired. However, not so tired that I didn't notice uneasiness in Aranck. I thought about asking him if he were okay, but changed my mind. We retired right after sunset. Despite my tiredness, I watched the moon rise. It was a full moon, and its brightness created a wide range of shadows and patches of light. I watched those for a time until sleep closed my eyes.

A fierce snarling growl and a scream woke me. I sat bolt upright, straining to see what was going on as my eyes adjusted to the moonlight. I saw Aranck thrashing around, and then I saw it—a horrible looking animal on top of him. I had never seen such a thing before. It wasn't a bear or a wolf. I didn't know what it was.

I grabbed my bow, placed an arrow, pulled it back, aimed, and let it fly. I prayed I didn't hit Aranck. I heard the arrow hit. Quickly, I pulled another arrow from my quiver, placed it, and shot it at the creature. Again, I heard it hit. Then I heard Aranck.

"Skunk bear. It ripped me pretty good. Build a fire, Cheveyo. Heat your knife. "

I had the fire going and set a good blaze. In its light, I could see Aranck bloodied back. I shoved my knife's blade into the fire. While it was heating, I used Aranck's knife to cut away what was left of his shirt. His back, razor-slashed, oozed blood. I used some of the water to wash the blood away. That didn't help. The slashes were too deep.

"You have to be strong now. Lay the knife blade on each of the cuts. I will tell you when to remove it and move to another. You can do this, Cheveyo."

I put some more wood on the fire to cause a bigger blaze and more light. Blood was oozing from his several wounds. I picked up my knife, laid it flat side down across one of the gashes. The smell of burnt flesh made me sick. His muscles tightened. I swallowed hard, trying not to vomit. Even though it was only a couple of seconds, I felt it was an eternity before he finally he said, next.

By the time I got all the slashes sealed, I was sweating. I began to shake. I felt cold. I placed more wood on the fire. Aranck passed out. I wasn't sure what to do. He stirred. I went over to him. It was then I noticed the teeth marks on his right shoulder. Panic struck hard. What am I to do? How will I find my way back to the cabin? I can't leave him here.

Tears rolled down my face, crossed my lips. Their salty taste jarred me. Aranck had me mark the trail as part of my lessons. Of course, you can get him out of here. Make a sled.

"No sled. I weigh too much for you to pull. Look for a tree branch to make a crutch," Aranck said. His speech was slurred.

He read my thoughts.

"Can you teach me how to read people's thoughts?"

It struck me that was a dumb question to ask, especially with him hurt the way he is.

"You have some bad bite marks on your right shoulder. They are still bleeding. Didn't you mention wood sorrel would stop bleeding?"

"Good memory. Get some sorrel out of our bags, crush it, and add a bit of water to make a paste. Apply that to the bites."

Once I had the sorrel plastered over the bites, I stocked the fire and lay down. Sleep would not come. I heard Aranck moan several times. The day opened its eyes. I got up, walked over to Aranck. I felt his head. He was burning up with fever. Carefully, I removed the remainder of his shirt; I had used to cover him. The claw marks swollen and pus filled made my stomach did a flip-flop.

Infection. What did he say stopped infection?

I searched for my notebook. It was a mess, covered with dirt and crinkled from my stepping on it. I couldn't read my notes. What draws out infection from a wound? Think.

"Wapato," I said aloud "Yes!

I dumped the contents of one bag on the ground. I found the wild potatoes and sliced several into thin pieces. I looked around, found a rock, and slowly crushed the potatoes. I cut a strip from Aranck's shirt. I scooped up the crushed Wapato in my hand, added a little water, stirred it around with my finger and then placed the paste on the deerskin, tied it into a knot, and then laid it next to the fire pit. The coals were still warm. While it warmed I put the other vegetables back into the bag. The rest of the Wapato I set aside.

The backpack made a good pillow of Aranck as I gently rolled him on to his stomach. I got the poultice bag from the fire pit and laid it across three of the worst looking slashes. I dabbed some of the still wet Wapato on the teeth marks. He groaned.

"I am going to look for a crutch and to bring back some more water. I won't be gone long."

Aranck did not reply. *What if he dies while I'm gone?* I shook my head to rid myself of that thought. *He's not going to die. He can't! What would I do?* I moaned.

Once I found a suitable stick for a crutch, I filled the water bag and headed back. The smell of the dead skunk bear assaulted my nose. Something had to be done with its carcass. Aranck was sitting up.

"You look like—"

"Shit. And I feel that way. What have you put on me?"

"Wapato."

"Good choice. You ever skin an animal?"

"No."

"Well, I guess this is as good a time as any to learn. The skunk bear's fur is good for a coat. Its claws will make a fine necklace. See if you can remove your arrows without breaking off their points."

With some effort, I got the arrows out. Next, I cut off its front paws. Rolling it over onto its back, doing as Aranck told me, I made a slit from its throat to its rear. The next part nearly got me, removing its guts. He told me to dig a deep hole. By the time I got that dug, I had my own waterfall of sweat pouring off me. I shoved the guts into the hole and shoveled in one layer of dirt. I severed the head and kicked that into the hole and covered it with dirt.

I stopped. Picked up the poultice that had fallen off Aranck's, back stoked the fire a bit, opened the pouch, poured some more water, stirred that around, and added some more smashed Wapato.

"Better put some more paste on those bites. Isn't there a tea that's supposed to be good for, what did you call it—immune system?"

I filled our one pot with some water and set it on the edge of the hot coals. It would take a while to boil.

"Tonight will be a bad night. My fever is high. You need to rest as soon as you have the skunk bear skinned. Do not become alarmed if I yell out. Be sure to keep the fire going."

I gave him a cup of the hot tea. He sipped that for a few minutes and then gulped the rest. He lay down on his stomach waiting for me to put on the refreshed poultice. I cleaned the bite marks and put on some smashed wild carrots as he suggested. Before eating the dried venison, I cooked a Wapato by placing it at the edge of the fire. I went back to the sunk bear. Removing the skin was slow going. Finally, I was done and I buried the remaining carcass. I packed the dirt down and rolled a large stone on top of that and then, using a bunch of ferns growing nearby to scrub my hands; I was ready to eat.

I sensed something was wrong and turned to look at Aranck. He was running at me with his knife in hand. I rolled out of the way. He lunged at me again, and I grabbed a chunk of wood, squatted low, and swung as hard as I could. He went down with a loud thud.

Scared, no frightened, I waited. He didn't move. *I've killed him*, I thought. Then I remembered the advice the naked Indian gave me: change your perspective and your perception will change. I inched my way around to face him. He was breathing. I reached out, took his hand, and cried.

"Cheveyo," he whispered. "What happened?"

"You went crazy and tried to attack me. I clobbered you with a chunk of wood. I am sorry. I think I may have broken your leg."

"No, it is not broken. You say I attacked you?"

"Yes, you were screaming in a language I didn't understand."

"My god, Cheveyo I didn't hurt you, did I? I am the one who is sorry. I apologize."

Feeling secure, I replied, "No problem. You hungry?"

I poked the fire back to life, laid in a row of Wapato, carrots, and leaks. I added some more corn flower buds to the pan of water and sat that in the center of the fire. After our meal, Aranck told me what to do with the skunk bear's claws. I cut them away from the flesh part of the paws, then put them in our one pot and boiled them until what remaining flesh fell off. Once they cooled down and dried, I packed them in one of the three bags we had with us. Sensing my disgust over using our only pan for the claws,

Aranck said, "Dig up a couple of good handfuls of sand, scrub the pot with that. Use some pressure. When you are done, the pot should not feel greasy."

***

We must have presented a sorry sight to my parents when we emerged a day and a half late. My mother put her hand to her mouth in disbelief.

"What the hell happened? Where have you been?" my father said

"It's not Aranck's fault that a skunk bear attacked him," I said. "It could have got us both."

"Did I ask you?" My father said.

"No." I sensed he wanted to hit me.

Aranck and my father stared at one another.

"Goodness, you do smell something awful. Go get some soap and wash up. And get out of those clothes. Take a clean set with you," my mother said.

That broke the tension.

I went inside, grabbed a bar of Lifebuoy, and some clean clothes. When I came back out, Aranck was leaving.

"See ya, Doc," I yelled.

"What's with the Doc business?" my father asked.

"He's a professor at a college in Maine," I said and hurried down to the lake. I stripped off my deerskins and jumped into the water. Despite the warm days, the lake water was cold. I shivered as I lathered up. I dried myself off, pulled on my clean clothes, and scurried up the bank to the log cabin.

"You had your fill of that Indian?"

My mother put her finger to her lips. I didn't respond.

He gave me a back hand, and I tumbled across the floor. I vowed right then that he would never hit me again without a fight. I was sure I would have a black eye. *Nice birthday present*, I thought.

My mother yelled, "Stop it. Stop it right now. You hear me, George?"

I could not go up to the wigwams or see Aranck for the rest of the summer. Fortunately, it was just a week away, and we would be heading back to the United States. During that time, I washed out my deerskins, making sure to stretch them, or they would shrink. Once they were dry, I rolled them into a bundle and hid them along with my bow, and quiver of arrows. I kept my knife. I strapped to my leg so it would be out of sight. Every night that last week, dreams interrupted my sleep. Dreams of half-naked Indians dancing in circles, a large bird screaming at me, and a skunk bear dancing. It had human legs and arms. I'd wake up sweating. Sometimes, I had my pillow over my head.

CHAPTER SEVEN

I said nothing during our return trip home.

Junior high school had a few interesting developments. Geraldine let me screw her. My size surprised her. I had my first fight at school. I was doing okay, but the gym teacher broke it up. He made us put on boxing gloves, and we went at it until we exhausted ourselves. After school, I caught up with him. His name was Bill.

"You fight good. You want to stop for a coke?"

"Sure. You buying?"

I bought the cokes. Afterwards, I walked the long way home which took us to his house.

"Oops. Guess I had better wait to go in. My mom's got company. She doesn't like me to come in when she has company," Bill said.

"That's my dad's car. Want to see what they are doing? I bet I can tell you," I said.

"What are they doing, Mr. Know-It-All?"

"Screwing."

We snuck into the house. They were in the den. My father was bare-ass naked and pumping up and down on Bill's mom. She had her legs up in the air.

We slipped out of the house and walked a couple of blocks.

"You won't say anything about my mom to the guys at school, will you?" Bill said.

"Not if you don't say anything about my father."

We knuckled our agreement.

Once I got home, I immediately changed my clothes and began my homework. I liked taking French. Algebra was giving me fits. I said nothing during dinner. No one asked me anything either. My father had his double shot of Jack Daniels after dinner. Just after dark, I was looking out my bedroom window. I saw him open the trunk of the car, pull out a bottle, and gulp some of it down. The trunk light shone on the bottle, and I recognized it.

I was sure there was going to be another argument. They were becoming a regular part of the weekly routine. It surprised me that there wasn't one.

The next day when I got home from school my mother told me a package had come for me. It was from Aranck. I tore the wrapping off the package as fast as I could. I finally got it open and inside was a note and a necklace. The skunk bear's claws. They were polished and carefully strung on a piece of rawhide. I looked at the drilled hole in each claw and wondered how he got a knot tied before and after each claw. I showed my gift and note to my mother.

"That's nice dear, but you better put that away so your father doesn't see it. He's not particularly fond of your Indian friend."

I made sure I had picked up all the wrapping paper and took it out to the garbage. I hid the necklace under my mattress. That night, once I was in bed, I pulled it out and looked at it. I mouthed thank you to Aranck and hoped he heard me. *Tomorrow, I will send him a letter*, I thought.

No need. I heard you, and you are very welcome. You are the one who killed the wolverine, Cheveyo. You earned the claws."

When will we talk; I mean really talk?" I whispered.

What bothers you, Spirit Warrior?

"Are you okay? I mean all those cuts and bites."

"They are healed. I asked you a question," Aranck said.

"He's at it again. You know what I mean. Other women. I think he hits my mother, and I think he wants to kill me."

"No, he does not want to kill you. He has problems, and he's not dealing with them very well."

"Problems? What kind of problems?"

"I'm not sure I can explain it to you. It's a thing that sometimes happens to men when they realize their mortality."

"I don't know. I do know this; I keep my knife with me whenever he is around."

"Stop that damn whispering and go to sleep." My father's voice bellowed from across the hall. "That kid drives me nuts."

That ended my talk with Aranck. The next day my father didn't go to work. He and my mother left the house before I went to school. When I came home at the end of the school day, my father told me my mother was in the hospital for another operation.

"She'll be there a month. You need to take hold here. You understand?"

"What's wrong with her?"

"Female business that didn't' get fixed the last time."

It was a very long month. My older brother came with his wife to see my mother. They stayed a couple of hours and then left. They said it was a long drive for them to return to their house— two and a half hours. My other brother stopped by. His wife worked at the hospital. My mother slept in my bedroom and I moved to a back bedroom. Said my father didn't' want to disturb her while she was recuperating. "Besides," she said, "it was closer to the bathroom."

I moved down the hall to the back bedroom, and there the wildest thing happened. I had just finished my homework, turned out the light, and snuggled into my covers. The temperature had dropped to just above zero and the heat took a while to reach the back room. It probably would have been better had I left my door open. Not only did I keep it closed; I locked it.

"Cheveyo, are you awake?"

I opened my eyes and there stood Aranck.

"How did you get in here? Do my parents know you are here?"

I sat up in bed, reached over to turn on the light.

"Don't turn on the light. If you do, you won't be able to see me. I am projecting myself to you. I am still in Maine. The college is closed because of the snow storm."

"How—how do you do this? Teach me how to do that?"

"You can do this. Close your eyes. Think about me. Take five deep breaths. Hold each one as long as you can. Blow out through your mouth, placing your tongue just behind your front teeth. Not too tight. When you blow your breath out your tongue should have a slight vibration. Do you understand? If you do, just nod your head."

I nodded my head up and down so hard it hurt my neck.

"Easy my friend. Relax. Close your eyes. I will count for you.

By five, I felt a slight quiver throughout my body and cold air on my face. I opened my eyes. I couldn't believe what I was seeing.

I was in Aranck's house, in a large room lined with bookshelves packed with books. A fire was burning in a large stone fireplace that rose up from the floor to the top of the ceiling. I looked around. He was sitting in a leather chair.

"Welcome. Your stay will be very brief. You now know you can travel through time. I will let you know when you may try it again. It's a gift from the Spirits. Don't abuse it. You must go back now. When you wake up, you will think all of this was a dream. It is not. Here is something for you to take back with you so you know it is not a dream."

He handed me a single claw from the skunk bear.

I was back in my bed. I reached over and turned on the lamp on my nightstand. I had the mark of a claw in my hand. I pulled back my covers and I found the single claw. I reached under my mattress to see if I had pulled one from the string. I had not.

His voice quietly penetrated my excitement.

"Do not use or attempt to use your ability to travel to spy on your father or friends. It is a very special gift to help others. Violate this rule and you will lose the gift for ever. Do you understand, Cheveyo?"

"Yes," I said.

I rolled over, pulled the blankets up over my head, and went to sleep.

When I woke up in the morning, I checked to see if the claw was under my pillow. It was.

Unlike some of my classmates, I seem to grow over the winter months. I grew a couple of inches in height and put on ten pounds. My PE teacher helped me with weights, so I was bulking up. I took to doing the cooking because my mother was still not completely over her surgery. A hired girl came in to do the house cleaning and laundry once a week. We didn't call her a maid. No one in town who had hired girls called them maids. None of them wore uniforms like the maids in the movies.

My mother was at her doctor's and my father, of course, was at his office, and I had a day off from school. It was the opening of hunting season and school always closed for that. I had fixed myself some lunch and decided I should offer some to Sharon.

As we sat at the kitchen table, eating tomato soup and peanut butter sandwiches, Sharon began rubbing my leg. I spread my legs apart. It wasn't long before she was rubbing something else. She began kissing me and I kissed her back and felt her breasts. I let my hand work its way down her thigh and up under her dress. She didn't have any underwear on. She pulled my zipper down and had me out, playing me. I wiggled around, got my pants undone and pulled them down. She straddled me and rode me up and down. Geraldine didn't do that.

I stood up with her legs wrapped around me and laid her down on the kitchen floor. She raised her legs up and around my neck. As I pumped away, she began groaning. It scared me and until she said, "Don't stop. You're wonderful." And I guess I was. That was my second time having sex. It wouldn't be my last with Sharon. I learned a lot about positions. She made the winter months easier to live with. Especially since my father was now having serious bouts of drunkenness.

One day in January when I got home from school, I noticed two suitcases sitting in the entryway. I heard parents' voices. I hollered "Hello."

"We'll be down in a minute." It was my mother.

I headed out to the kitchen for an after-school snack. My mother's fur coat lay on a chair along with her pocketbook. On the next, was my father's coat and hat.

"You father has to go to a sanitarium. It will be very late when I get back."

"What's wrong with him?" I asked.

"Something's wrong with his lungs. They want to run more tests. I will call you from there when I am ready to come home."

My father came into the kitchen, put his coat on and then his hat. He was pale.

"I'm ready. Let's go." Turning to me, he said, "You behave yourself. You hear?"

On their way out, the back door my mother stopped and said, "Oh dear, I nearly forgot. Sharon will be here shortly. She'll spend the night, in case I have to stay over."

A wave of excitement flowed over me as I followed them out the door and waved at them. No sooner had their car disappeared out our long tree-lined driveway, Sharon drove in. We immediately went to bed. This time she took me in her mouth.

Nine o'clock came, and my mother had not returned. At 9:30, the telephone jangled. She would not be coming home until tomorrow. The snow was accumulating, and she didn't want to drive in that at night. She wanted to talk to Sharon. When they finished talking, Sharon hung up.

"What did my mother want?"

63

"She wants me to make sure you take your shower before you go to bed, and you are not to stay up much longer. Ten o'clock is your bed time. Race you to the shower," she giggled as she grabbed my dick.

My mother arrived the next day around noon. My father would be staying at the sanitarium for a couple of months, maybe longer. I watched her hand Sharon a twenty.

"Sharon dear, would it be possible for you to move in here for the next couple of months? I'll pay you."

I nearly shit my pants. I couldn't believe Sharon would be sleeping right next door to me.

"Well, I suppose I could. I'll have to go home and get my things and tell my folks I'll be working here for a while."

"Wonderful," my mother said. Then to me, she said, "You go with her and help her get her things. I am beat. The roads were a mess. I will be glad when this winter is over."

"What time do you want to go," I said to Sharon.

"Right after I fix your mother a cup of hot tea. I think she could stand a shot of rum in it. You got any."

We did. Once my mother had finished her tea, she curled up on the davenport and went to sleep. Sharon and I left. She knew a back road, and we stopped there for a while. She said I fit her good.

***

Things were pretty quiet with my father away. My mother went to visit him once every week. While she was gone Sharon, and I popped into bed. Only once did my mother ask me to go with her. My father said little to either of us. He looked thin and older. He coughed a lot.

I noticed that Sharon was gaining weight. And so did my mother. She offered some of her old dresses because those Sharon had were too small. One day when I got home from school, Sharon was gone.

64

"Sharon had to leave, dear. Her aunt, who lives on the other side of the state, had a bad fall and Sharon has gone to take care of her. I have to go and get your father. The hospital is releasing him. We'll be home tomorrow. I'll call you before we leave there."

"Did Sharon say anything before she left? I didn't know she had any relatives other than her folks. Did she say when she will be back?"

"No dear. Well, yes—yes—she did. She said she enjoyed working for us."

My parents arrived home mid-afternoon, and my father immediately went to bed. He was really thin. During the next month, he seldom came downstairs. In my mind, I was sure he was dying. However, as April came around, he began to look better, and I heard him talking to my mother about returning to the Baskatong. He thought it would be good for him to be on the water. My middle brother showed up and helped him load the trailer and the boat. The weeks my father was in the sanitarium, he never came to see us. I understood from their conversation that he had gone to see my father. No one mentioned that to me. It didn't take me long to figure out why he was there to help. His five-year-old son was going with us. Just great, I thought. I will end up babysitting, and I won't have much time with Aranck. I need to try to contact him.

One part of their conversation really caught my attention. I heard my brother say he heard our hired girl got herself knocked up and her folks had sent her out of town until the kid was born.

I ran into the house and ran up the stairs to my room. I felt sick on my stomach.

CHAPTER EIGHT

My father was really into showing my nephew how to fasten a lure on a line, how to cast and to reel in a fish. He used a heavy sinker to play the role of a fish. He purchased a new life jacket for Bradley. My mother altered the jacket so it would fit. My father insisted Bradley try it on. Satisfied with the fit, my father said to my mother, "Did you stock in some extra candy?"

"Yes. I got the kind he likes."

"What about soda pop?"

"Yes, I got an extra carton of Cola."

"Did you bake those chocolate cookies he likes? Better make several dozens."

"I already have. Don't worry so much."

"What about clothes. Did his father bring over warm clothes? Early spring can be chilly."

"Oh, for heaven's sake George, stop fussing. You're driving me nuts."

"Well, I want his first trip to the Baskatong to be perfect."

Man, guess I know where I stand. Maybe they aren't going to take me. Can't leave me with Sharon. She's gone, I thought. So, he's going. Make the best of it. To that end, I said to my mother, "Wonder if Bradley would like to have a couple of my old coloring books to take. I think I have a couple, unused. They are in a box up and in the attic. Do you want me to get them?"

"Good idea. He'll need to be entertained. Unlike you," she paused. "Of course you were two years older when we first took you there. Two years makes a difference. Can you dig out some of your games and toys? Pack them in this bag. Leave a coloring book out for the car."

I found the coloring books, puzzles, and some toy trucks. I even found a box of unopened crayons. I kept those and one coloring book out for the car. I handed the bag to my mother.

"Have you got your things packed? Be sure to put in enough underwear and socks. We're going to be there an extra month."

"I will."

Outside, I found my father with Bradley. They were playing catch.

"You want me to get down one of my fishing poles for Bradley?" I said.

"No. I got him a new reel and pole."

"Okay," I said and went back into the house.

It was while I was in the kitchen that I spotted a new tackle box. It had Bradley's name on it. After dinner, my father went into his office. My mother finished packing clothes and food. I got out a map of the United States and Canada. Bradley and I were lying on the floor as I traced where we were going.

"It's a long way," I said. "Are you excited?"

"Yes. It's fun being with you," Bradley said and put his arm around me.

My father walked in.

"Come here, Bradley. Come over to grandpa."

"In a minute. I'm looking at a map," Bradley said.

"Come over here, now"

"Better go," I whispered.

I got up and went to my room. I tried to send a thought to Aranck. I didn't get a response. Next, I tried to visualize him. Again, I detected nothing. Sleep, fitful as it was, didn't bring any messages. Four AM finally came and we had breakfast, loaded ourselves into the car. I carried Bradley to the car. He was still in his PJs. I put him in the back seat.

"Put Bradley up front with your mother and me," my father said.

I did as I was told.

"And pass up the blanket. You don't need it," my father said.

I passed it over the back of the seat. My mother took it and wrapped it around Bradley.

Finally, we were underway.

Fourteen hours later we arrived at our log cabin. It was dark. A quick check showed no winter damage or leaks. I built a fire in the stove and filled the kerosene lamp with oil and lit it. My father went to bed. Bradley was sound asleep and covered up on my bed. Hmm, I wonder if he's doing to sleep with me. I don't think my father packed a fold up army cot. I got down my bow and quiver of arrows and my deerskin clothes. I tried to unfold the clothes. They were stiff. Then I realized I wouldn't be able to wear them because I had grown. I helped my mother bring in the bags of clothing, boxes of canned and dried foods. This time, I noticed there was a whole case of Jack Daniels. My father would unload the fishing gear, boat, and motor.

I took a flashlight and went behind the cabin to see if my canoe and rowboat were still there. They were and appeared to be in good shape. I hung my bow and quiver on a peg just above my canoe. I laid my deerskin clothes over the back of the canoe. Tomorrow I would bury them. I tried to see if the wigwams were there, but it was too dark for me to make sure. Hopefully, Aranck will be there.

The smell of cooking food woke my father and he, in turn, woke Bradley. Vegetable beef soup and crackers tasted wonderful. My father downed his whiskey and went back to bed. The night passed without incident. And yes Bradley became my bunk buddy. Actually, he's a pretty good kid. A woodpecker woke me with its loud pecking on our metal stovepipe. I looked at my wristwatch. Six AM. The sun will soon be showing itself. I can see if the Indians are back. I slide out of the bunk, slipped on my clothes except for my shoes. I carried those and my socks with me as I carefully opened the only door to the cabin.

A blast of chilly air hit me. I shivered as sat down on the single step and put my socks and shoes on. A heavy mist covered the lake, spooky like. A loon gave its crazy laugh as it prepared to take flight. I heard the whir of its large wings. I started to walk up to where the Indians usually pitched their wigwams when I saw the sun peeking up on the horizon. Spellbound, I watched it get brighter and the sky exploded into brilliant golden yellows and reds. Little Baskatong was calm, and my quartz mountain glistened in its mirror. Despite my chopped-liver-family status, I felt wonderfully alive. And just for a moment, I thought my soul took flight with the loon.

Hurrying along the overgrown path, I strained to see the wigwams. "Something is running and it's big," I said.

I stopped. Pulled my ever-present knife from its sheath. I stood very still, struggling to calm my heart. It was a bull moose and he was in a hurry. He was so close I felt his body heat. I waited thinking there might be others. Then it hit me. Wolves! My god. I froze. Nothing. I continued to wait. Still nothing. Wonder what spooked that big guy. I got to where I could get a clear view. No wigwams. My heart sank.

I hurried back to the cabin. I sat down on the stoop and fought back the tears. I heard the door open. It was my father.

"Give me a hand getting the boat down."

We got the boat and other gear unloaded. I helped him drag the Dundee down to the lake. He put the motor on the rear end, made sure it was secure, filled its tank with gas, and then started it. It kicked in on the first pull of the rope.

"Breakfast is nearly ready so don't go off. Are you taking Bradley with you?"

"He awake?" my father said.

"Yes. Now come up."

"Am I to come, too?" I asked.

"What?" My father said.

"Am I to come up to breakfast or do you want me to stay with the boat?"

"Come along. Bradley is going out with me. You help your mother."

There was a big fuss over what clothes Bradley should wear and of course, the life jacket. I felt sorry for him. He wasn't allowed to walk down to the boat. My father carried him. I watched as he pushed the boat away and started the motor. Back inside, I asked my mother what she wanted me to do. I should have known.

"Go get some water," she said.

I took my bow and quiver of arrows with me. I remember all too well the skunk bear. The spring growth had begun even if there was still some ice left on the lake. I was glad most of the bugs had not emerged from their winter. I filled the bucket and now because I am bigger I no longer sloshed it.

As I left the forested area, I heard them. Then I saw them. The Indians are back. I sat my bucket of water down and ran to them. I looked for Aranck. He was not with them. I spotted his sister, Chepi. I waited for her to recognize me. She didn't seem to know who I was.

"I am Cheveyo. I was here last year."

"You have grown much. How are you and your parents?"

"I am fine and they are fine. Thank you for asking. Is Aranck with you? I have not seen him."

"He has not arrived. He is teaching."

I thanked Chepi and told her I would bring my nephew for her to see. Had I been thinking clearly I would have realized Aranck was only here at the end of May. I never knew how he got here. Or the others as a matter of fact. There was no car and no horses.

Things went smoother than I had figured they would. Bradley loved being in the boat, and my father loved having him there. My mother, if she didn't go with them, spent her time knitting and reading. When I told her, the Indians were back she seemed pleased.

I spent my time in the woods, practicing my herb and edible plant hunt. I practiced building a fire without matches and using vines to make rope. I didn't hunt for animals. Our second week there a plane swooped down, low flying over the lake and right at our cabin. It was so low I could see the pilot but not clear enough to know who it was. He banked to the right, came out over the lake, and then right at the cabin again. He waved this time and threw something out of the window. It landed within a few yards of where I was standing. I ran to the spot. It appeared to be a military canvas bag. My mother had caught up with me by that time.

"Be careful it might be a bomb or something."

I gave it a shove with my foot, and it rolled over. There in bold white letters was my name. I whipped out my knife, slit the heavy string holding it together, and pulled it apart. Inside was a new set of deerskin clothes for me, pants, shirt, and moccasins. I held the pants up to my waste and then the shirt to my chest. Perfect fit. I sat down on the ground, sat on a bunch of sand spurs. I moved real quick. The moccasins were also a perfect fit. There wasn't a note in the canvas bag. But, I knew they were from Aranck.

I gathered up the bag, clothes and moccasins and headed back to the cabin. Inside, I tried on the pants and shirt. There was a short fringe along the bottom of the shirt, open neck with rawhide laces. I stuffed my hands in the pockets and that's when I discovered the envelope.

"What's that?" mother asked.

"It's a letter from Aranck."

I read the letter and then gave it to my mother to read.

"Well, goodness. Isn't this nice. He remembered you have a birthday this summer. I wouldn't talk about him too much in front of your father. He doesn't seem to like him."

"Yeah, I know. And he doesn't seem to like me very much either."

I hadn't meant to say that, but there it was. Out in the open.

"What an awful thing to say. Don't ---,"

"It's true and you know it. I am just excess baggage."

"That's not true. It's just hard for him to understand you."

"He doesn't have that problem with Bradley. Or haven't you noticed? He seldom speaks to me, and he never calls me by my name."

"You sound like your jealous and of your own nephew. I am ashamed of you. Don't let me ever hear you talk this way again. You understand."

I looked down at my feet and nodded my head. It would have been better had they never had me, I thought.

I picked up my canoe, carried it to the launch area the Indians used, slid it in the water, stepped in, and headed for my white rock mountain. Wonder if I could live here, I thought as I dragged the canoe under some bushes. I decided to climb all the way to the top, something I had not done before. As I began my climb, I noticed little indentations in the rock and realized they were for climbing.

At the top, I stood up and looked out across the expanse of sky and water to our cabin. A bit to the north, I could see the three wigwams; the same number as last year.

A flash, a jagged sizzling ring of lightning danced its way around me. Too terrified to move or scream I remained frozen in place. The hair on my head and arms stood up as a tingling sensation shot up through my legs. Maybe I am getting my wish after all. Do I really want to be unborn? My arms, on their own, spread out above my head and my left hand pointed left and my right pointed right like a preacher does when he's praying.

I found my voice and screamed, "What do you want of me?"

"Your soul!"

"Help yourself."

"I already have," boomed the voice.

"I guess that's it for me then. Will the birds eat what's left of me?"

Roaring laughter filled my ears. The vibrations sent shock waves through me. I nearly fell over.

"What's so damn funny?"

"You are not dying. You are that you are. Many things will come to you."

"Things? What kind of things?" I said, feeling bolder.

"They are not to be named. They are gifts. Use them wisely."

A huge clap of thunder rolled across the sky. I felt the island shake. I sat down before I was knocked down. For several minutes, I sat very still.

My skin on my feet and legs felt hot. I stood up, dropped my pants to check my legs. No burn marks. I checked my feet and found no sign of burns. Even my hands felt warm. I definitely changed my mind about living here and climbed down from my lofty perch, pulled my canoe out from the underbrush, and headed back to the cabin. I swung out far and then into the launch site and pulled my canoe up on the shore with the other canoes. I stopped dead in my tracks. There, painted on the front of my canoe was a bald eagle and a bolt of lightning clutched in its talons.

My mother said nothing more about expressing my feelings of being excess baggage. I am glad I didn't say I heard her and my father arguing over the fact that I was not planned and was unwanted. That brought a pang. I wonder if my child has been born and if it's a girl or boy. I wish Aranck was here. Maybe next week he will arrive.

CHAPTER NINE

My parents and Bradley went fishing this morning. They did not ask me to go. I decided to go on my own. I selected two lures from my tackle box. A front spinner and a rear spinner. I was careful in laying the fishing pole in my canoe. I paddled to the north end of my island. Dropped a line and let the canoe drift. I had a hit. I worked the lure just enough to tease. I waited. Another bump and this time I yanked hard to set the hook. It broke water. I had a Great Northern and by the looks, a large one. It immediately tried to dive into deep water and in doing so it spun my canoe around. I secured my pole, grabbed a paddle, and straightened the boat. I then began the slow process of reeling him in. I grabbed it just behind the gills and pulled it in. I removed the lure, and then cleaned the fish, rinsing it in the lake.

I returned to shore, scaled the fish, and rinsed it again. At the cabin, I built a small fire in a sand pit, wrapped the fish in wet juniper branches containing berries, and waited for the fire to turn to hot coals. I laid the fish in the center of the fire and spread a few of the hot coals on top.

So occupied with my cooking I didn't notice my parents' return. Bradley made the announcement by running over to me. He wrapped his arms around my shoulders.

"What are you cooking? Smells good."

"A fish. Did you catch any?"

"No. Grandpa and grandma didn't either. Can I have some fish?"

"Sure, when it's done."

My father came over then.

"Bradley, come away from that fire. Why did you let him get close to that fire? You know better than that. Put it out."

"I'm cooking a fish I caught. It will be done soon," I said.

"I don't give a rat's ass what you are cooking. Put that fire out and do it now."

"How long before the fish is done?" my mother said. "It smells wonderful. Don't you think so, George?"

"Just make sure that fire is out."

He stomped off and slammed the screen door as he went inside.

"You probably shouldn't have got that fish. You know how your father prides himself on being a fisherman. Anyway, when it's done, bring it in. I'll open some canned vegetables to go with it."

I didn't bother to tell them I had fresh vegetables cooking along the fire's edge. I lost my appetite. I figured the fish was done, pulled it off the hot coals, removed the juniper, placed the fish on a turned over cake pan. I placed the vegetables around the fish and then put the fire out by shoveling dirt from the fire pit over the remaining coals. I then patted it down. I took the food into the house, sat it on the table and left.

"Where are you going? Aren't you going to eat?" mother said.

I didn't answer. I took off running. I don't know how long I ran or exactly where I was on Little Baskatong. Nothing looked familiar to me. I felt the hair on the back of my neck stand up. I was lost. The sun was setting. I would be dark soon. I fought the urge to panic. Guess he's right. I am a mess-up. What a jerk. I didn't mark out a trail.

I gathered up some dry grass, twigs, and some larger pieces of wood. I used a pointed stick to dig a fire pit. I piled the dirt around the pit to create a shelter. Using my knife, I cut some cedar bows, enough to make a bed. I looked for an oak tree. Found one close in and climbed up part way. I found a reasonably straight branch, cut it off, and let it drop to the ground. On the ground, I stripped off the leaves and small branches. Once I had one end sharpened to a point, I had myself a spear. It was still light enough for me to gather a few edible berries and other plants. I lit the fire by rubbing two sticks together and blowing on it to create a small flame. The Small pieces of dry grass worked great as my tinder. It caught, and I added a few small twigs. They caught, and I added some larger pieces. I ate the berries and leafy plants. Mosquitoes could be bad this time of year, so I placed two small branches of cedar on my fire to create smoke.

I gathered up several cedar branches, loosely wove them into a blanket. The rest I spread out on the ground near the fire, but not so close to catch on fire. I added a couple more pieces of wood to keep the fire going and then curled up under my cedar blanket. I made sure I had my knife and spear close by.

The sound of a low flying plane woke me. The sun was up. Birds fluttered in nearby shrubs. I dug a hole and relived myself. I had remembered fern leaves for TP. I covered the hole. I walked toward the water to get a drink and to see if I could spear a fish. I pushed my way through some thick underbrush and there glistening in the morning sunlight was a seaplane. A man was climbing down from the cockpit. His back was to me so I couldn't see who it was. He opened a compartment along the side of the plane, reached in and pulled out a large duffle bag, then a second and third. He turned and when he did I yelled at the top of my voice.

"Aranck!"

"Who calls my name?"

"Cheveyo," I hollered.

He waded ashore, tossed a bag to me, went back, and retrieved the other two.

"What are you doing here? You are a long way from your cabin. Do your parents know you are here?"

"It's a long story. Right now, I am lost. I forgot to mark the trail."

When we got to my campsite Aranck stopped. A smile brightened his face. He placed his hand on my shoulder.

"You have done well and you have grown. I sense you have much to tell me. We can talk once we get this gear on a sled. It's just the other side of the plane. You fetch that while I unload the rest of the stuff I bought with me."

The sled, two long poles with animal skins stretched over it, was under some bushes. I met him at the plane and helped load two boxes and together we pulled it to my camp and loaded the duffle bags. We made some birch bark tea flavored with dried lemon leaves. It did not quiet my stomach.

"Have you eaten? If not, we will eat before we leave."

I shook my head. Aranck got up from his squat and began walking around the area, stopping here and there to gather some vegetation or to dig something out of the ground. In no time, he had a breakfast. While we ate, I told him about Sharon, catching my father with my friend's mother, and about the blow up back at the cabin.

"I don't understand. Even if they didn't want me, they could at least be nice. God, you should see how my father carries on with Bradley."

"Who's Bradley?"

"He's my five-year-old nephew. My parents brought him with us for the summer. He's a neat little guy. My mother claims I'm jealous. I'm not, honest."

Tears flowed. The more I tried to stop crying, the more I cried. During my crying binge, Aranck said nothing. Finally, the tears dried up. I vowed I would never cry in front of him again.

"Sorry. I didn't mean to lay all this crap on you. So flying in is how you get here."

"Do not feel guilty about showing your emotions. You have revealed much about what kind of man you are. I can talk to your parents if you like."

"No! My father doesn't like you. They would forbid me seeing you. I think I would rather die."

He stood up, picked up one of the sled's poles, and indicated that I should do the same. I was glad to have something physical to do. We had walked about three miles when I realized I had not told him about the lightning on the quartz mountain.

Aranck stopped. Turned and looked at me.

"Did it leave any marks on you?"

"Well, I looked at my feet and hands. Nothing more."

"Would you mind removing your shirt?"

I removed my shirt. He whistled.

"What?" I said trying to look at my upper arm.

"You have been marked. There is an eagle's talon holding lightning. You, my friend, are a very special person. The Spirits have chosen you and you will do wondrous things. I am honored to be in your presence."

"You're just saying that to make me feel better," I said, hoping that it was true.

"Let's put it to a test. You game?"

"Sure. What should I do?"

"Well, we know we can transfer our thoughts and we can visualize each other."

"Can I visualize Sharon?"

"I don't think that would be a good idea. You need to let that go. Hold out your arms from your sides, straight out, and squat on the ground. I will join you but not with my arms out."

I did as he said. I heard a whistle, and then, the flutter of wings. I nearly fell over as an eagle landed on my right arm. I looked at it and it opened its mouth. I understood what it was saying. "Thank you," I said and it flew away.

"Did you see it?" My arm felt sticky.

"Yes, a bald eagle. You are much honored. Did you understand what it said?"

"Yes. It told me it was my spirit guide and it would always be with me."

"Uh huh. So, it is true. You are chosen."

"Aranck, I am sorry for not saying thank you for the new clothes. How did you know my size?"

"I guessed when we did the visual. They fit good."

CHAPTER TEN

An hour later we arrived at the wigwams. I worked my way back to our cabin, coming up from my boulder. My mother was on the stoop. She looked like she had been crying.

"Where have you been? I've been worried sick. Your father is ill. I think we need to pack and go home."

"Is he drunk?"

What a nasty thing to say about your father. I swear I don't understand you either."

"Mom, you know very well he has been hitting the bottle. It doesn't help to pretend it isn't so. If he's really ill, let me go and get Aranck. Remember, he's a medicine man."

"Oh dear, I don't know. He is having such a difficult time to breathe."

"I'll be back," I said and took off on a run.

Aranck surprised me when he told me to heal my father myself. However, I convinced him he should come back with me.

"Besides," I said, "He won't dislike you so much if you make him better and maybe he won't object to my visiting you."

Aranck gathered up a few things and a leather bag decorated with porcupine quills and beads.

"Medicine bag," he said. "Bring that small duffle bag. Thanks.

We broke into an easy trot. On the way, neither of us spoke. My mother was waiting on the stoop.

"Thank you for coming. I don't know what to do." She held his outstretched hand.

Aranck took his time looking at my father whose raspy breathing was irregular. Even I could see that. Next, he placed his hands just above my father's bare chest. They hovered there and slowly began to move around, stopping and then continuing. Aranck's hands began to tremble, slow at first, gradually increasing in speed until they were nearly invisible.

"I need a cup of hot water, Cheveyo. Can you get that for me?"

"I'll get it," my mother said.

She brought the hot water; Aranck opened his medicine bag, pulled out a smaller leather bag, and emptied its contents into the water. It turned to a yellow thick paste.

"Mustard. I need a heated towel or cloth to make a poultice."

My mother heated a towel over the wood-burning stove and brought it to Aranck. We both watched him lay the paste in the towel, fold it over, and place in on my father's chest. He covered him with the blanket. He reached over, opened the bag I had brought in. My eyes nearly popped out of my head. It was the wolverine's fur. He placed that on top of my father.

Speaking to my mother, he said, "This is the skin of the skunk bear your son killed to save my life."

He pulled his shirt off and showed my mother his scared back.

"Oh my god," my mother said, holding her hand to her mouth.

"Had your son not shot true I would be dead. I owe him my life. He is a brave man. Few survive an attack by a wolverine."

"I, we had no idea. My goodness. What is it, you call my son?"

"Cheveyo. It's Hopi, and it means spirit warrior. And that he is."

We waited four long hours. During that time, we heard my father groan. Aranck changed the poultice every hour on the hour. Around three o'clock my father sat up and looked around.

"Where's Bradley?"

"I'm here, grandpa."

"Hello, George. How are you feeling?" Aranck said.

My father blinked, trying to focus. "Aranck?"

"Yes. You had a high fever. I want to give you something to drink. It will help you."

My father did not respond. He lay back down, closed his eyes. I went outside, and Bradley followed me. He was really worried. We sat down on the stoop.

"Aranck will make your grandpa well," I said.

"I hope so. Tony, can I ask you a question?"

"Sure. What do you want to know?"

"Why doesn't grandpa like you?"

I nearly shit my pants. I didn't know what to say or do.

"What an odd question." It was my mother. "Of course your grandfather likes Tony. What in the world made you think of that?"

"Well, he never talks to him like he does me, and he doesn't take him fishing with us."

"He knows I like to go fishing in my canoe the Indians made for me, so he doesn't ask me to go," I said.

The look of relief on my mother's face said it all. I have heard her say 'out of the mouths of babes comes the truth.' I felt vindicated. I struggled not to say to her, see I told you so. The three of us went back inside. Aranck asked for some whiskey. My mother got a glass and poured it a quarter full.

"Fill it half way," Aranck said.

Once he was satisfied as to the amount, he accepted the glass but instead of drinking the whiskey, he began to add things from his medicine bag.

As he stirred the contents around, he said, "The whiskey will help him sweat, the herbs I added will help him fight the infection in his lungs. I would like to add this to hot water. May I?" He nodded toward the teakettle sitting on the stove. "And do you have sugar or honey?"

"Yes, both. You are making what I call a hot toddy."

"Correct."

I thought she and Aranck looked at each other a bit long and then I was sure she smiled at him. There was a slight flush to her face. I had never noticed how they acted toward one another before. Anyway, my father downed the drink, wiped his hand across his mouth, and then lay back down. My mother covered him with the wolverine robe.

"It's late afternoon and I haven't given Bradley his lunch. Will you stay and eat with us?"

"Cheveyo and I have some hunting to do. Feed the boy and yourself. We'll have some fresh meat when we come back." Turning to me he said, "You got your bow and quiver of arrows?"

"Yes."

In my excitement, I nearly ran through the screen door. I flung the door open and raced around to the back of the cabin where I had them stored. Coming around the corner to the front of the cabin, I heard my mother say, "So you are a college professor now."

I thought that was odd since I had told her he was a professor and why 'now'.

"Yes," Aranck said.

"I had forgotten that. What college did you say?"

"A college in Maine. I see you are ready, Cheveyo."

I waved good-bye as we took off at an easy trot. About an hour out, Aranck held up his hand, put a finger to his lips. I watched him steady his breathing and I did the same thing. He signaled we should move very quietly northward. He had explained where I should aim the arrow if we came upon a deer. We circled and came upon three feeding deer. One was a six-point buck. I selected an arrow from my quiver, placed it, aimed, and let it fly. Two of the deer scattered. The buck bolted, ran a short distance, and collapsed. We would have venison steaks for dinner.

"Aranck, can I give one of the hind quarters to your family? What will we do with all of this meat?"

"It would be nice if you gave meat to my sister and the others. We will dry the meat and make it into jerky. The skin will make a nice coat for you. Back at the cabin I again built a fire. The steaks slowly cooked over an open fire along with some wild vegetables. My father ate a small piece of the steak and a couple of the vegetables. As for me, I ate two steaks and a second helping of vegetables.

After dinner, I asked Bradley if he would like to go on a canoe ride. He was excited. The sunset was unusually colorful with lots of bright reds. My mother called it a blood sky. We were gone about forty minutes. As I pulled the canoe on the bank and turned it over, my father met me. He was screaming and shaking his fists at me.

"You stupid jerk. That's exactly what you are, a jerk. Taking that little boy out in that canoe. He could have fallen overboard."

He pulled back his arm to hit me.

"Stop it! Stop it, grandpa. Don't hurt Tony."

My hand felt for my knife. *Just let him hit me, and I will slice him good*, I thought.

"Mind your own business, Bradley. I'm going to teach him a lesson he won't forget."

He grabbed me by the shirt collar and pulled back his fist to hit me. I looked directly at him. He had a stricken look on his face. He let go of my shirt, dropped his fist, and collapsed.

Bradley screamed.

My mother and Aranck came running. Seeing my father on the ground, she bent down, looked up at me.

"What have you done? Oh, my god, is he dead?"

"Tony didn't do anything. Grandpa tried to hit Tony. He's a bad man. I don't like him anymore."

Tears were flowing down my mother's ashen face. Aranck bent down and gently removed her from my father. He held her for a moment and then passed his hand over my father's face. He opened his eyes.

"What happened?"

"You fainted," I lied.

I heard Aranck's voice in my head. He was asking me if I had decked my father. I told I did not. A loud call from an eagle as it took flight from a nearby tree.

"Ah, your spirit guide protected you. You are very blessed."

We helped my father back to the cabin and put him to bed. I fixed him the rest of the hot toddy and took it to him.

"Thanks," he said

"No problem."

***

My lessons, and that's what I now called them, with Aranck continued throughout the summer. I learned how to make a lean-to shelter, to set snare traps, and gather moisture from foliage. Aranck and I had a camp out and included Bradley. I was surprised on my fourteenth birthday with a cake and a card from my parents and Bradley. There was a hundred-dollar bill inside. Aranck took me for a ride in his plane. Even let me fly it for a short time. Physically, I had grown another inch, and I felt other changes taking place in me. My hearing became more acute, and I began to see things in the dark—energy radiating from trees, shrubs, and animals. One thing may help explain my father's aggressive behavior. He had stopped smoking. By the end of our second month on the lake, he had mellowed somewhat and as a consequence, things between us had neutralized.

CHAPTER ELEVEN

Freshman year in high school brought a new round of experiences. My height bought me a place on the basketball team. Using the training hunting with a bow gave me; I soon set a record of dunked baskets. The seniors, older and only a tad bigger than me, did not give me any grief. In addition to being a good team player, I had something else that held them in awe—a certain part of my anatomy was bigger than most of theirs. The word got out among the senior girls and a couple of them actually asked me to drop my pants. I did for one. She dropped hers. We were at her folks' camp. Man, she sure had large tits. I had a three pack of rubbers the coach had given me. We went through the pack.

My father did not take up smoking again. His drinking bouts now seemed to be the last weekend of the month. I'm not sure how my mother accomplished it, but she seemed to be able to contain him. Once he went into a crying jag, babbling something about wasted lives.

The first week of December was mild. Temperatures went to freezing only twice. Light snow covered the ground. Chains were put on the Buick. The week before Christmas was another story. A howling blizzard Christmas Eve brought more snow and high winds. Snapping trees and exploding transformers made the town look like a war zone. As I looked out our living room window, a snowplow worked its way up our street. Within a few minutes, a car crept along the road. A large crack filled the air. It sounded like a shot from a high-powered rifle. A tree came down right on top of that car. A second car swerved and ended up in a ditch and a third came to rest in our front yard.

I bolted out the front door. Stopped at the car in our yard to see if anyone was hurt. None were. I went to the car with the tree on its roof. A woman was slumped over the steering wheel. I pulled on the door. It wouldn't give. The smell of gasoline filled the air. I was sure the car would catch fire. I ran back into the house, found a hammer, and used it to smash the car window. As I did the car burst into flames. I pulled the lock latch up, yanked open the door, grabbed the lone driver, and pulled her out, slung her over my shoulder, and rushed her to our front porch. As I sat her down, I realized it was Sharon.

My mother and father were on the porch by then.

"It's Sharon," I said.

"Bring her in. George, go see about that other car. And be careful!"

We both went. No apparent serious injuries. Two people were just shaken up. We had them come into the house while we called for a wrecker and the police. The driver of the car in our yard spoke to my father and mother.

"That's one hell of a brave kid you got there. He saved the woman's life."

"He did what anyone of us would have done," my father said.

"Where's Sharon?" I asked.

"I helped her upstairs. She's in your old room. Dr. Brown is on his way. It will take him a while to get here. The roads are bad."

"What's wrong with her?"

"She's got a nasty head gash and feels dizzy. It might be a concussion."

I took the steps three at a time. I didn't bother to knock.

Her pale face and blue lips scared me. I didn't notice any breathing, so I leaned over and put my ear to her mouth. She was barely breathing. I put my hands on her head. They got hot and turned red. They hurt but for some reason, I did not remove them. I felt I was experiencing the pain Sharon was feeling. She opened her eyes.

"Don't try to speak. You have been in a car accident and hurt your head. Doc Brown is on his way."

"I feel fine. Honest. Your hands felt so warm, wonderfully warm. I have to tell you something before anyone else comes in."

"I know about our baby," I whispered. "What happened to him or her?"

"A boy. I had to give him up for adoption. There just was no way I could keep him. And you were too young to marry me and couldn't support us."

Tears tumbled.

"I understand. It's just I wish I knew. You know, I could have been there or something."

I felt the urge and the heat building somewhere other than in my hands.

"You have really grown up. Handsome, too. I need to call my parents and tell them I wrecked their car."

"You didn't wreck your car. A tree got you. I'll call your folks and tell them"

"There you are. I wondered where you had gotten yourself off to. Have you been pestering Sharon?" mother said.

"He healed me. He put his hands on my head and healed me."

"What on earth are you talking about, dear?"

"Do you see any gash in my head?" Sharon said.

My mother turned on another nightstand lamp, leaned over, and parted Sharon's still bloodied hair. She gasped.

"You are right there is no cut. But there is all that blood, and I saw how deep that cut was."

"Could you give me a wash cloth and some warm water? I'd like to get this blood cleaned up," Sharon said.

"I'll get it," I said.

"Don't go being a pest. Get a pan from the kitchen and put some warm water in it. I'll get a wash cloth and towel."

"He's not a pest, Mrs. Wells. I'd like him to stay for a while if you don't mind."

"Alright dear, but don't let him talk your ears off."

Dr. Brown arrived while I was getting the basin and warm water. He said Sharon should stay put for a couple of days. The police and wrecker had arrived, pulled the car out of the ditch and the car out of our yard. The street department sent out a crew to cut up the tree limb that fell on Sharon's car. The wrecker hauled it away. I nearly forgot to call Sharon's parents. They were not happy. I had my mother talk to them. It was agreed Sharon would stay at our house for the next few days. That meant she would be with us for Christmas. I was beside myself.

My mother fixed some chicken soup, and I took it up to Sharon. I waited while she ate. My mother knocked on the door, entered. She had a slice of chocolate cake for both of us.

"I am going to stay here. I can sleep in my chair. I'll get a blanket and pillow. Doc Brown said she should be watched for any sign of quivers or difficulty in breathing."

"Well, alright, but don't keep her awake all night talking about your escapades in Canada, you hear. You go on out so she can get into a nightgown. I'll bring you one of mine, Sharon. I think it will fit."

I stepped out into the hall. My mother came back with a nightgown, robe, and slippers, a pillow and blanket. I waited until she left and then went into the bedroom.

"You really have grown. It's not necessary for you to sit up all night. I'm fine," Sharon said.

"I don't mind. You are sure you are feeling okay?"

This healing thing threw me for a loop. I wonder if that's one of my 'gifts'.

"Yes, I'm fine. Come sit beside me on the bed. What things did you get into in Canada?"

While I told her about Aranck, the wolverine, and the sunrises and sunsets, she began to rub my leg, gradually moving her hand to my crotch. I rolled over on to the side of the bed, got up, locked the door, pulled off my clothes, and slipped back into bed. She had the nightgown off.

I whispered, "You going to get pregnant again?"

88

"No. I can't have any more kids."

I felt disappointed. And I wasn't sure why. One hour later I had spent myself and I remembered to get up and unlock the door.

My mother found me on the bed, with a blanket pulled up around my head. Her presence woke Sharon. I watched her put her finger to her mouth and whisper, "He's sound asleep. Can I help you with breakfast?"

"No, but thank you anyway, dear. I have it prepared. You come along when you are ready."

"Wonderful. I want to take a quick shower if you don't mind."

"Of course not. There's a set of clean towels by the hamper." As soon as the door clicked, I was out of bed and followed her into the shower. I felt her heat I held her tight to me as the water gushed over us. I exploded and I felt her shudder.

At breakfast, I couldn't get my fill of flapjacks, ham, and eggs.

Sharon's folks arrived just as we finished breakfast. They took her home. I never saw her again. Her words haunted me. How do I know if I am a healer? As far as I am concerned I didn't do anything special.

Aranck. Call him. I thought.

My parents gave me a phone for Christmas with a line separate from the house phone. I called and he answered on the first ring. I told him what happened.

"So, how do I know if I am a healer? Do I just go around healing people? Can I heal my father's binge drinking?"

"Whoa! One thing at a time. You have been given gifts. Healing may be one of those. Only time will tell. You don't go around healing people. If you try to do that, people will call you a crackpot and ridicule you. Instinct will guide you. I don't think you should attempt a healing on your father. He has to want to change."

"Boy you are a big help," I said. I didn't hide my disappointment.

"Be patient. You will know soon enough. Whatever gifts the Spirits have given you also brings a responsibility to use them wisely. You will be tested and the choices you make will determine what the outcomes of your endeavors will be. Do you understand?"

"I guess so. You're telling me to play it close to my chest. I got to go. My mother is calling me. Thanks."

I ran down stairs. My father was on the floor.

"I can't get him up."

I reached up under my father's arm pits and pulled him up. He was barely breathing.

"Is he drunk?"

"I wish you would stop saying that."

"Look, mom, I know he gets drunk. I don't smell any booze. Tell me what happened," I said as I carried my father to a couch.

"I heard this thud and found him on the floor."

I felt his forehead. I checked his neck for a pulse. It was barely noticeable.

"You better call Dr. Brown."

For some reason, I changed my mind and told my mother not to call the doctor. I took his head in my hands. They began to vibrate slowly at first and gradually increased to a light tapping. Their warmth increased and they turned bright red. My hands moved to his throat and hovered there. By now they were bright red.

My mother watched, wringing her hands in her apron.

My hands stopped vibrating and the redness disappeared. I got up from the edge of the couch and as I did my father opened his eyes.

"What? What's going on? "

"Shush. You fell flat on your face as you walked into the kitchen. Tony carried you in here."

"How do you feel?" I said.

90

"Actually, I've never felt better. Why are your hands bleeding?"

"What?" I looked at my hands. They were bloody. "I guess I scraped them across the floor trying to pick you up."

"Better have your mother put some disinfectant on them."

"That's okay. I can do that." I said, leaving the room.

"George, when Sharon was hurt, I know I saw a hole in her head and saw her brain." He healed her. I watched him with you. He held your head in his hands, and they got very red and then he moved them to your throat, and they began to bleed. He healed you. George, I think we need to talk to him about this."

"Fine, but right now I want a cup of coffee and a slice of your apple pie. I am starving."

***

Upstairs, in my room, I called Aranck. His voice was strange, breathy. Then I heard a woman's voice. A smile snuck its way on my lips. Well, what do you know? He just got laid, I thought.

"Mind your own business," Aranck said.

"So?"

"So—why'd you call? I thought we agreed we'd talk only once a month."

"I did a second healing a few minutes ago. My hands bleed."

"Hmm. Explain what you did?"

I told him the details and waited for a response.

"Looks like you are a trembler. Sometimes, the hands vibrate so fast they force the blood through the skin. You must be very careful, Cheveyo. Healers, especially powerful ones, sometimes take on the illness of the person on whom they did the healing. Be sure to cleanse yourself. Burn the sage and smudge it all over you, bathe and then drink a cup of Echinacea tea. This is very important. You need to protect yourself. Do you understand?"

"Yes. I am lighting the sage as we speak. I do have Dried Echinacea. Will that work for tea?"

"It will work just fine. Drink the tea for three days."

"Who's your friend?"

"None of your business."

Aranck hung up. There was a light knock on my bedroom door.

"Come in."

My father stuck his head in and said, "Can we talk? Hmm, what's that smell?"

"Sage. It's for purification," I said, pointing to the easy chair in the corner.

I sat down at my desk and waited.

"Your mother tells me you did a healing on me and that saved my life. Can you explain that?"

"I'm not sure. It's only happened twice, Sharon and now you. When I was on the quartz mountain and the lightning came down and sizzled around my feet, it travelled through me and out of me. Voices come to me and tell me things. One came from a bald eagle and it said I had been given gifts."

My father sat very straight, looking at me in a way I had never seen him do before. His eyes seemed much larger and his mouth was slightly open.

"And these gifts, do you know what they are?"

"No. I asked Aranck and I know you don't care for him, but he knows stuff. I just talked to him and he said I was a healer, one whose hands vibrate and the vibration caused them to bleed. In your case, you had a very high fever and a severe throat infection of some kind. The heat from my hands killed the infection."

"Remarkable. It's not that I dislike him, it's just a feeling that all is not as it appears to be. Do you know why you were chosen to be a healer and to receive gifts, whatever they may be?"

"When he and I went into the deep woods for the two weeks, I had a vision. I told Aranck about it and he said I am blessed and that I was a chosen. That's all I know."

"Did you really kill that wolverine?"

"Yes, I did. I was so scared. I was sure we were both going to die. I don't know how I managed to get a second shot but somehow I did. And when I was sure it was dead, and I looked at the rips it had made in Aranck's back, I puked my guts."

"Thank you."

His thank you nearly got me. He so seldom has ever said that to me.

"Dad, can we just keep this healing stuff between you and mom? People will think I am some kind of freak if the word gets out."

"Of course. I don't see a need to talk about it."

He left and I sat dumbfounded at my desk for a long time. Maybe, I thought, he doesn't hate me, after all.

Finally arousing myself, I went down to the kitchen and made my Echinacea tea.

***

The next afternoon my brother, his wife, and Bradley came to our house. They exchanged gifts with my parents and then my parents gave Bradley his gifts. John's wife, Beverly was a nurse at the local hospital. John managed a men's clothing store. My mother served drinks and snacks. Once, Bradley, had all of his gifts open he said, "Where're Tony's gifts."

"Oops, guess I left his gift at the house," John said. "Sorry, Tony."

"No problem." I knew he was lying.

"Bradley began to cry.

"I want to go home," Bradley said.

"Why? You just got here," my father said.

"Because my present for Tony is there."

"No problem, Bradley. I have something very special for you. Something from the Baskatong."

Bradley's eyes lit up and the sniffling stopped. "Where is it?"

I handed him a little box. He ripped the ribbon off, opened the box, and looked at me, puzzled.

"It's a claw from the wolverine I killed. Carry it in your pocket. It will keep you safe," I said.

"Don't feed him crap like that. All he talks about is the thing you supposedly killed," John said.

"It's true. Tony killed that beast and saved Aranck's life. That's the skin from the wolverine on the back of your chair," my father said.

"Well, I don't want him putting any those crazy ideas of hunting with a bow in Bradley's head."

Bradley began to cry again.

"Stop that damn bawling. Right now. I tan your little ass but good," John said.

I got up, left the room, and went upstairs. As I left, I looked at Beverly and sensed she was not well.

The next day, just after nine, the phone rang. It was the hospital. Beverly had collapsed after helping a doctor deliver a baby. When we got to the hospital, John was already there. She never woke up. I stayed out in the hallway with Bradley. My parents took him home with us.

Once we were home my father asked, "Why didn't you do a healing on Beverly?"

"She was already dead."

The week following Beverly's funeral my brother went on a trip with a woman. He took Bradley with them.

So much for grieving, I thought.

CHAPTER TWELVE

For my sixteenth birthday, my parents gave me a car, a Chevrolet BelAir convertible. It was bright red with black upholstery and white sidewalls. I had just passed my driver's exam and had gotten my license. I was in such a shock because my birthday is late summer. The shock was so effective I forgot to drive it to school. At lunch time, I ran home, picked up the keys, and drove back to school. On my way, I cranked up the radio to listen to "Little Darlin'."

I was in my first afternoon class when the principal, using the PA system called me to come to the office. I'd not been called to the office before. Now the whole school knew I was in some kind of trouble. I thought maybe I had violated a rule by driving to school. Then I thought something had happened to my mother. The school secretary told me to take a seat. She disappeared behind another door.

"You may go in now," the secretary said.

"You father wants you to meet him at his office after school today," Mr. Atwood said."

"Sir, has something happened?"

"I don't think so. I am sure your father would have said there was a family emergency. Here's your pass to return to class."

"Yes sir." I got up and left.

On my way back to class, I tried to visualize the inside of my house to see if things were normal there. For the life of me, I couldn't think of any reason my father would want to see me at his office. The visualization didn't work.

I thought the last three classes of the day would never end. Talk about something dragging on and on. As soon as school let out I didn't take time to show off my new car but drove directly to my father's office. It was on Main Street. He owned the whole building. It was three stories high and made of Vermont marble. His office was on the top floor and overlooked Main Street. I took the elevator up to his office. His secretary immediately told him I had arrived.

"Come in and shut the door."

I did as he asked and then sat down in front of his large oak desk. He cleared his throat.

"I have something here for you. It's from your grandfather."

"What is it? I thought grandpa was dead."

"He is deceased, but he left this for you when you reached sixteen. I guess you are close enough to have it."

The cold in his voice made me shiver.

He handed me a large white envelope with the name of a law firm on the return address. I opened the envelope. It was a legal document of some kind. I wasn't sure exactly what it all meant. When I saw the figure of one million dollars, my eyes nearly popped out of my head.

"I don't understand. Is this saying grandpa left me a million dollars?"

"Yes. It's a trust fund. You will get so much a month until you are eighteen, and then you will get the whole amount. As you can note in the documents you will be getting a five hundred a month.

"Whew!" I said.

I still couldn't believe what I was hearing. My hands shook and I dropped the document on the floor. I bent down, picked it up, and waited for my father to continue.

"That convertible is also from your grandfather. His specific instructions were to give you a red convertible. I don't approve of a fifteen-year-old having a car. I can't do anything about it. It's your responsibility. Not your mother's or mine. You understand?"

Ice cycles filled the room.

"Why—why didn't you tell it was from my grandfather instead of letting me believe it was from you?" *I should have known better,* I thought.

"A word of advice, not that you will accept it without checking in with your Indian friend. I suggest you open a bank account and put a good part of that monthly in a savings account. Use your money wisely. Don't squander it on your friends. In fact, I wouldn't mention this inheritance at all."

"Did my brothers get this when they reached sixteen?"

"No."

"Do they know about this trust fund?"

"Again no. I strongly suggest you not tell them."

"Do you know why they were excluded?"

"Your grandfather never discussed it with me."

"Are you doing the same thing for Bradley?"

"That's between your mother an me."

"This is so hard to believe. Did you know he was doing this?"

"No."

"And my car?"

"Didn't know anything it until the bank called me yesterday. They simply had the car delivered to the house."

"I'll put the money in a bank."

"Use the bank that was your grandfather's. That's where the trust is set up. Because the bank is a privately owned institution this trust fund makes you a significant player in the bank. You might be asked to sit on the Board. That will really set your brothers off."

"Hmm, you mean as in Board of Directors? Do I have to do that?"

"I suppose not. Don't be in a big hurry. You have time to think it over. Besides, the bank may not offer you that position. I have to admit I'd be surprised if they didn't. That's it. You can go now. I have clients waiting. Oh, and go pick up Bradley when his school is out. I don't want him walking to our house."

I left the office and crossed the street to the bank and opened an account. The president of the bank asked me to step into his office.

"I assume George has explained the very large trust fund and the living expense," Mr. Appleby said.

"Yes sir, he did. I will put part of the five hundred into a savings account; the one I just opened."

"That's good. There is one other matter, Mr. Appleby said, leaning forward, "the bank's Board of Trustees has voted to offer you a seat on the board. It's quite unusual for someone your age to be offered such a position."

"My father mentioned that possibility. How soon do I have to let you know if I will accept that offer?"

Mr. Appleby's eyebrows shot up. They were bushy.

"Take as much time as you wish. There's no hurry. "

"Thank you. I'll talk to my parents and let you know," I said getting up to leave.

We shook hands.

I wonder if my dear brother, John knows about this trust fund. If so, that may be why he doesn't like me. Maybe my father feels he should have gotten the money. These thoughts nagged at me. An inner voice told me to keep my mouth shut about the inheritance. Since my experience with the lightning on my quartz mountain, I now make it a practice to listen to my inner voice. *From now on, be careful*, I thought.

Bradley was waiting for me at his private school. He loved the car. When I drove into our driveway, John was already there. He looked at the car.

"Where'd you get that?"

"An early birthday present." I decided not to say from whom.

"You sure are spoiled rotten. I don't see why you had to have a new car. A used one would have been good enough."

"Well, I didn't see why you needed to have our father buy you a house, either. Talk about spoiled rotten. Look who's calling the kettle black."

He stopped. Looked at me.

Little brother wasn't so little anymore.

"Get in the car, Bradley."

They left. I got back into my car and drove to the next town, stopped in at Stephen J. Watkins' office, a lawyer, and had a will drawn up. I also left a statement in a sealed envelope that if something happened to me, the police should investigate my father and or my brother, John. I paid the lawyer twenty-five dollars. He didn't question my age. I had two copies of my will made and a copy of my letter. I sent them to Aranck. On the inner envelope, I wrote 'open only in the case of my death.'

***

We left for Canada, and the Baskatong right after school was out in May. Bradley didn't go this time. There were just the three of us. We stopped at a dinner for our evening meal. My father made a couple of trips to the men's room. I smelled the booze and I'm sure my mother did. On the way out to the parking lot, my father tossed me the keys.

"You drive. I'm tired. Watch the speed limit. When you get to the Canadian border let me know."

He climbed into the back seat. My mother rode up front. As I drove along, I glanced in the rearview mirror, and I could see him drinking. He was carrying his booze in a flask he kept in his coat pocket. I now understood the reason for the extra bottles of Jack Daniels. He was going to spend the summer drunk.

It was just a bit after midnight when I pulled into Customs. I handed the agent my driver's license. I answered his questions about where we were going, and how long we'd be there. He waved us on through. With my mother's help in giving me directions, we made it through Montreal and headed due east. During this time, my father slept. He woke up when I eased the Buick to a stop in front of our cabin. It was four AM.

I took my time turning the car around. I wanted to see if the wigwams were there. They were not. In a couple of weeks, I thought, they will be here. And I can talk to

Aranck about going to a college in Maine after I graduate next year.

My father woke up. Just as I finished taking the boat down. He climbed out of the backseat, hung on to the door to steady himself.

"Didn't I tell you to wake me up when you got to the Border? Can't you do as you're told?"

"George, Tony did just fine. Look, he's even got your boat off and ready to put it in the water for you. You want some breakfast or do you want to go to bed for a couple of hours? Of course not, you've been asleep for hours."

"Coffee," he said.

"I think some food, George. Actually, I'm hungry. I'm sure Tony could stand some hot food."

I unloaded some of the food stuff, set afire going in the stove, and brought in two gallon-bottles of water we had brought with us. Within minutes, my mother had a breakfast of flapjacks, eggs, and bacon. After breakfast, my father went to bed. So did I.

Bird song woke me. I rolled off my bed, opened the door, and went to the outhouse. On my way back, I checked to see if my canoe was still there and if it had survived the winter. I stood it up on its end, so I could check for any holes. There were none. I pulled my bow out and walked to the front of the cabin. My father was in his boat and had shoved off. The motor kicked in, and he took off with the throttle full open. I didn't see any fishing gear in the boat. *Guess he's just trying out the motor,* I thought.

I quietly checked the box containing the liquor. All the bottles were there, and none of the seals had been broken. I couldn't help but wonder if he had booze stashed somehow on the boat. I helped my mother finish the unpacking, and hung up my clothes on the wooden pegs by my bed.

After two hours, my mother began to worry. She went out to the bank. Her eyes darted from one part of the shoreline to another. Then to the open water, looking for a boat. She came back inside and immediately busied herself with sweeping the cabin floor for the third time.

"You want me to go out and look for him? I checked the liquor bottles, and none are missing."

"Wait a bit longer and then we'll both go."

I heard his motor cut off and went out to see if he needed some help mooring the boat. My mother was right behind me.

"George Wells, where have you been? I've been worried sick."

He knocked her down and pulled back a leg to kick her. I stepped between them. He swung at me. I blocked his punch and gave him a right uppercut to the jaw. I had remembered the lesson in boxing when I was in junior high school. He fell to the ground. I bent over him to hit him again. I felt all the anger and frustration swell up in me, and I pulled back my arm to pummel him.

"No, Tony. Don't," She was sobbing. "He didn't hurt me. I tripped."

"Stop making excuses for him. He's drunk and he's mean, "I said and headed down to the boat.

"Damn," I said as I found an empty bottle of whiskey. I lifted up the boat seat. There were two more bottles. I opened each and poured their contents into the lake. Wonder if the fish will get drunk. I ran up the bank. My mother was helping my father into the cabin.

I waited for a while and then went in. She had him on the bed and was taking his shoes off.

"Mom, I think you better make a cold compress for his jaw. It's going to be real sore."

While she was busing getting a towel, I leaned over my father, shook him a bit. He opened his eyes.

"Listen to me very carefully. If you ever strike my mother or me again or even attempt it, I will beat you into the ground. This drunkenness has got to stop. If you don't stop I will tell her about all the women in town you have been screwing. I will begin with your secretary, the minister's wife, my friend's mother, and my French teacher. Do you understand?"

He mumbled something.

"I didn't hear what you said. Answer my question."

"Yes," he mouthed.

"Good."

"Good what, dear?"

"His jaw is not broken," I said as I placed my hand on his jaw

I felt the heat build in my hand. I looked into his dilated eyes. In a flash, I saw; no read, all of his thoughts. I finally understood the reason why he didn't like me. I took the cold clothe and laid it over his eyes.

"How about something to eat?" I said.

I didn't tell my mother I had put him under, and he would remain that way for a while. I had to ask her a question. I waited until we had finished eating. I took a deep breath.

"Mom, who is my real father?"

"What an odd question. What made you ask such a thing?"

"George is not my real father, and that's why he dislikes me. You didn't answer my question."

She began to cry. She shook her head back and forth. I got up from the table and got a box of Kleenex.

Between the sniffling, she managed to say, "I am so tired of all of this. It's time for the truth."

"Which is?" I said, trying to encourage her to continue.

"Several years ago, actually seventeen years ago, your father and I were at Bangor, Maine. We spent the summer there. I caught him with another woman, a waitress where we ate our meals. I was so mad at him, I went into the bar. Had a couple of doubles. I woke up the next morning in the bed with a man I had met at the bar."

"Does this man know he has a son?"

The door opened.

"He does now." It was Aranck.

CHAPTER THIRTEEN

"Is that why you have shown me all these things over the years? Because I am your son and you have known it," I blurted.

"Yes, that is true."

"Why—why didn't you tell me?"

"It was not up to me. It was your mother's choice."

"So, I'm a bastard."

"That's not a nice thing to say," mother said.

"A god damn fucking accident," I continued.

"Just stop that right now. Don't you dare use that filthy language in my presence ever again! I could have given you up or had an abortion. I kept you and despite what you think, I do love you."

I was about to say more when a message came to me from Aranck. Have you forgotten your own child? Didn't you find out you had a son by accident? It seems each of us has our own little secrets.

I looked at Aranck. I felt him searching me. A noise from outside caught our attention.

"There's someone outside," mother said.

"Could be a wolverine. Better let me check," I said.

"It is not a wolverine. Come in. I want you to meet a fellow professor's daughter," Aranck said.

My eyes popped out of my head. She was movie star beautiful. I felt my face flush. *She heard everything about me,* I thought.

"This is Julie Henderson. Her parents will arrive in a couple of days. They are at a conference in Washington. Charlotte, I thought you could put her up for a couple of days. I see my gang has not arrived."

"Of course. We can fix a bed on the floor for Tony and she can have his bed. You don't mind do you, dear?"

I didn't mind.

"Good. I want to take Cheveyo into the deep woods for a couple of weeks. My sister will come down and get Julie when she gets here."

He walked over to the bed where my father was lying and squatted down beside him.

"George, do you mind if Cheveyo goes with me? You are the one who has raised him and provided him a home all these years. Had I known, I would have provided for him much sooner."

George sat up in bed, rubbed his jaw. Turned at looked at Aranck. And for once he seemed to understand. He cleared his throat. My mother brought over a glass of water.

"George has taken a—." She stopped. "No, that's not true. George tied one on and is sobering up. Come in, Julie. Have you and Aranck had anything to eat?"

Julie dropped a backpack and a duffle bag on the floor. Looked me up and down, lingered a moment and smiled

"What may I do to help, Mrs. Wells?"

I pulled out my backpack, stuffed some clothes in it, picked up my bow and quiver of arrows and headed toward the door.

"I'm ready. See you in a couple of weeks."

"Doc, I don't see why I can't go. I am a Botany major and I need the experience of plant identification. I here to turn in a paper on plants I've identified as well as mounted specimen."

"Well, I don't know. It's not like walking along a wooded trail during daylight hours."

"Aranck, I'm sure she'll be fine. We have some great plants here. So you are in college?" I said.

"Yes. I just finished my freshman year. How about you?"

"I just finished my junior year in high school. After next year I hope to go to the college in Maine. Is that where you attend?"

"No. I'm in a school in Ithaca."

"Impressive."

"Come and sit. Foods on the table," Charlotte said.

It was when Julie sat down that I noticed stiffness about her movements. She didn't just sit down; she sort of slid into the chair.

"Do you have an injured leg?" I asked.

Julie looked up from her steaming plate of food, looked directly at me and said, "I have braces on both legs. I had polio."

I understood Aranck's concern. How can she bend down and examine plants, I thought.

I realized she was speaking to me.

"I asked if my braces make me less attractive, and if you think I can't be a field botanist."

I caught a glimpse of a smirk on Aranck's face.

"Less attractive, no. Do I think you can't be a field botanist? Time will tell. Do you have physical exercises you do to strengthen your legs?"

"Yes, and I have an ointment I rub on them every night. Doc tells me you are a healer. Will you try to heal me?"

I dropped my fork full of food on the floor. I looked at Aranck. "What?"

"You are a powerful healer. I thought you wouldn't mind trying to help Julie."

"And what if I fail? What then?" I couldn't believe he expected me to do this. I am not even sure what it is I do.

"Failure is an opportunity to learn. There are no guarantees. Julie understands this."

"Will you try to help her?"

"Of course. It's just- - -"

"Just what?" Julie said.

The challenge in her voice didn't set well with me. I won't be goaded.

"Just this, I have no control of whatever it is that I do. It's not something I turn on and off. You have to understand it is a big gamble. You can't have any expectations."

"So. The docs never expected me to walk but I did. Expectations? You want to bet your life I do."

"Okay. Can your braces come off? If so, can you walk without them?"

"They come off; I can hobble a bit. Why?"

"Go over to the bunk on the side wall. Sit down, and take your pants off, and your braces," I said.

"You've got to be kidding. I'm not taking my pants off."

"Have it your way. No pants off, no braces off, no healing." I said.

"It's alright dear. I have a robe you can slip on. I'll help you," Charlotte said. "Besides, I'll be right here."

"Not so fast. I have a question for Aranck," I blurted.

"And that is?"

"You are a shaman, why haven't you healed Julie?"

"Doc did a healing. And if he hadn't I wouldn't be walking at all," Julie said.

"No need to be defensive. I have a right to know. Damn it, Julie, give me a little slack here. I just found out Doc as you call him is my father, and he's told you about me."

She sat on my bunk. My mother was helping her off with the braces. She looked up over my mother's bent back.

"Did I miss something along the way? Aranck, you are Cheveyo's father?"

"Yes, you were still outside. Let's not get sidetracked on other matters. Clear your mind and do as Cheveyo instructs," Aranck said.

As I approached my bunk, I received a message from Aranck. Don't look at her as a sweet piece. She is your patient. Healers don't have sex with their patients.

I felt my face turn red hot.

"Okay, I am ready. Let's get the show on the road," Julie said.

I sat down on the edge of the cot. I placed both hands just above one leg, making sure not to let them touch her leg. Both were shriveled. At first, I felt nothing; no tingling or heat. My fingers began vibrating and then actually tapping her leg at such a speed, I couldn't see them. I felt my hands had separated themselves from my arms.

Julie's scream stopped my hands. I felt sick to my stomach. I got up, walked out onto the stoop, and then went around the back of the cabin. I puked my guts out. His hands clasped my head, and I felt the spasm calm.

"Holly shit! What happened?" I said.

"Healers often pick up their patients' inflictions. I will give you something when we go back inside. You ready to do the other leg?"

"Yeah. Let's get at it."

At Julie's side, I said, "I am sorry for not warning you. Are you okay and do you want me to continue?"

"I'm fine. I didn't feel much in that leg, but I sure do now. Yes, do the other one. I promise I won't scream."

I went through the same procedure. First nothing, then all hell broke loose. My hands disappeared. Julie grabbed the edge of the cot and clinched her teeth. The tapping hands lasted a bit longer this time and when they stopped they were dripping with blood. My mother was the one who screamed this time.

Aranck grabbed a couple of towels, soaked them in the bucket containing our drinking water, and wrapped my hands in each. I felt dizzy. As I stood up, I fell forward. He caught me and helped me to a chair.

"Breathe deeply and slowly."

Once I was calm I went back to Julie. She looked flushed. Aranck handed me a jar.

"Arnica cream. Rub it on her legs. It sooths muscle pain."

As I rubbed the cream on her leg, Julie leaned forward, wrapped her arms around my neck, and kissed me on the forehead.

"You want to have sex with me?" Julie whispered.

"Sure, what guy wouldn't," I whispered back.

107

"Even with these legs?"

"It's not your legs that hold interest," I whispered.

"You can, if you want," Julie said.

"No. You are my patient. The offer is highly appreciated I said. Then in a louder voice, I said, "Let me help you up and let's see how you are."

Julie eased herself up on the side of the cot, wrapped the robe around her, moved her legs, and with my help very slowly stood up.

"You want to try to walk? If so, hang on to me. You don't need to fall and break a leg."

"Okay. Let's try it," Julie said.

Two steps and a pause. Three steps and then four.

"Let go of me and see if you can take a couple of steps by yourself," I said.

Julie did. She burst into tears.

My mother and Aranck clapped their hands. I joined in.

My father rose himself from his drunken sleep. "What's all the noise?"

"Welcome to the world, Pop," I said.

I had no idea where the Pop came from. I'd never called him that. Maybe, I thought, I should call him George since he's not my father. This is just too much. I feel like I'm going to freak out. Maybe I wanted Aranck to know what he had missed.

Aranck's voice walked around in my head.

Consider how lucky you are in having two fathers. A lot of young men would be glad to have just one. Step outside with me.

I excused myself and went outside. Aranck followed.

"Come; let's walk down to your favorite rock. We can talk there."

We walked in silence. At the boulder, I climbed up and squatted. Aranck followed. We sat there, two statues surveying the water world in front of us. He was the first to speak.

"It must be a shock to you; yet, I believe last summer you suspected I was more than your Indian friend. It took me quite a long time to locate your parents and you. The Inn where we met burned to the ground and consequently any registration records.

"The place burned down?"

"Yes, the people who owned it rebuilt it. Strange as it seems, it was and is called The Wells Inn."

"Like my last name. Wow."

"I thought all was lost. One day, I got a phone call that the registration ledger of the Inn existed and was available if I still wanted to look at it. Can you imagine my excitement? I still did not know you existed. I wanted to find the woman I fell in love with the moment I saw her. There has not been another woman in my life that held my heart and soul."

"When did you find out I existed?" I said.

"The page on which your mother's name was written was badly charged but I made out two things: Wells and the name of the town of residence. It took me another year to find that town and to verify who she was. I hired a private investigator to watch George. He was sleeping with every woman he could find."

"You haven't answered my question," I said.

"I am getting there. I decided to go where she lived. One day, I saw your mother and she was walking with you along the main street of your town. I got out of my car and spoke to her. I frightened her at first. When she recognized me I thought she was going to faint. It took me a bit of doing to assure her I was no threat. I looked at you and I knew you were my son. I asked your mother to join me for a coffee this time since the last time we got tanked. I told her how much I loved her and asked her to marry me. She refused. I then begged her to let me be a part of your life. She told me about going to the Baskatong Reserve. I arranged to be there. I was really pissed when I found you were not with them. I met Charlotte at the water hole. We had sex, wonderful sex."

"Great! Just great. My father's whoring around and my mother's knocked up by an Indian," I said.

"Don't get smart mouthed. I am trying to tell you something. Hate me if you will; don't disrespect your mother. You got that, Cheveyo?"

"Yes sir, I do."

"Good. I arranged to meet you the following summer. Do you remember?"

"Sure. That was wild."

"I have not stopped watching over you and loving you. I could have used the information I had on George's extramarital affairs to blackmail him, but that would have destroyed your mother. George began to suspect you were not his son early on and those were the fights you heard. You have any questions, about anything, ask them and I will answer them."

"What am I supposed to do? Continue to live with my mother and my father—George knowing how he hates me or go off on my own. I have not heard you say you want me to live with you."

Tears flowed and I struggled to gag my sobs. Aranck waited until I stopped crying.

"George doesn't hate you. He resents you, but he is the man you have known as your father. I am still very much a stranger, not that's the way I want it. I would love to have you come and live with me and you are welcome to do so. There is another consideration."

I stood up, tossed a stone into the still lake. Its glassy mirror reflected the shoreline. I watched the ripples flow outward until I no longer could see them.

"What's the other consideration?" I said.

"Your mother. She needs you more than ever. I don't know if George will stop drinking or not or if he can. If he doesn't he won't live long. His business is falling off, clients are leaving him, and he's not getting new ones. Your brothers are too involved in their own lives to help."

110

"Do you know about my new convertible and the million-dollar trust fund I have?"

"No. Is the trust totally in your name or in what is called jointure?" Aranck said.

"It's in my name only. It's at my grandfather's bank. He's dead and he's the one who set the trust up for me and ordered a new car for my sixteenth birthday. I can use that money to take care of her."

I had made a decision and didn't realize it. Aranck brought it up.

"So you will stay with your mother and George."

It wasn't a question.

"Next year, I want to go to a college in Maine. Can I come and live with you then?"

"Of course. Why not plan on coming up for the Christmas holidays?"

"I'll be there."

"We better get back. We have some walking to do before nightfall," Aranck said.

I felt wonderful. He had that way about him, making me feel good.

CHAPTER FOURTEEN

Aranck and I insisted Julie put on her braces and that she have a walking stick. Instead of hiking, we packed two canoes. Aranck took the lead, leaving Julie and me in my canoe to follow. We headed to the Big Baskatong. The sun was setting when we made landfall. It's golden red streamers floated lazily across the western sky. Ducks, undisturbed by our presence bobbed up and down on the water a short distance from shore. The sandy beach would be our campsite for the night.

It was my responsibility to provide the evening meal. I went fishing while Aranck and Julie set up camp. Within twenty minutes I had a beautiful Great Northern Pike. I cleaned and scaled the fish and brought it to the campsite. Aranck had a fire going and had an array of fresh wild vegetables. Because it was still early in the season, berries were not available. However, I was to learn how to provide a natural sweet for desert. After instructing Julie to remain at camp, Aranck had me follow him into the woods. He carried with him a three inch round stick he had set on fire.

He stopped at a tree, pointed to a bee hive.

"Oh no, you don't. You must be kidding. You expect me to climb that tree and get honey," I said.

He laughed.

"Here rub this on both hands, up to your elbows and then rub it across your forehead, around your ears and neck. It will cover your smell. When you get to the top, hold this smoking stick just at the entrance to the hive. The bees will fly out. Be sure you wrap your legs tight around the tree to hold on. Once the bees are out, reach in and grab a handful."

"Great, just great. How am I supposed to get the honey down here? Just drop it and you are going to catch it."

"You put it in this little bag," he said as he put its strap over my head. "Insert your hand very slowly into the hive.

The bees won't sense a threat. Here's a strip of rawhide, use it to tie your smoke stick to the tree.

I climbed the tree, one limb at a time. Pausing each at each limb. At about twenty-five feet I shoved the smoking stick up to the hive. Almost instantly, the bees swarmed out. I didn't move. There must have been hundreds of them.

"Wait a couple of minutes. I'll tell you when to go after the honey. Remember, do it slowly," Aranck shouted.

The bees going crazy with the smoke swarmed all around me. A couple lit on my hand, stayed for a second and then flew off. They didn't sting me. I inched my way up a bit more and waited for the signal.

"Now," Aranck said.

I got two good handfuls into the bag and then untied the smoke stick, and came back down that tree as fast as I good.

Aranck took the smoke stick, swung it around a couple of time until it glowed. Smoke spiraled upward. He dug a hole with his hands, shoved the stick into the hole, packed sand around the stick, and stomped it down.

"We need to move quickly while the smoke still distracts the bees. Once we are out of the immediate area we will be safe," Aranck said as he broke into a run.

I was right behind him.

At camp, we found Julie had her braces off and was rubbing her legs. To my inquisitive look, she explained, "Tingling feeling in both legs."

"Good sign," Aranck said.

I poured the contents of my bag onto one of our plates. A couple of bees flew away. I broke off a piece of the comb and stuffed it in my mouth. It was delicious. I passed the plate to Julie and Aranck

While still licking his fingers, he got up, grabbed a pan, and went to the water's edge. He climbed in a canoe, and crawled to its rear end, dipped the pan and returned to the fire.

"For tea," he said as he sat the pan directly in the center of the small fire pit. "Mint and honey tea. Put some Feverfew and Echinacea in it for Julie. You'll find some in my medicine bag."

I found the leaves, sniffed each, and tasted each to make sure I had the right leaves. I didn't crumple the leaves or powder them. I put two of each in a cup for Julie. Once the water came to a boil I poured it into her cup. She put in the honey. I poured the water into the other two cups, added the mint and honey. *This is the life*, I thought looking out over the water and up at the sky.

A star shot across the sky, making an arc. The ugliness of the fight with my father and his kicking my mother disappeared and I felt at peace. That wasn't all I felt. A certain definable stirring made itself known. *Be still*, I thought.

Aranck's voice brought me back.

"You will need to lay down some plants to avoid getting bit by ants, chiggers, and mosquitoes. You see that green plant, with green ribbed leaves spiraling up the stem? That's false hellebore and it's a natural insect repellent. Cut enough leaves for the three of us."

He followed me and then went into the woods. He stopped beneath a cedar tree, reached up, and cut a medium sized branch. I watched him as he went back to our campsite. He began sweeping an area with the cedar branch. His next move surprised me. He dipped the end of the cedar into the fire pit and dragged the flaming branch over the area he had just swept.

I had a large bunch of leaves. Instead of laying them in the area where Aranck had just burned, I dropped them on the ground. Went over to my backpack, rummaged around. I pulled out my notebook and began to write.

"What are you doing?" Julie said.

"I keep detailed notes and little sketches of the plants as Aranck introduces them to me. This false hellebore is a new one. If you are here to learn plants, it might be a good idea if you did the same. If you need a notebook, I got a couple extras."

"I'm impressed. I'd like a notebook. It's the one thing I didn't bring."

Aranck had the leaves spread out and I noticed he had his backpack as a headrest in the middle. I got the message and placed my backpack to his right leaving the left for Julie.

"Potty time," I said.

"See that tall plant with the broad leaves. It's mullein. Use that for toilet paper. And don't forget to dig a hole and cover it," Aranck said. "And face up wind."

"I brought a small spade. You can use that to dig," Julie said. She caught my concerned look. "Don't worry, I can squat for that."

She laughed and so did I.

We finally settled down and went to bed.

Chirping birds and the flutter of wings woke me. Aranck was already up. I rolled over, gave Julie and shove. While Aranck busied himself with breakfast, I decided to give Julie another healing. This time I didn't have to tell her to take her pants off.

My hands vibrated and turned red, but not so fast this time and no bleeding. I felt Aranck's eyes upon me. That wasn't the only thing I felt. I felt her heat. I ended the treatment with an Arnica rub. I watched as she pulled her socks back on and then her pants. When she was done I said, "I'd like you to walk for a while today without your braces. As soon as you tire, we'll stop and put your braces back on. Is that okay with you, Aranck?"

"Perfect. Don't overdo, Julie. You have nothing to prove to either one of us. Cheveyo has come on to you pretty heavy. Give his latest healing time to work."

I wish he would come on to me. He's so cool. What a body! Julie thought as she adjusted her walking stick and backpack.

It was a nice surprise to see how well Julie kept up. Secretly, I hoped I would need to do another healing. Two hours into the deep woods, Aranck signaled to stop. We were in an open area, several yards in diameter with a fabulous canopy of trees creating a dome through which bright blue-sky shone. We made short work of setting up camp. While Julie was relieving herself, I spoke to Aranck.

"Do you think I should try another healing on Julie?"

"She has done remarkably well. I suggest you wait a couple of days. We are in a sacred power place. Tonight I will take you on a journey to the Spirit World. You have a teacher waiting to receive you."

"What do you mean journey to the Spirit World? Are you talking about ghosts?" Julie said as she walked into the open area. "Don't tell me you two are going to try to scare me."

"No. And actually, you will not be involved. You can be an observer. As part of Cheveyo's training, I will instruct him on how to journey to the other worlds. It is there he will meet his spirit teacher."

"Other worlds, Doc? Come on. You are supposed to be a scientist," Julie said.

"He's not kidding. I've been there once before. I was twelve," I said.

"The world we are currently in is the present ordinary reality. Then there is the Upper World where kindly spirits live and the Lower World where not so kindly spirits live but who will help if asked in the proper way. Even in our present reality, there are spirits; some good and some bad," Aranck said.

"And you really believe this, and you believe you can travel to these worlds, as you call them?" Julie said.

Aranck did not reply. However, I heard him. We have a visitor. Be prepared.

I heard the snapping of tree branches and heavy breathing. There were no other sounds in the area. It seemed that all time had stopped.

116

A large burly figure charged into the open space. He carried a club. He stopped in a half squat, turned slowly around and all the time swinging the club. I could see glazed eyes reflecting our fire.

Julie screamed, and he lunged for her. Before either Aranck or I could interfere, he had her by her long hair. She thrashed and kicked him. He howled, and she jerked free. It was then I saw her small knife. Before she could get away, he had her again, pulled her to him.

"Mine!" He yelled.

Clutched in his hand was a machete, and he had it pressed against Julie's throat. He slowly backed away, growling all the time. Aranck stood up.

"She's not yours. She's mine," he yelled, throwing his arms up in the air and bringing his clinched fist back to his chest. A challenge.

There was an ear-splitting scream as the thing threw Julie aside. He ran at Aranck. There was a brief tussle, and Aranck flew through the air. I heard a crack. It started for me. I stood still. That confused my attacker just enough. I held my right hand up, drew a clockwise circle, and shoved it at him. A bright blue flash shot out from my hand. He fell to the ground, writhing in pain. Bunt hair and flesh filled the air.

"Doc. My god, please don't be dead," Julie sobbed.

I walked over to where Aranck lay and gently pulled Julie away. I kneeled down, placed my hand on his chest.

"He's alive. I think he has a broken rib," I said.

"You're sure," Julie said, wiping away tears.

"I'll soon find out."

"It is broken, Cheveyo," Aranck mumbled. "It hurts to breathe.

I did a healing. My hands vibrated at a furious speed. Blood flew from them. Nearly exhausted, I managed to check Julie and was glad to find she was not hurt. I went to the invader.

I gingerly removed his weapons. I wasn't sure if he was dead or not, and I wasn't about to lean over and give him an opportunity to rip off my head. Instead, I took a small branch, stuck it in our fire until it caught and then passed it close to him. He did not move. Still not sure, I cut a couple of stakes and drove them into the ground and using strips of rawhide from my backpack, I tied his hands to those stakes. Only when I felt he was really secure, I knelt down to check him out.

Not sure as to what he was, I soon realized he was dressed in animal skins and in keeping with those skins, he smelled. I got his fur coat open. He had a nasty burn on his chest. Getting up, I got my sample case and found some chickweed. I mixed that with water to make a paste. I spread that on the wound. He was awake. He spat at me and screamed when he realized he was tied down. I held up my hand, palm outward. Terror filled his eyes. I turned my palm inward and placed a finger on my lips. He seemed to understand.

I stoked the fire, checked on Aranck and made up a bed for him. I pulled out a shirt from my backpack, tore it into strips and wound them around his chest. I did that because I wasn't sure how well my healing had worked. That's something I must ask about, I thought. I spread out my bedroll and then went to check our guest one more time. I decided to tie his feet to stakes and I tied one end to one of my feet. If he got wild during the night, I would feel him trying to get loose.

"What about me?" Julie whispered.

I opened my blanket, and she crawled in. *I don't think there will be any visiting the Upper World tonight, I thought.*

She had my pants open before I could even roll over. I never knew anyone could get naked that quick, but she was. Her smell was wonderful and her touch sent shock waves throughout my body. I was ready and with two easy thrusts, I was all the way home. I let her have her way and set the pace. I slide my hands down her backside and pulled her into me and forced her to stay still. She felt my vibrations and began to shudder. Unable to hold back, I exploded. And so it was throughout the night.

Somehow, before morning we managed to get our clothes back on.

CHAPTER FIFTEEN

Morning brought a huge shock. The man who attacked us was gone. And so was Aranck. To make sure I wasn't dreaming I found the stake holes but no stakes. Aranck's bed was still warm. Maybe he let the man go, but then where are the stakes? I really drove them down into the ground.

"Wondered when you two were going to get up," Aranck said as he strolled into the open area of our campsite. And then I heard him in my head. *I thought you understood no intimacy with patients.*

I felt my face flush. I was sure it was bright red. I felt if I had been caught with my hand in the cookie jar, except in this case; it was with my pants down.

"Where's the creep I tied up? Did you release him?" I said changing the subject.

"No, I didn't."

"Strange. How are your ribs?"

"You did a good job. I think you can take this wrap off."

I used my knife to cut through the knot I had tied to hold the cloth in place. Aranck breathed easy as it fell away.

Julie walked into the campsite. She put her arms around me and kissed me.

"I really thought I was going to remain a virgin all my life. Good god, here I am a sophomore in college and still virginal."

She stopped talking. Looked at Aranck. Putting her hands on her hips, she said, "Well, don't tell me you didn't expect us to get it on. Really Doc."

Aranck's face turned red this time. Taken aback by Julie's matter of fact attitude, I suddenly felt used, and our sex cheapened. *Lesson learned*, I thought. I walked off to relieve myself and to cool down. I was pissed. I didn't realize I had not gone to our designated spot until I came face to face with our attacker. He was hanging from a tree. I could see my rawhide strips wrapped around his neck.

"Aranck, come quick!" I yelled.

He came roaring through the bush with Julie right behind him. She screamed.

"This is how I found him. How did he get up there, spread-eagled like that?"

"We need to return to your parents' cabin. I can call the authorities from my plane. Come. We need to pack up. Hurry," Aranck said.

The urgency in his voice propelled me through the bush. Julie was right behind me. I immediately began slinging stuff into bags. I didn't care whose stuff went where. Aranck took the lead, Julie followed, and I brought up the rear. I had my bow and an arrow in place. We slowed to an easy trot. Two hours later I noticed Julie was limping. Her legs were giving out. I caught up with her, passed her, stopped, and bent down.

"Get on my back. Be quick."

I was surprised there wasn't an argument. With a little adjustment, we were again on our way. Aranck stopped, came back to us, and took our backpacks. He slung them over his shoulders.

"If we can keep this pace we'll hit your cabin just at dusk. You okay with that?"

"No problem. Let's go."

"Aranck, is that thing what they call Big Foot? I just read about it before we came out here?" Julie said

"No. He is human. I opened his animal skin coat," I said.

As predicted, we arrived at the cabin just as the sun began to set. My parents were shocked to see me carrying Julie. I let her down, and she trotted over to them.

"I'm fine, Mr. and Mrs. Wells. Oh, no! My braces. I left my braces."

"We'll get them later," I said.

"Where's your Indian friend?" George said.

"He's gone to his plane to notify the Royal Canadian Mounted Police. We were attacked by a crazy and then found him hanged,"

I took a long look at my father and sensed he had actually stopped drinking, at least for today. Even though he was pale and a bit shaky, he seemed less aggressive.

"Goodness. Any of you hurt?" Charlotte said as she put her arms around Julie.

"Aranck got a broken rib," Julie replied. "But Cheveyo healed him, just as he has healed my legs. Isn't it wonderful? I mean my not needing braces."

"Yes, that's wonderful, dear. Are you two hungry? I got a pot of homemade soup simmering on the stove?"

Actually, the warmth of the cabin felt wonderful. Sleeping out and on the ground in May is not the warmest thing one can do.

"Oh dear, Julie, I nearly forgot. Your parents have arrived. I am expecting them for supper. Don't worry, there's plenty to go around."

"Great. Is there anything I can do to help?"

"Pop, you got a few minutes?" I said.

"Yes, I guess I'm not needed around here."

"Let's go for a walk and watch the sun set. You game?"

As we walked out the door, I put my arm around his shoulders. I felt him stiffen and then relax. My fingers came to rest just at the base of his skull. He turned his head and looked at me.

Smiling at him, I said, "It's hard for me right now. You know, to find out I'm a bastard and then to find out the man I thought was just my friend is actually my father."

We stopped walking, faced out toward the water to watch the sun setting.

"I want you to know something. It's true my mother could have had an abortion. But she didn't. You could have divorced her, but you didn't. Together, you raised me. Thank you."

"Well, I—we never discussed it. I knew though."

"Sharon had a kid, a boy. I am his father."

"Good god! Does your mother know?"

"No, and I think this should only be between us. Sharon put the baby up for adoption, and she claimed she didn't know who adopted him."

"Why are you just now telling me all of this?"

"I guess I'm trying to tell you I understand resentment. I resented Sharon for not telling me I was the father of her kid. I got over that. I hope you can get over resenting me."

There was a long silence. Too long to suggest anything other than rejection. I turned to walk back to the cabin.

"It's just so damn hard, knowing my wife slept with another man, and he knocked her up," George said.

"But it's okay for you to sleep with other women, most of them married. How do you think their husbands feel?" And what about that waitress in Maine? And how your wife felt when she saw you?"

I tried to keep my voice calm and not accusing; just factual.

"Of course, you are right, you know. I am a first-class ass."

"Naw. Just over sexed," I said laughing.

"What's so funny?"

"I watched you bang my friend's mother.

"Good god."

"You sure hung in there. What about it; can we have a truce?"

"Truce it is. But would you mind not calling me Pop. That's something you drink."

"How about George? That ought to shake up my half-brothers."

"George it is."

We hustled our butts. We could hear loud voices. Julie's parents arrived. Aranck was back. George introduced me to Tom and Mary Henderson. He introduced me as his son. I winked at him.

"Isn't he absolutely gorgeously wonderful?" Julie gushed. "He has saved Doc's life and mine from that awful creature in the deep woods. More important, he healed my legs." She slipped her arm through mine and gave me a hug.

Professor Henderson looked at me with one eyebrow raised.

What he didn't see was her pinching my ass. I was sure my face turned red. I wonder if she's told her parents Aranck is my real father.

After an awkward pause, Professor Henderson said, "So, Tony, can you explain all this healing business? How do you do it?"

"No sir, I can't. I will tell you this, and I mean no disrespect; it's not a freak show. Aranck can probably explain it."

"Aranck? Who's that?" Mary Henderson said.

"Doc here," I said realizing I didn't know his other name. I heard him. Joseph Redwing.

I looked at Aranck and gave him a slight nod to let him know I understood.

"Goodness can't that wait? Soups ready," Charlotte said.

A second announcement wasn't necessary. I picked up a bowl and a second one for Julie. My mother filled both. I grabbed some homemade bread already buttered, and said, "Come Julie. Let's go out and sit on the stoop."

We ate in silence. I used my last bit of bread to soak up the remains of my soup.

A quarter-moon took command of the sky. One thing about this part of the country it gets dark quick. Twinkling stars began to pepper the area over the lake. Julie snuggled close to me.

"It's beautiful," Julie said her voice low and soft.

"You want to go for a walk? Just a short walk if your legs are okay?" I said.

"Sure. Can we walk down by the water? You know Tony; I will never be able to thank you enough." She leaned over and kissed me on the cheek.

There was a cough behind us. It was Professor. Henderson.

"Maybe you shouldn't be sitting out here. The night air is cold."

"It's alright, daddy. Tony and I are going for a walk down along the lake. Want to come?"

"No. Just don't stay out too long."

The screen door squeaked shut. For some reason, it only squeaked when it shut, never when you opened it.

We hadn't walked far when the night sky became a dazzling light show.

"Oh, what is it? I've never seen anything so beautiful," Julie said.

"The Northern Lights."

"Tony, can I ask you a question?"

"Sure. Fire away."

"Did you kill that man? I saw you hold your hand up, and he fell to the ground screaming. I smelt burnt hair and flesh."

"No I didn't kill him. I think Aranck believes there is something evil back there in the deep woods."

"Did he kill him and string him up in that tree like that?"

"I am sure he did not."

"Whoever did it would have to be very strong."

"I do know he wanted us out of there and quick. I think we had better get back."

"Yeah, my parents are worry warts. I am totally surprised they let me come here."

"Glad they did," I said.

I pulled her to me, kissed, tasting her. She returned the kiss.

"Don't want you to forget," I said swatting her on the butt.

"Good god, Tony, your eyes are glowing. Just like the night sky," Julie said.

"That's because I am in heat, or hadn't you noticed."

"Julie, come in now. You've been out there long enough, Tom Henderson said.

We scurried up the bank. Just before we reached the cabin I said, "Julie does your father boss you around like that all the time? Gee, you're in college."

"Uh huh, and it's about to stop. Drives me nuts. You'd think I was in elementary school."

"Do yourself a favor and don't make a big scene."

***

We were barely inside when Tom Henderson began berating Julie, yelling at her.

"Didn't I tell you not to stay out there? You've been gone over an hour. Pick up your gear we're going home."

"You mean up to the wigwams?'

"No, back to Maine. First thing in the morning."

"Well, daddy, I'm not going. I am here to complete a field course in plant identification and I have a paper to write. I am staying."

"What did you say? Don't get smart with me. You'll do as I tell you or - - -"

"Or what, daddy? I am an adult and you have to stop bossing me around. And stop embarrassing me. I didn't hear you say thank you to Cheveyo for fixing my legs or for saving my live or to his parents for giving me a place to stay."

"And just where were you staying? I only see two beds in here."

"Don't know what's sticking in your craw, Tom, but you are out of line. Cheveyo and I camped out at the edge of the woods," Aranck said.

"I'm not sure about all this pretend Indian stuff." Turning to George he continued, "What with this Cheveyo business and the Indian clothes? Good god, he's white."

"I never knew you resented me and after all these years of being friends. I've not hidden my Indian heritage," Aranck said.

"Aw come on, Mr. Henderson. You can't be serious," I said.

"Keep your mouth shut and speak when you are spoken to," Tom bellowed

"Wrong thing to say. You are in my house, Mr. Henderson and you don't speak that way to my son," my mother said.

"Come Mary, Julie I told you to get your gear. We are leaving. Now!"

"And you want to go and stay with Doc's sister? She an Indian, too." Julie said.

"Are you arguing with me?"

"What's happened to you? You are acting like you're on some kind of drug of something. Look at me, daddy. And listen to what I am saying. I am not leaving here."

Tom Henderson pulled back his fist. Before he could release it, I put up my right hand, drew a circle clockwise, and thrust my hand toward him. There was a flash, and he hit the floor. He sat there, stunned. My father went to help him up.

"Leave him alone," I said.

"Oh my god, Tony, have you killed him?" Julie said.

Tom sat up, shook his head, and looked around. "Whew, what happened? I feel like crap." He plopped back down. His eyes dilated and wild.

"Did Tom eat anything other than the soup tonight?" Aranck said.

"Well, yes he did. He grabbed up some of those lovely mushrooms that were on the bank near where we landed our plane. He washed them off in the lake and ate them. He did say they had a slightly bitter taste.

"Psilocybin. Hallucinogenic mushrooms. Charlotte, do you have any mustard or mustard seeds?" Aranck said.

"I have mustard."

"Good I need a glass of warm water and add a tablespoon of mustard to that, stir it around."

Within a couple of minutes, Charlotte had the water and mustard mixture. She handed it to Aranck.

"Tom, drink this straight down. Don't stop to taste. I believe you ate crazy mushrooms. From what Mary tells me, it has been just about long enough. You may have gotten a couple of mushrooms causing mycetism poisoning. You need to vomit. I'll need some towels. Put them in boiling water. Cheveyo, get a bucket. When you have that, better go outside and dig a hole. Once Tom is done vomiting I need to give him a strong laxative."

Taking a lantern with me, I went outside and dug a hole, a good foot and a half deep. I went back inside grabbed my old tree stump stool and took that out by the hole. I made sure it was not wobbly. It won't do to have Professor Henderson fall into his own shit, I thought. On the other hand, it might serve him right for being such a jerk. Naw, I don't wish that on anyone.

Twenty minutes later, Henderson was vomiting his guts out. When that subsided a bit, Aranck placed the hot moist towels on Henderson's stomach. These he changed every ten minutes. Well into a full hour, Aranck fixed a quart of warm water with sea salt. He gave that to Henderson to drink. My mother produced a straw from somewhere and gave it to him to use.

Two hours later Tom Henderson stopped vomiting and pooping. He settled down and was lying on my bunk. His raspy voice indicated he needed liquid. Aranck made a tea he said would replenish the fluids.

"I sure am embarrassed as hell, Joe. I've made a fool of myself in front of your friends. Where's that young man, Cheveyo as you called him?"

"I'm right here. I hope you are feeling better, sir."

"Not sure about that at the moment. I apologize to you for my very bad behavior. I, my wife and I, are so grateful for what you have done for our daughter, strengthening her legs."

That wasn't all I did for her, I thought.

A hooting penetrated our cabin.

"Chepi," Aranck said going toward the door.

She had come to see where her guests were.

"Have they not come to record the old stories? I am tired," Chepi said.

"Come in, Chepi," Charlotte said. "It was a long walk for you and at this late hour."

Aranck stepped back from the door to allow Chepi to enter.

My mother offered Chepi the rocking chair and brought her a glass of whiskey which she accepted.

"Didn't any of the men walk down here with you?" Charlotte said.

"No. Only two left. They are feeble. The others dead. Been a long winter. This will be my last summer here. Old age has got me."

I looked at Aranck and saw the concern on his face. He watched Chepi sip her drink. Usually, she tossed it down in one gulp. For whatever reason, I will never know, but I went over to Chepi and moved her rocking chair closer to the stove. In doing so I touched her hand. It jerked as a spark jumped from my hand to hers. She looked up at me, eyes wide, fearful. I knelt down beside her, took both of her hands in mine.

My hands warmed, and she felt their heat. She tried to pull back, but I held her hands firmly in mine.

"Chepi, it's okay. Nothing bad is going to happen to you. I can tell you this; this is not your last summer here."

My hands cooled, and she relaxed. I looked at Aranck and tried to send him a message. Her heart is weak.

I heard him. Thank you for helping my sister.

"It is very late. We need to leave so they can get to bed," I said.

"Mary you and Tom take our bed. Julie will sleep in Tony's bed. I'll make a place on the floor for George and me. Tony, get down those deer hides from the rafters and spread them out for me."

Aranck and I would camp out doors, but not until we had Chepi safely back to the wigwams. This year instead of the usual three, there were only two. My father insisted we sleep in the car. We now had a Buick Roadmaster station wagon and there was enough room for the two of us when we let down the tailgate.

The night was a very long one for me. I had so many questions and so few answers. I wish I understood this healing thing and this business of putting people down with the palm of my hand. It's been my right hand. I wonder what would happen if I used my left hand. And drawing a circle in the air, clockwise with my hand is strange. The bleeding of my hands during a healing scared the shit out of me. That was so unreal. Fact is I have trouble telling the difference between what is real and what isn't. Maybe I am hallucinating all of this. I am not sure at what point I realized Aranck was mind-talking to me. I don't know what else to call it. I am positive I heard him say, Quiet your mind. You will have your answers.

I sure hope so.

CHAPTER SIXTEEN

Loon talk and the whir of wings woke me. The sun peaked over my quartz mountain. I needed to relieve myself. Easing my way out of the Buick, I headed for the outhouse. On my way back, Julie was waiting for me.

"Are we going to go back into the deep woods? I really do need to complete this assignment. It's worth three semester credit hours."

"I don't know. I am sure Aranck wants to wait until the Mounties arrive. I know that something spooked him. He may feel that it's not for us to go back there."

"Well, what am I to do? In our hurry to get out of there, I left the few samples I had. I'll have to start all over again. College is not cheap. I hate to think of costing my folks all that money.

"There are a lot of places to go. We can go to one of my favorite spots."

"Where's that?"

"Right there in front of you. I call it my quartz mountain. We can canoe over if you like, gather some samples, and bring them back so Aranck can help you identify them. I think my mother brought wax paper with her. We can use that to press some of the leaves."

"Great. I brought a gathering bag and several old dishtowels to wrap specimens in. I have material with me to set up a dryer. Can't wait to get started. Thank you, thank you."

"Ah, there you are. How did you sleep? And is Aranck alright?" Charlotte said.

"He was up when I got up to go the outhouse."

"How is Professor Henderson?" I asked.

"He's still asleep. Mary is up." Hello Julie. Did you sleep well?"

131

"Hi, Mrs. Wells. Yes, thank you. May I help you get breakfast ready?"

"Thank you. That's sweet of you, dear. Come along while I get some things ready for George. He wants to go fishing today. What's that awful noise? "

I listened and heard a rumbling sound.

"It's a truck. Sounds like it's constantly down shifting. Strange."

Two large trucks pulled up in front of our cabin. A man in a Royal Canadian Mounted Police uniform got out of the truck.

"Hello, the cabin. I'm looking for Dr. Joseph Redwing."

"Right here," Aranck said climbing up the bank from the lake.

Several other officers emerged from the trucks. The number even surprised Aranck. The rumbling noise and the loud voices woke my father. Within minutes Mary and Tom Henderson came out.

"I am Captain Louis Fonteyn, Royal Canadian Mounted Police. I would like to first establish a procedure for interviewing all those involved. Who first discovered the body of the deceased?

"I did," I said.

"And you are?"

"I am Tony Wells."

"Did you recognize the deceased?" Captain Fonteyn said.

"I did not."

"Attacked your campsite. Explain," Captain Fonteyn said as he whipped out a notebook and pen.

"I gave all that information when I called it in. It might be a good idea if we went to the area. Animals may have gotten to the corpse." Aranck said.

"I am merely verifying information and that is necessary," Captain Fonteyn said.

"You can ask your questions as we walk. It's a two day trip." Aranck said. "It will take a few minutes to pack."

"Very well. There were three of you at the campsite. All of you will accompany me."

"I don't think the young woman who was with us should be subjected to what might be there," Aranck said.

"I am going, Doc. Besides, I need to retrieve my braces. I can give them to someone who needs them."

Julie hurried back into the cabin. I followed her. I grabbed my canteen, filled it with water, and slung it over my shoulder. The rest of our gear had not been unpacked. I double checked to make sure I had everything. Julie was already out the door. She stopped gave her parents a hug.

"I don't like it. You going off with all those men. Who knows what's out there. I'm going with you."

"Tom, I don't think that's a good idea. Besides you need to start recording the stories from my sister. Good time to get that going," Aranck said.

"See you in a few days. And don't worry. With that army with us, I am completely safe," Julie said."

***

As soon as we reached the clear area of our former campsite, we again set up camp. Julie found her braces and immediately put them in her backpack. Her collected plant samples were of no value. The Mounties bivouacked some distance away.

"I'd like you to show me where you found the body," Captain Fonteyn said.

"Sure. Follow me," I said.

Aranck, Julie, and two of the Captain's men followed us further into the deep woods. We'd gone about thirty yards. The buzz of flies told us we had arrived. Captain Fonteyn ordered two of his men to cut the body lose. Two more began to search the area. The men carefully lowered the corpse to the ground. Its hood fell away and it was then I saw the marks—talons.

"How can that be? I know eagles are strong, but a full-grown man weighed down with heavy animal skins, impossible," I thought.

I felt Aranck's hand on my shoulder. I turned to look at him. I heard him and yet his lips did not move. "Don't mention your sacred birds, the eagles to the Mounties. They might not understand."

"This campsite seems to have been messed up. Did you have a fight with the dead man?" Captain Fonteyn said.

"Yes. He attacked Aranck, broke his rib, and tried to drag Julie into the woods."

"He didn't attack you?" Captain Fonteyn said.

"I tackled him and knocked him to the ground and then I punched him in the face. He rolled free and ran way. We grabbed our gear and returned to the cabin."

"You are very lucky. If our information is correct, this is a wanted killer and an escapee from the Centre de détention de Québec. He has killed and raped half dozen women. So if you killed him, you did the country a favor."

"Well, I didn't kill him and neither did Aranck," I said.

"So, he just climbed the tree, spread-eagled himself, and then strangled himself to death? I don't think so," Captain Fonteyn said. This time, his voice contained a hint of a threat.

"I'm hungry. How about some chow." Julie said. "Better pick some vegetables before it gets dark. Cheveyo, you want to go with me?"

Grateful for the opportunity to escape the questioning by the Captain, I quickly agreed. I picked up a gunny sack, a digger, and made sure I had my knife.

"You got your notebook with you? We can still get some samples for your class."

"Wonderful," Julie said.

We headed in the opposite direction from the corpse. We hadn't gone more than a few feet when Aranck came up behind us.

"Don't mind if I tag along do you?"

"Of course not. You can help me spot some plants on my list I have to identify," Julie said.

"Cheveyo, I am sorry that our first trip to this sacred ground didn't work out. I had hoped you would have been able to commune with the spirit world and locate your next teacher. It has been defiled now."

"It can be cleansed, Doc. It can be cleansed." That was the second time I had called him Doc.

Julie was thrilled over the number of plants she found, identified, and made notes on. I cut some for her to seal in the wax paper. We picked up a good supply of wild carrots, potatoes, leaks, and cabbage.

"You ever eat frog's legs?" Aranck said.

"Yes. They're great," I replied. "How about you Julie, you ever eat frog's legs?"

"Good lord, no."

"Well, you are in for a treat," Aranck said.

We came to a small mossy pond. Within a few minutes, we had a bag of frogs. I noted Aranck had enough to invite the Captain to eat with us.

The evening meal was great. The frog legs were unbelievable. Captain Fonteyn ate with gusto. Gradually, the small chatter turned to the case at hand. What happened next is impossible to explain. We were comfortable around our small campfire. A brilliant flash of light shot across the night sky. For a few seconds, it was daylight.

I stood up, raised my arms, spread them apart, and looked up at the sky. I drew a circle around Aranck, Julie, and Captain Fonteyn. They didn't seem to notice my movements. I sat down, legs crossed, and back erect. An image began to form. Unclear at first, the image slowly defined itself. We were watching the attack by the animal skin man. His movements were ape-like. Unlike a movie projection, I could see right through the images. I could see Aranck, Julie, and the Captain watching the images.

The sequence of my putting the attacker down was clear. The image shifted to the woods, and I watched in awe as a dark shadow folded itself over the man. My ears ached from the hideous scream he made. He rose up into the air and just seemed to hang there, spread-eagled. Straining, I could see the leather strips holding him. My whole being shuddered as the next images came into focus. A long talon emerged from the black shadow and pierced the man's throat. I heard him gurgle and saw him struggle for a few seconds, and then become still. The shadow lifted. I heard its wings. A voice boomed from all space:

"We are always with you."

I unfolded my legs, stretched them out. Captain Fonteyn cleared his throat. Aranck looked at me with a question on his face. Julie wiped her eyes in disbelief.

"And now we know what happened," I said.

I had no idea where that came from. They looked at me.

Captain Fonteyn stood up. "Can you explain what just happened?

"Yes, Cheveyo, what just happened? I saw something grab that man and the next thing I saw was him trussed up in that tree," Julie said.

Before I said anything, I looked at Aranck. He shook his head ever so slightly.

"I don't know. I saw that guy grab you Julie and Aranck knocked down."

"Yes, I saw that and saw the dark shadow cover the victim and then string him up."

"Strange, but then this is a sacred site and the spirits may not have liked its violation," Aranck said.

"Well, whatever we experienced, it certainly gave an explanation. I need to rejoin my men. Thank you for a great meal. I'll see you in the morning," Captain Fonteyn said.

136

Julie busied herself with making the cedar beds. She tied the trances together and double laired them, soft side up. I swept the area and used a burning branch to get rid of any bugs. I noticed she had placed our cedar boughs together. I also watched Aranck set up his sleeping area some distance away.

This time out I had rolled two blankets and brought them with me. I put one down on top of the cedar branches and the second on top of that. I sat down, removed my boots, pulled off my pants and shirt, and rolled into bed. I opened one side for Julie. Once under the blanket, she pulled off her slacks and blouse. She snuggled close to me as I let my hand begin a slow circular massage of the spot between her legs. Like a small kitten, she purred in my ear. I felt her hands slip into my shorts. Her touch was electric. With a couple of wiggles, I had my shorts off and pressed against her. She pulled up a leg, and I was home. Slow thrusts soon brought her to a boiling point, and I felt her shudder. I exploded. I rolled over on my back, and she mounted me. I let her have her way with me. She finally spent herself and fell asleep. I gently removed her and got up.

I pulled on my clothes and moved over to the fire. Its coals were still hot, so I added a few small branches. They flamed immediately. I added two larger pieces of wood and waited for them to catch. Picking up my backpack, I left for the deep woods. Along the way, I stopped and relieved myself. Not sure of where or why I was going; I moved as quietly as possible. Every few minutes I stopped to listen. No animal sounds. The forest was eerily quiet. I barely heard my own breathing. Not even a night bird was about.

By the set of the moon, I guessed I had walked a good hour. I was feeling tired and thought I'd sit down and rest. As I brushed some leaves into a pile, I realized I was standing in a small patch of moonlight. I sat down and began to take deep breaths and slowing exhaling them. My heart beat slowed, and I relaxed. I'm not sure what I noticed first: the sweet smell, like Jasmine or the shift in the moonlight. Whichever it was, I became very aware of not being alone.

The moonlight shimmered into a discernible shape, almost human. I looked right through it, seeing the shape of the trees. For some reason, I was not afraid. I felt totally at ease. A slight breeze caressed my face. It was touching me. The touching continued down my chest, my stomach, and into my privates. There the touching stopped.

"Who are you? What do you want of me?" I asked.

Beautiful music from nowhere, yet from everywhere surrounded me. I began to cry. Deep sobs wrenched my gut. The music stopped and so did my bawling. Why I was crying I have no idea. God what a baby. Glad no one else was here to see me, I thought.

A voice, a soft baritone resonated around me. It was more singing than speaking. It wanted me to look up at the heavens. A massive sworl unfolded, creating an inverted vortex. The blue-green-purple color radiated. I felt something touch my face and for a very brief moment, it burned.

The voice spoke to me again and this time I understood. The musical notes became words.

"You have been given much. Use your gifts wisely. Use them to heal others and to protect yourself, family, and loved ones. Never use them for revenge. If you do, those powers will destroy you. If you need us call us by saying Utpadyate." [3]

"Who are you? Where are you from?"

"We are pure spirit manifested by the All. We are from everywhere."

The image disappeared; all was quiet, and the smell of sweet jasmine filled the air. I remained very still, deeply breathing in the perfume. It was intoxicating.

"You had me worried. Why did you go off like this?" Aranck said.

I was so absorbed in my breathing and trying to understand all that had just happened I didn't hear him approach or sense his presence. *I won't be careless again,* I thought as I stood up to greet him.

"I am sorry for causing you concern. Where's Julie?"

"I'm right here. And I am really pissed. It's not funny scaring the shit out of us like this."

"Something's not right," I said.

"You got that right," Julie said.

"You don't understand. I should have sensed your approach, and I missed both of you. I know Aranck walks the woods real quiet, but even so, I should have heard him."

"The Mounties are not happy about your disappearance," Aranck said.

"They have no need to remain here. They know what happened. How Captain Fonteyn reports it is his problem. Let's help Julie find the rest of those plants on her list. I think there are several right here," I said, pointing to some plants with flower buds. I hoped the shift in the subject would work. I didn't want to talk about what had just happened to me.

"You're right. What a find," Julie said as she began taking samples and making notes on each one. Within an hour, she had nearly every plant on her list. Aranck checked her list and thought the rest could be found along the shoreline of the Baskatong. We headed back to the campsite. There, the Mounties, packed and ready, began to move out. Captain Fonteyn stopped to speak to me.

"Young man, I don't know what you did, but I am not going to report we had a visual of the incident. I am simply calling it a suicide. I do have one question."

"Fire away," I said.

"Who owns this acreage?"

Before I could give an answer, Aranck spoke up. "Cheveyo owns close to a thousand acres."

"I thought the Reservoir was government," Captain Fonteyn said.

"It is. The land west and northwest including where we are, belongs to Cheveyo.

I am not sure whose mouth dropped further, Julie's or mine. I said nothing. Forty-five minutes into our hike back to the cabin I asked Aranck what he meant. His reply threw me for another loop. He said I was now the shaman, and the land belonged to the gang's shaman. I stumbled and nearly fell flat on my face and would have if he had not caught me.

"How can this be?" I asked.

"I have stepped down as the shaman, and you are my successor. The land continues in the gang's name with its shaman as the owner. I was giving you this for your birthday. Some other members are coming for a ceremony. They have heard of your feats and are anxious to meet you. I will ask Tom and Mary Henderson to record this ceremony of passage."

My head spun. So much to try to understand. Aranck and I were so absorbed in our conversation; we didn't notice Julie slowing down. I trotted around Aranck and came up alongside of her.

"Julie, are you okay?"

"My legs are bothering me. Tired I guess."

"It's late afternoon. Let's stop and make camp. We can be back at the cabin tomorrow by midday," I said.

Aranck looked like he was ready. We stopped under a large hemlock. Its lower branches made a nice canopy. While Aranck dug a fire pit and lay in the wood for our evening fire, I gave Julie's legs another healing. My hands grew red and tingled but did not go through the trembling they did before nor did they bleed. I wasn't sure what was going on.

"Aranck, what kind of poultice can we fix to wrap around Julie's legs?"

"Let's see what plants are nearby and maybe some of them can be used. I didn't bring my medicine bag."

He left the fire and began to look around. I heard him say "Ah."

"Here we go. Stinging Nettles. They will make a good poultice."

As I watched how he handled the plants, I heard the Mounties. I wondered where they had been since they left before we did.

"Hello, the camp. Captain Fonteyn here."

"Where have you been?" I said.

"We got lost. I smelt your fire and headed back this way. The aurora borealis is giving our compass fits. Can you give us directions?"

"Of course," Aranck said. "If you stay straight with Sirius you will arrive at your vehicles. It will take you south."

"Thanks. One thing, though. Would you mind not mentioning we got lost? Have a good evening," Captain Fonteyn said.

"No problem," I replied. I had to turn my head and bite my finger to stop from laughing. Some Mounty, I thought.

We had a very light meal. Julie went to bed early. We changed the poultice twice. I laid one finger in the middle of her forehead. She closed her eyes and went into deep sleep. I had no idea where that move came from. Her going into deep sleep gave me a chance to tell Aranck about my experience back where they found me.

I looked over at him, squatted by the fire. I tried to tell him, but no words formed. Finally, I heard him in my head.

"You have been chosen by the Spirits, Cheveyo. You have been visited by Mi'Kmuesu [4]. Very few have the privilege of actually seeing the kind of spirit you describe. It was truly a messenger from the Great Spirit, the All as you called it."

"That may be true, but I still have no idea about these gifts. Just now, I put Julie into a deep sleep and I didn't know I could do that. And another thing, I know that Sharon's baby, my son, is dead. He was born dead."

"Are you sure about that, Cheveyo?"

"Yes."

141

"How do you know all of this?" Aranck said.

"It told me, the Spirit. And he gave me a word to say if I ever needed help and they would be here. He made it plural. And for all I know, I could have done that guy in and strung him up."

"Your gifts are being revealed to you as the need arises. How many and what they are I do not know, but I do know you are powerful, very powerful."

"That's another thing the Spirit told me. I am never to use my gifts for revenge. If I do they will destroy me. Can I change the subject?"

"Of course."

"What goes on during this ceremony you mentioned? And should I have gifts and food for the guests? How do we know the number of people coming?"

"Whew, you sure have the questions. It will be very serious, much drumming, dancing. There will the passing of the pipe, plenty of talking, and the changing of the guard, so to speak. It will certainly set well with the members if you provide food. I do not recommend serving alcohol. In terms of gifts that is up to you."

"I have the wolverine claw necklace and a few extra of its claws. I also have the wolverine's skin, and the two arrows I used to kill it. I can catch fish to bake and gather natural vegetables. Maybe I can ask my mother to bake fruit pies."

"That is good, my son. That is very good. I will hunt with you and let us see what game we can catch. And now, it is late and we have a long walk tomorrow. At least your bed will be warm."

"I will not sleep with her tonight. Instead, I will sit and watch over her."

Aranck raised an eyebrow.

"So?" I said.

He managed not to smile. Despite his efforts, I saw the corner of his mouth curl upward.

142

Fortunately, the night passed without incident. The morning saw Julie up and refreshed.

"How are your legs?" I asked.

"They feel great. I think I just overdid. I guess I will have to remind myself there is a limit. That limitation has made me think that perhaps I shouldn't be a field botanist."

"That's what I'd call a major change. Did you hear that, Aranck?"

"Yes. And I agree with Julie's assessment. If not the field botanist, what would you like to do?"

"That's a good question, Doc. I really have no idea. I am starving. What have we got for breakfast?" Julie said as she continued to get ready for the return to the cabin.

Within an hour we had eaten and packed up. We made good time and arrived back at the cabin midday. Julie immediately began to build her plant press. That was new to me. I knew the Indians hung bundles of herbs to dry. She had retrieved a large cardboard box my mother had broken down and put aside. Julie cut several two-food long squares from the box. Over the first square she placed a newspaper, also scrounged from our packing. On this, she carefully laid a row of plants. She placed a number beneath each plant.

"What's the number for?" I asked.

"It corresponds to the number in my notebook. That way, I know which plant is which and can then correctly label them for my paper."

"Impressive."

She soon had her plants laired and a final piece of cardboard in place.

"I need something to flatten this down and some rope to tie it tight," Julie said.

"No problem. Give me a couple of minutes."

I went around back and found four cedar shakes and took those to Julie. I gave her three rawhide strips. I split the shakes in half and placed them across the stack and then tied them as tight as I could. She had her plant press.

143

My mother came out from our cabin. A worried look crossed her face.

"Tony I need to talk to you."

I got up and walked with her toward my favorite rock.

"I am concerned about your father. He's not eating and he's losing weight. His pants are a size too big."

"Is he drinking?"

"No. We emptied all the bottles. And I did check his hiding places, including the boat. I just don't know what to do. There are no doctors around for miles and miles and even then I don't know how well trained they are."

"Do you want me to try a healing session with him? I'll do what I can."

"At least we'd be doing something. I have almost decided to pack up and leave. I can help with the driving."

"I can't leave, not right now. Aranck is having a special ceremony for me. People will be coming from Maine, some of the other New England states and from Nova Scotia. Let me ask Aranck to help with the healing. We should know with a couple of days if it worked. If not, then I will ask him or Dr. Henderson to fly you to Montreal."

"Will these people need to be fed?"

"Yes. I thought you might make blueberry pies. Julie and I can go up along the path and pick a couple of buckets."

I have to admit it's nice to have one of my parents confide in me.

We hustled to the cabin. I located Aranck sitting down at the water's edge. He was in a deep discussion with Dr. Henderson. I quickly explained my mother's concern. He agreed we both should do a healing but not in the cabin.

"Where do you want to take him?" I asked.

"Tomorrow morning as the sun comes up bring him to your rock. There we will call upon the Spirits to heal him."

***

144

My mother had George up early. He was already on the stoop when I crawled out of the Buick. His skin had a yellowish pallor about it. He nodded as I walked up to him. Aranck appeared out of the early morning mist. Together, we helped my father walk to the rock. We had to make frequent rest stops.

"Before we begin our healing session, I would like the sun to be a bit higher in the sky," Aranck said. "Cheveyo, test the rock for its warmth. If it feels warm to the touch we'll help George to the top."

I climbed up, touched the rock. It still had some warmth from the day before. I slide down and went over to my father, picked him up, and put him over my shoulders. I kicked off my moccasins and began a slow crawl up the rock. My father hung on with his arms and legs wrapped round me. Aranck followed.

At the top of the boulder, I lay my father down on his back and told him to close his eyes. Aranck had a small bundle of kindling with him as well as his medicine bag. He started the fire, lit a bundle of sage, and smudged George. He then squatted down and looked at George. He then leaned forward and placed his ear on George's chest.

"His breathing is shallow but I didn't hear any rattling in his lungs. His coloring suggests he has a case of jaundice. Probably the heavy drinking caused it. If his liver is diseased I am not sure how much we can do. I just want you to be prepared for failure."

"You mean he can die?"

"Yes. And Tony, he has to want to live. Do you understand?"

"I understand."

"Good. I will do the chant and call upon the Spirits to help."

He pulled out a small drum from his backpack. Handing me a pair of rattles he continued

"You play these. Shake them in sync with my drumming. Listen to my prayer, memorize it. When I chant, you chant. Any questions?"

I had none.

He stood up, stripped off his clothes. Most women would call him handsome and actually he was. I hoped I'd look as good when I reached his age stripped. He faced East. I faced the East. He began to pray.

"Oh, Spirit of the East, place of the rising sun, and sign of new beginnings we ask for your wisdom and help in healing our sick brother, George Wells."

Turning to the South, he said, "Oh Spirit of the South, site of passion, of fire, of creation, and of inspiration we ask that you join us in healing our sick brother. Bring your warmth to his body so he may walk in good health."

Turning to the West, he said, "Oh Spirit of the West, home of the setting sun, and of water. Bless us with the knowledge to heal. We ask that you join us as we come together to heal George Wells."

Turning to the North, the last of the four stations, Aranck said, "Oh Spirit of the North, seat of quiet, of stillness, and of solitude. We ask for your guidance and help in stilling the troubled soul of George Wells. We ask you to join us here today."

Aranck stood still, his arms still upraised to the sky. I failed to notice we now faced due North. We turned and faced the rising sun. He sat down, legs crossed. He picked up the drum and slowly began to drum and to chant.

"Yeha-Noha." [5]

I picked up the rattles, shaking them in time with his drumming and chanted with him.

"Yeha-Noha."

I had no idea what that meant.

Aranck stopped drumming and I stopped shaking the rattles. Neither of us moved as rumbling crossed the water. I felt a soft wind blow across my naked body and yet the water below me did not move.

I leaned over and as I placed my hands on George's abdomen I whispered "Utpadyate."

A bolt of lightning flashed across the sky yet there were no dark clouds. It struck the ground and circled the rock, making the water bubble. I was sure I heard it sizzle. Aranck keeled over. My hands vibrated over George's abdomen so fast I could no longer see them

A red glow floated over him and he cried out.

My hands were dripping with blood. I felt faint and struggled to remain conscious. Aranck was on his stomach. I didn't know if he was alive or dead. A groan from George told me he, at least he was alive. A woman's scream pierced my brain.

It was a struggle to open my eyes, and when I did I saw Mrs. Henderson standing by the rock. She was screaming, "They are naked and dead. They've killed each other."

I managed to stand up, wobbly and dizzy.

She fainted.

"Thank you," I whispered to my protector.

CHAPTER SEVENTEEN

We managed to get our clothes on before Doc Henderson and my mother arrived. With Aranck's help, I got George down from the rock and headed back to the cabin. My mother revived Mrs. Henderson. If anyone had been watching they would have sworn they were watching a bunch of drunks.

After getting George to have a cup of broth, we helped him into bed. Aranck made a liquor of turmeric and crushed mint leaves in water. He added a tablespoon of honey to ease the taste

"Charlotte, make sure he drinks this three or four times a day. It will help the jaundice."

Surprisingly he didn't put up a fuss. While this was going on, Julie hovered over her mother who sat fanning herself.

"Julie, you want to go with me and pick huckleberries? My mother has agreed to bake pies for the people who will be arriving throughout the rest of the week."

"Great. I don't believe I included a sample of the huckleberry bush in my collection. Let me get my collection bag and I'm ready to go."

I was anxious to get away for a while. I still wasn't feeling quite right. I wish I understood what happens when I do a healing. It seems to me that I am not in control.

"And you are not," Aranck said. "The spirits are. You are a conduit for their actions."

"So, calling myself a healer is not really correct."

"Technically, you are correct, but to the public one is a healer. Speaking of public, do you plan on letting the word out that you are a healer?"

"I don't want to do that. I don't know enough. Do you agree?"

"First of all, you know what there is to know. All the answers to your questions are within you. I agree you should not go public right now. You have several other things to get out of the way."

"Yeah, you're right about that," I said.

"You two mind if I tag along? I need to go up to my sister's wigwam."

"You'll have to pick huckleberries," Julie said.

Aranck didn't pick many berries. He seemed preoccupied. Julie whispered she had gotten her period and there would be no sex.

"Gee and I thought you saw something more in me than just a stud."

She swatted me on the butt. Her eyes alive with mischief

"I like you anyway," I said.

Aranck had reached the wigwams and was busy talking with several men squatted in front of the wigwam belonging to Chepi. They stopped talking when they became aware of Julie and me. They did not speak to us, and that creeped me out. We waited until Chepi came to the doorway. She was dressed in a deerskin and high matching boots. Her dress contained lots of black-and-white porcupine quills. Unlike the men, she was delighted to see us. She had not met Julie before.

"Very pretty, Cheveyo. She makes a good woman for you."

Julie blushed. I guess I did, too. I offered her a quart jar full of berries.

"Chepi, my mother will be baking berry pies. Do you know how many people will be here for the ceremony?"

"I don't know. Maybe a hundred, maybe more."

"Whew! That many? I see some have arrived," I said, tilting my head toward the outside.

"Big shots," Chepi said as she spat on the ground.

"Julie and I had better pick more berries, Chepi. We'll see you later."

149

We took the berries back to the cabin and then headed out again. My mother was shocked about the potential number of people. Instead of pies, she decided on large pans of berry cobbler. I still didn't understand how we were going to feed all the people that might show up. Chepi's "maybe a hundred, maybe more" bothered me. What if no one shows up other than the three men who were talking with Aranck? Then what will we do will all the food?

That fear was short lived. The honking of horns filled the air. A dozen vehicles loaded with people sped by our cabin and in a dust-bowl skidded to a stop at the wigwams. A quick count gave me an estimate of seventy people. Immediately, after jumping out of the vehicles, the people began setting up tents and building fires. I watched Chepi greet each of the women, and assign them things to do.

From the woods, north of the wigwams came another group on horses dragging sleds behind them. One man was dressed in traditional native regalia, including a beautiful head piece. Aranck hurried over to him. They exchanged greetings and continued to talk for several minutes. Chepi stepped through the entrance of her wigwam and suddenly burst into a full run toward the new arrivals. The man in the regalia, bent down took her in his arms. I stood very still, turned my right ear toward them. I could hear them speaking to one another but could not understand the language. Chepi broke away from her native tongue and said, "Welcome father. We are honored by your presence."

As the old man on the stallion rode in to the encampment, everyone stopped talking. Even the three men who earlier had engaged Aranck stopped talking. Aranck and his sister, Chepi walked beside the man on the horse. I know everyone thinks of Indians and painted ponies, but this horse was a beautiful shinny chestnut.

"Julie," I whispered, "They are headed right to us."

My mother, George, and Dr. and Mrs. Henderson came out of the cabin to see what the commotion was all about. It surprised me to see George up and about.

150

The old man pulled in the reigns on his mount and stopped. The horse nuzzled me. Neither Aranck nor Chepi spoke. The man dismounted and stepped in front of me.

"Je m'appelle Mundoo [6] et je suis votre grand-père. Je suis heureux de vous rencontrer. J'entends vous êtes un grand puoinaq."

For once in my life, I was glad I had stuck it out with my French lessons.

"Bonjour, grand-père. Parlez-vous anglais?

A broad smile spread across his weathered lips, as he extended his hand to me.

"Yes, I speak English. I have heard a great deal about you. I am anxious to hear your stories."

I shook his hand. He had a strong grip and held my hand for a few seconds. Our eyes locked for a moment, and then he released my hand.

"It will be my honor, grandfather."

I felt awkward introducing him to my mother and George. It went better than I expected. Introductions to Dr. Tomas and Mary Henderson went well. Last but not least, I introduced Julie.

"She will make a good woman for you, Cheveyo." He laughed loud and long.

I watched Dr. Henderson to see his reactions. It wasn't good.

"Julie is my friend, grandfather; not my woman."

That statement surprised me. I had not thought in those terms before. She definitely was not my woman.

I heard an audible sigh of relief from Dr. Henderson.

Grandfather Mundoo put his arm around me and indicated we should walk to the wigwams. On the way, he asked me about my several healing experiences.

"My father, Aranck says the Spirits heal through me. You know, like I'm a wire and their energy travels through me to the person who needs to be healed. I don't know what will happen when I begin a healing. I wish I had some better understanding."

151

"You explained it very well, grandson. How do you feel about finding out who your biological father is?"

"That's hard to explain. I have known for ever that George resented me. When I found out he was not my father, it explained a lot about him. I liked Aranck the first time I met him. It's ironic, don't you think?"

"How so?"

"Well, I had wished he was my father. And he is."

Mundoo laughed. I liked his laugh. It came from deep within him.

"If you had a wish, Cheveyo, what would it be?"

I didn't answer right away. We reached the wigwams. His horse nudged my back.

"I would wish George would stop his drinking and that his business would grow," I finally said.

"That says much about you. I like that. Come inside, I have something for you."

Mundoo dropped the reigns of his horse. It stayed put, content to graze on the grass. He pulled a bundle from the horse.

"Come," Mundoo said as he handed me the large bundle.

Inside Chepi's wigwam, I opened the bundle. It contained white leather pants, a white leather shirt with black fringe. Burned into the top right side of the shirt was lightning. White moccasins, a white headband with an eagle's feather, and a necklace of black stones. I looked at Mundoo and realized his eyes, like Aranck's, were blue as were mine. Strange, I thought, blue-eyed Indians.

"Try them on," Mundoo said.

He noticed my hesitation.

"Don't mind Chepi. She's seen naked men before."

Picking up a necklace of black beads, he continued, "This is made of obsidian and it is from the bowels of the earth. It is your power stone."

He then placed the head band on me, adjusted the eagle feather, and stepped back to admire his work. There was a

152

bright flash. Mundoo took my picture with a Polaroid. He showed me the photo as soon as it developed. Not bad at all, I thought.

"Grandfather," I said, "Thank you for the beautiful gifts. I am very honored."

"You are very welcome. There will be many more."

"I have two questions. Am I to continue to wear these new clothes or should I remove them and save them for the ceremony? Also. . ."

"Whoa! You've already asked three questions," Mundoo said, laughing. "Save the new clothes for the ceremony. What's your next question?

"I understand when I receive a gift; I should give one in return. I don't have enough to give all of these people," I said, pulling off my pants.

"Your father realized that and has brought appropriate gifts for you to give."

"I will ask him about that. I do have something for you grandfather," I said, pulling the skunk bear claw necklace out of the leather pouch still attached to my old pants.

I removed my new shirt and put on the old one, and rolled the new ones back into a bundle.

"These are the claws of the wolverine you killed to save your father's life?"

"Yes."

"I am the one who is honored. I thank you, Cheveyo. I will wear them with great pride."

"What gift will you give your father?"

"I have given him my gift," I said.

"And what is that?"

"His life."

"So you have."

My answer surprised me. I hope it didn't sound what my mother called 'high and mighty'. Sometimes things don't come out the way I mean them. I said good-bye to Mundoo and Chepi and headed back to the cabin. As I walked along

I wondered if Aranck would explain to me what the ceremony was and what he expected of me.

CHAPTER EIGHTEEN

I didn't have long to wait. Aranck caught up with me.

"We need to talk. In two days, your ceremony will take place. There is much to do. Walk with me to your favorite rock, okay?"

"I've been wondering when you were going to tell me what I need to do," I said.

As we walked along a bevy of quail took flight. It was the first I had seen since we had been spending our summers here. I guessed there were at least a dozen birds. Sure will take a lot more than that to feed the group gathering, I thought.

"I want you to know I am immensely proud of you, my son. And again, I am so sorry I did not know of your existence early on. The ceremony is very important and how you present yourself will tell the gang much about you and will determine their acceptance of you as their new shaman," Aranck said, putting his arm around my shoulders.

"I am honored to be your son," I replied. Stopping, I turned to him, sure that my face was red, and said, "That was a dumb-ass thing to say. I had no choice in the matter."

Aranck roared. He laughed so hard he had to stop walking.

"What?" I said.

"You. I do appreciate the complement. Thank you."

We arrived at the boulder, climbed up and sat down. A Great Northern Pike jumped out of the water. I thought that was unusual. Pike generally don't bother with small water bugs. They eat smaller fish, frogs, and even ducks. It was then I saw the cause of the jump, an otter. And that was different. All the time I have spent in the woods and in the deep woods I've not come across any otters in the streams on small ponds.

Sensing my puzzlement, Aranck pointed to the far end of the lake. "Watch, just at the edge of the water."

I strained to see what he was pointing at. Movement caught my eyes, and I focused— Otters.

"You suppose they have been there all along?" I said

"Probably. I don't recall seeing you at that end of the lake."

"We'll go there after the ceremony, Aranck, said.

"What about the ceremony? You know; you are driving me nuts."

"Our people have some beliefs or rules of protocol. Like any people, not everyone follows or obeys them. There are several you need to know."

"Okay. Great. What are they?"

"We believe in non-interference. By that I mean we respect and accept the beliefs of others. Second, respect is given to all creations; that is, to all life forms. We respect animals and when we take one to nourish us, we give thanks to that animal's tribe. We believe that everything in life happens for a reason and that each person has a purpose for existing, and each person is responsible for discovering what that purpose is. We believe that whatever a person gives to others will return, and this includes kindness as well as respect. There are several more [7], but these set your core. Think upon each; make each a part of your soul."

"How does this fit into the ceremony? I want to know what I am to do.

"Patience is another rule you need to learn," Aranck said.

"Crap on this. What if I had done that with you when you were bleeding to death? What if I had said be patient while I do this or that?"

"That was different. A life was a stake, several lives in fact."

"No, it is not. We are talking about my life here."

"Cheveyo, I will present you to the gathering as my son and as my successor as shaman. I will tell them of your

156

bravery, skill as a hunter, finder of good medicines, and one who is wise beyond his years. You will be dressed in the outfit your grandfather brought you. Drums will beat, flutes will play, and those who have gathered will get up and dance the medicine wheel. During this time, you will say nothing. My father, Mundoo will offer me the pipe. I will take two drags on it and blow it out over the crowd. I will then hand you the pipe, and you will take two drags, holding it, and then blow it out to the crowd. "

"So, why haven't you told me this earlier?"

He ignored my question.

"You will then offer the pipe to the ranking chief. When you do, hand the stem first, cradling the bowl in your right hand. Once that is done, those present will bring you gifts."

"I told Grandfather I didn't have enough gifts to go around. He said you had taken care of that. Mind cluing me in?"

"One of the trucks is loaded with blankets. You will distribute one to each adult male."

"What about the women? Am I not to gift them, also?"

"For each of them, there is a wool shawl."

"How much do I owe you for all of those gifts?"

"Nothing. They are my gift to you."

"And after the gifts what will happen?"

"It will be story time, a sing-a-long. You must prepare something to entertain them."

"And food, I am sure the berries Julie and I picked won't be enough to go around."

"The guests have brought things to make. There will be much food. You and I could go hunt for a deer or moose if you want."

"Let's go. I'll pick up my bow and quiver of arrows."

We had gone about an hour into the woods. Luck was with us. I brought down a doe

Even though I knew some people like the heart, liver I decided not to tote them back to camp. I buried the guts.

Stopped for a minute. I remembered one of the rules Aranck had told me.

"Thank you for giving me one of yours, so I could feed mine," I said.

I wasn't sure if that was the right thing to say or not. Aranck just nodded.

At the campsite, we turned the deer over to Chepi. Immediately, two men came forward and skinned the animal, cut up the meat. It disappeared among the various fires. I thanked the two men and gave them the deerskin. For a minute, I thought they were going to kiss me.

On our way down the now well-worn path to our cabin, Aranck said I should spend the night in prayer and come morning, I should go to Chepi. She would do a purification. The big blow came next.

"You are too fast. Only a small about of water," Aranck and just as we opened the door to our cabin, he said, "and that means no sex."

"Well, shit!" Then I remembered Julie said she had her period and couldn't.

Julie looked up at me, raised an eyebrow, and went back to her plants. She was sorting them.

Her parents and George and my mother were engaged in a game of bridge. My mother folded her hand and got up from the card table.

"You want something to eat? Won't take but a minute to warm something. How about you Aranck, have you eaten?"

"I am fine, mom. I have to fast in preparation for the ceremony tomorrow. I will be staying down at the rock all night."

"Nothing for me Charlotte. In the morning, Cheveyo will go to my sister, Chepi for purification."

"Purification? Oh dear, that sounds anonymous," my mother said. "You mean to give him a laxative?"

"Well yes," Aranck laughed. "She will burn sage and smudge it over him. Next. Chepi will rub him down with special oil, from head to foot. Once he has emptied his bowels he will bathe and dress for the ceremony."

"Great, Joe. I'll have my cameras ready," Dr. Henderson said, calling Aranck by his other name.

"No way. You will not photograph me naked let alone taking a crap. End of discussion," I said.

"Of course not. Some aspects of the ceremony are private," Aranck said. He had a big grin on his face.

"Great. I'm off to the rock to pray."

I'm not sure how to go about praying but time will tell. At least, I hope so.

I took two folded blankets with me. One to sit on and one to wrap around me. Nights still were chilly, and an early-morning frost was not unusual. I made myself as comfortable as possible as I sat facing east. I eventually dozed off. At some point, I gradually became aware of someone's presence. I raised my head, opened my eyes. There was an indefinable shape of light hovering just off the water; a violet glow. Shades of Melville's Moby Dick, I thought.

A tinkling sound like a small wind chime floated up from the water. The light vibrated in sync with the sound, and it changed into a butterfly

"Who are you? What do you want?" I whispered.

"I am from Sirius, the dog star. Hold out your right hand so you can receive my gift."

"Gift? What kind of gift?"

"Hold out your hand. Be quick. My time here is very limited."

I held out my right hand. Nothing.

"Close and open your hand."

I closed my hand, making it into a fist and slowly opened it. A small fire flamed in my palm yet it did not feel hot. Nor did it burn me

"Close your hand like you have a ball in your hand. Throw it."

I threw the invisible ball in the water. Flames shot out, and I heard the sizzle.

"Use your gift wisely."

With that, the light flashed across the eastern sky.

To make sure I was not dreaming I stood up. I closed my right hand into a fist and opened it. A flame appeared. I closed my hand again threw an imaginary ball. Light flashed down to the water. Again, I heard the sizzle.

I wondered what I was to do with such a thing. What is its use?

"It is a weapon of defense. Very few of your kind have been given such a gift. Be careful with its use."

The voice seemed to come from everywhere and all at once. I shook my head. The sun was making its presence known, and I realized I had to relieve myself. I slide down the boulder and hurried along to the outhouse. Then I went to the water's edge and washed my hands and face. The water was frigid. It'll be late morning before the lake begins to warm; I thought as I scampered up the bank and headed to Chepi. My stomach complained the whole time.

Chepi was waiting for me. After a brief greeting, she said, "Take off your clothes and sit by the pot. You know the place."

I removed my clothes. She lit a bundle of sage and slowly circled me. She then handed me the bundle and had me smudge myself from bottom to top, even under my arm pits. While I was doing this, Chepi placed a large white sheet over several animal skins.

"Lay on your stomach."

She poured something into her hands and then gently rubbed it over my back, down my butt and legs. It smelled wonderful. It felt even more wonderful.

"Chepi, what is it you are putting on me?"

It's a mixture of herb and plant oils. Roses, chamomile, black pepper, spruce, juniper. Roll over. "

I clinched my fists and hoped I wouldn't get a boner if she touched my cock. Talk about embarrassing. I was grateful I didn't. My fingers ached from clinching them so tightly. I started to open them and remembered my new gift. I placed each hand along the sides of my legs and slowly opened them. No flames. *Hmm. I wonder how it works.*

Sleep took hold of me. Voices woke me. I realized it was Aranck and Chepi.

"Wake up, Cheveyo. Drink this. I have dug a hole behind the wigwam for you to use. There is an open flap at the back for you to go out. No need to dress."

I drank the concoction. It was Goldenseal. Within minutes, I headed out the back flap. Three more trips and I was done. I felt weak, and my disposition was anything but pleasant.

"Look," I said. "Enough is enough. No more. I am hungry."

I took a few steps and nearly fell over. The wigwam swirled around me. Aranck grabbed me and held me up.

"Here, drink this. Slowly," Chepi said. "It's honey and water." Slowly, Cheveyo."

I finished the honey and water. Chepi then gave me a bowl of soup and again admonished me to eat it slowly. I did. I began to feel better. At least enough to realize I was still bare-ass naked. I reached over to get my clothes but Aranck said, "Not those. Put on the new ones from your grandfather. He will be here soon to escort you to the gathering."

"What about my mother? And George?"

"You may introduce them," Aranck replied.

"And Chepi? Should she not be recognized? She is my aunt, is she not?"

"Yes, that is also up to you."

"Dr. and Mrs. Henderson and Julie?"

"If you want to do that?"

"Well, they are your friends, and you invited them here. I think you should do that," I said.

I was pulling on my pants when the flap of the wigwam flew open. It was Mundoo. He was dressed in full regalia. His headdress of beautiful feathers fell to the ground. The necklace of wolverine claws hung on his neck. A red fox tail hung from his belt.

I got into the rest of my clothes. Wish I had a mirror to see how I look.

The rhythmic beat of tong-tong drums filled the early evening air. Somewhere, off, in the distance, a flute's sweet notes joined the drumming. As it gained momentum and taking the lead, the flute joined in accompanied by many chanting voices. I felt the hair on the nap of my neck stand up. My heart throbbed against my chest.

Aranck and I followed Mundoo through the crowd. As we passed by, I heard only low murmurs, nothing really clear. Small children clung to their parents, and the few teenagers stopped talking. Once we arrived at the edge of the crowed, we climbed up a three-step ladder to a flatbed truck, decorated with colorful ribbons. Mundoo turned toward the crowd, raised his right hand high in the air.

He spoke to the crowed for a good thirty minutes. Sometimes he shifted into his native language. And the crowd of about 200 people would laugh. Finally, he introduced Aranck. During his talk, I kept trying to think of something to entertain the crowd. The jokes I knew wouldn't work here. I felt there wasn't a need to repeat the stories of my healing since Aranck was talking about them as well as my hunting.

I felt a tap on my backside. Aranck had finished speaking and was prodding me to speak

I introduced my mother.

"I would like you to meet the man who raised me and gave me a home, George Wells."

George nearly fell over. He stood and waved his hand. I introduced Chepi. She simply nodded her head. I told the crowd and the elders I was honored and humbled. The sun had set, and the people were getting antsy. So I announced it was time to eat. I still had not thought of something to entertain the crowd once the meal was over. While I was stuffing my mouth with meat, one of the young girls came up to me, rubbed her breasts against me and let her hand slide between my legs.

"I will come to your tent."

"I don't have a tent," I stammered.

"Yes, you do. See," she said, pointing toward the lake.

There was a wigwam next to my boulder. I swear it was not there earlier.

An older woman came up, grabbed the girl by her wrists.

"Behave yourself. He is the shaman. Stay away."

I was about to say something, but the sound of the tong tong drums rose up above the noise of people talking and laughing. Aranck came up to me and told me it was time for me to entertain the people. I followed him to the center of the large ring of seated people. Firelight shone upon their faces. Three chiefs sat with Mundoo.

I stopped in front of two of the young men and asked them to extinguish the fire. They did. I stepped into the center. I raised my arms, drew a circle in the air. A beautiful rainbow of colors appeared as I continued to move my right hand. It took a full minute for the group to realize what was happening. Ohs and ahs filled the air.

I drew a circle from my head to my toes. The crowd gasped as I turned into a bright blue light.

"Fake. Fraud." Someone yelled from the group.

I stopped the light around me. Headlights on some of the vehicles turned on.

"Who is it that calls me a fake and a fraud? Show your face," I called out.

A man slowly stood up.

"I challenge you. According to our law, I can, and I do. Again, I say you are nothing but a fake, a cheat. You are not a real Indian."

My face felt hot. My anger was building. From somewhere in my memory I remembered the spirit in the deep woods told me I would be tested. I wondered if this was one. Aranck appeared at my side as did Mundoo.

"Ah, just as I thought. You can't stand alone. You have to have your father and grandfather come to protect you. It won't do you any good."

The crowd divided itself leaving the challenger standing alone. Aranck started to jump down from the flatbed. I reached out and stopped him.

"No. You and grandfather stand back."

The man stepped closer. He had a gun in his hand. People scattered, some running behind parked vehicles, others fell to the ground and covered their heads with their hands. He pulled the trigger but nothing happened. The gun had jammed. He frantically checked the gun. He aimed it at me again. I clinched my fist and opened it. A flame appeared. I closed my hand again and then threw a ball of fire at the man. It struck him and he screamed. The echo of a gunshot disappeared into the night as the air filled with the smell of burnt flesh.

Aranck jumped down from the truck and ran to where the man stood. There was just a pile of smoldering ashes. I followed. Aranck looked at me; his eyes wide, and his mouth agape.

"Good god, Cheveyo."

That was all he said; he turned and walked away. I felt like a piece of shit. Rejected, totally is more like it. That was short lived.

"You have seen the shaman. You now know his power. Does anyone else have a challenge?" Aranck shouted. "If so, let it be peaceful."

No one stepped forward. I was relieved. Sensing the need to break the tension, I opened the back of a truck holding the blankets and shawls.

"I bring you gifts in honor of my mother and father."

The two men who skinned the deer stepped forward and began to distribute the blankets to the men. Chepi took the shawls and gave them to all the women, including the one who threw herself at me. I noticed George, and my mother left. The Hendersons and Julie left. I wonder how much he got on film.

"It is fitting that you retire. There is a new wigwam for you down by your boulder," Aranck said.

"Who put it up and when?"

"I did while you were being purified. Be on your guard, Cheveyo. Sleep well."

"Why is the wigwam away from the others?"

"The shaman always lives apart from the people."

I reached out, clasped his arm with both of my hands.

"Good night," I said.

I totted slowly to my wigwam. I kept wondering why the man tried to kill me. And if there would be others.

I pulled the flap back and crawled into the blankets. I lay on my back, comfortable under the blankets. Uncertainty plagued me as I sought to understand all that had happened in the last couple of days. I shoved my arms and hands up under my head, stretched my legs, and humped the air. Slowly, I looked around. My bow and quiver of arrows hung on a pole as did my other deerskin clothes. Just over the entrance was a painting of a bald eagle.

"How can this be? It's pitch dark out and there's no fire or light in here; yet, I see everything. And it's an eerie green.

I sat up, did a 360. I picked up a spear whose feathers were eerie green and stepped outside. I wanted to see if they had been painted with florescent paint. Everything outside had an eerie green and I could see the heat rise up from the trees. I shook my head. Nothing changed. I went back in, lit my fire pit. I watched as the flames came to life. They were normal. As the area brightened, the eerie green disappeared.

I forgot to wind my wristwatch so I have no idea what time it is. I guess by the position of the stars I saw when I was outside it must be after midnight.

I watched the fire die down. I had only torched a couple of small pieces of wood. The area once again became eerie green. I crawled back under the covers.

I heard the flap open and felt a rush of cool night air. She stood there, motionless, letting her eyes adjust to the dim glow left over from the fire. She turned closed the flap, dropped her dress, and crawled her way over to me. I opened the blankets and she slid in.

Her heat was unmistakable. She began kissing me as she rubbed her breasts on my naked chest. I eagerly sought her mouth and returned the kisses, holding some. She slipped her hand between my legs and gently massaged me. With a quick roll and one shove, I was all the way in. With a few long slow plunges, I brought her to a boiling point. She fainted. I removed myself, sat her upright, put her over my shoulder, and walked down to the water. A couple of splashes of cold water revived her.

I carried her back to the beach and sat down. She mounted me. Between gasps, she managed to tell me her name. It was Ann of the Doe Eyes. Just before sunrise, we returned to my wigwam, she dressed and left. Even though the water was cold, I went for a swim. I could see underwater and fish scurried as I splashed around. I climbed up the bank, wrapped a towel around me.

I smelled my mother's hotcakes and hunger made itself known as my stomach emitted a loud growl. I headed on over to the cabin.

Tom, Mary, and Julie Henderson were packed and ready to fly out as soon as the light permitted. George was in unusually good humor. After breakfast, and the goodbyes to the Hendersons and the promise of a copy of my installation ceremony, I asked Julie to take a walk with me. As we went out the cabin door, I put my arm around her. The screen door didn't squeak as it closed. Dr. Henderson was standing on the stoop watching us. This time I didn't let his presence intimidate me. I pulled Julie close to me, bent down and kissed her.

166

She wrapped her arms around me and returned the kiss.

Dr. Henderson coughed. Julie turned and went back to the cabin. I waved goodbye as they backpacked back to their airplane. I felt alone. Totally alone. I went inside and asked George if he would go fishing with me. Much to my surprise, he agreed.

I used the canoe. At first, George wasn't comfortable, but that soon passed as he hauled in a beautiful Walleye. We each caught two more after that and then I headed back to the cabin. As we approached the landing, he said, "I owe you more than I can ever repay. That was the damn descent of you to introduce me to those Indians the way you did. I am proud of you even if you are not my son."

"We can be friends and I will always respect you for keeping me for sixteen years. Do you plan on telling your sons about me? Who I am and what I am?"

"You want me to?" George said.

"Would it serve any good purpose? I don't want to say anything about this shaman business at school. The less said the better. What do you think?"

"There's no need for your brothers to know anything. And I agree with you about not saying anything at school. Concentrate on your studies. You'll be going to college. You want to go to college where Julie goes? I think she's sweet on you."

He chuckled and gave me a wink.

CHAPTER NINETEEN

I walked up to Chepi's wigwam to see Aranck. He was not there. Chepi offered me coffee and then handed me a sealed envelope. She seemed to expect me to open it so I did. It was from Aranck. He said he had taught me all he knew and that he had never experienced such power as he had witnessed coming from me. He also told me he loved me. I folded the letter and put it in my pocket.

"Thank you, Chepi for the coffee," I said as I stepped out into the open. I heard the motor of his plane. Within seconds it came into sight, flew low over the compound, and dipped its wings and then headed East.

"When do you leave, Chepi? How do you travel?"

"We walk to the main road. There a car picks us up and takes up to Maniwaki. We stay there for a few days visiting old friends. Then we take a bus to Montreal. From there we fly to Bangor."

"Why don't you fly with Aranck? Certainly, his plane is big enough for the two of you?"

"He has too much stuff on board"

"I will drive you to the where you meet your friend. Fact is I can drive you into Maniwaki. Or my folks will," I said.

"That would be nice. I will get things ready."

"What do you do with your wigwams?"

"A friend comes just before the first snow fall and takes them down and stores him in his barn."

"Take care, Chepi. I'll come by tomorrow to see you and Dave Crow."

Loneliness really engulfed me. I cried all the way back to my wigwam. "Don't know why he didn't say goodbye personally instead of a letter," I said out loud. An inner voice replied, maybe it was too difficult for him to say goodbye. Maybe like you, he would have cried and he would have felt embarrassed. Isn't that why you are here, now?

"Yeah, that's probably it," I answered myself.

Admitting that didn't make me feel any better. I got up, took down the bow and quiver, spears, clothes. I rolled up the animal skin blankets and tied them together. I took these things outside and then began the slow process of dismantling the wigwam. I tied the poles together, rolled the skins, and tied them into a bundle. It took several trips to get all of it to the cabin.

"George, will you help me put this stuff up in the rafters?"

"Of course," George said. "I take it you didn't want to spend the rest of the summer by yourself."

"Aranck has left. Chepi and Dave Crow are packing to leave. No point in my staying by myself. I told her that I would drive them out to the main road. They have someone coming there to pick them up. Is that okay?"

"Of course, dear. You want something to eat?" Charlotte said as she held open the screen door.

"Not right now, mom, but thanks anyway," I said.

We got the stuff up in the rafters of the cabin. I went outside, walked around the cabin looking for any holes. I patched a couple holes with wet sand and grass. I hoped the field mice didn't get in and ruin my gear.

Lonely doesn't even begin to describe the way I felt. I took to roaming the woods, traveling deeper and deeper with each trip. Because food had no interest for me I lost weight

After breakfast one morning my mother said, "Tony, I am worried about you. You aren't eating properly. You are gone for hours and sometimes for days. Your father and I think we should pack up and return home. I agree with him, and we think you should go and see the family doctor."

"Your mother's right, son," George said. "I'd hoped you would explain that business of killing that man. I think it's strange no one seemed to consider reporting it to the RCMPs."

"First of all, I think most of the people there thought it was entertainment. If you recall, no one indicated they knew who he was or when he had arrived. "

"You might be right about that. But I smelt the burnt flesh. I know you incinerated that man," George said.

"A spirit came to me during my fasting and praying time. She gave me the gift of fire balls. I clinched my right hand into a fist and slowly opened it.

My mother gasped.

The flame in the palm of my hand burned brightly. It was about four inches high. I made a fist again.

"Come out onto the stoop with me," I said.

Once outside, I threw the ball of fire at the lake. It rolled around the water's edge, sizzled, and died out.

"And it didn't burn your hand?" George asked.

"No, but man it sure fried that guy with the gun."

"How do you feel about killing a human being?" George said.

"Honestly? I felt like a piece of shit. The thing that is so wild about this is I was told there would be challenges."

"Who told you that?" my mother said.

"While Aranck and I were in deep woods with Julie, I went off by myself. A Spirit visited me and told me that there would be those who would want to destroy me."

"Oh dear. That's not good. Why would anyone want to destroy you?" my mother said wringing her hands in her apron.

"I have no idea. I can tell you this. I am very blessed to have the Spirits looking after me. One is always with me and acts as my guardian. By the way, just to let you know it was all very real, here's the gun that man had. It's still loaded so be careful."

"Do you think it's a good idea to be handling it? Fingerprints," George said.

"You're probably right. I hadn't thought about that," I said laying the gun down on the ground.

I clinched my fist, created a fireball, and threw it down on the gun. Then I took a stick, turned it over, and threw another fireball. I waited a few minutes for it to cool. Using the stick, I picked the gun up and flung it in the lake.

"That should take care of that," I said.

"Well, I can tell you this, Tony, I am impressed," George said.

I nodded my head and shuffled my feet.

And so after years of war, not really, maybe indifference is a better word, there is a peace between us. It surprised me my mother and Aranck didn't try to get together. He is younger than George and actually better looking. I spent my last few days at the Baskatong helping in winterizing the cabin, dragging my canoe, not the one given to me earlier, a bigger one, into the cabin. We created a hoist, turned the canoe upside down, and hoisted it to the ceiling. I didn't want mice building their nests in it. I went outside, stood the old ladder up against the side of the building, and climbed up on the roof. Lying on the roof was a large stone. I placed in on the chimney. The stone would prevent birds from nesting inside and keep out bats.

I watched George pack the large ice chest with a fresh layer of ice and making sure the fish was well covered. I don't know who came into the area and cut the ice out of the frozen lake, but there was always ice, covered over with sawdust, in the 'ice house'. The ice house was not much more than a lean-to made of split logs. I asked George about it, and he said a man from the village of Maniwaki came in with a horse and sled. Maybe it was the same guy who would take down Chepi's wigwam. George said he always left him as ten spot and a bottle of hooch.

In keeping with George's driving habits, we got an early start. In a way I was glad.

The journey home was totally uneventful. I drove most of the way.

CHAPTER TWENTY

My last year in high school went along smoothly. I dropped out of sports and concentrated on my studies. I still did not reveal anything about my experiences at the Baskatong. And I didn't reveal anything about the million-dollar trust fund. Some of my former friends commented on my withdrawal from many of the social functions. I drove up to Ithaca once to see Julie. She had a boyfriend. She introduced me as a high-school student and the son of her parents' friends. I let it drop and asked about her plant collection. After a very long hour, I left and returned home

I had thought about Sharon but decided not to renew old acquaintances.

I started stopping by George's office after school. My mother now worked there as his secretary and receptionist. It seemed to please them that I showed an interest in the business. Actually, I was making sure it was a going concern. The two of them seemed happier than I can remember.

One day while I was at the office, I told them that I was driving to Maine to spend Thanksgiving with Aranck. That didn't set too well, but I convinced them that I should be with my father.

I took two days off from school to give me a head start. According to my map, I would have to spend one night on the road. I withdrew a thousand dollars from the bank. I kept half, putting some in my wallet and some in my pocket. The rest, I hide in the trunk of my car. I left at four in the morning, a habit I picked up from George and all our trips to the Baskatong.

The trip through Connecticut was busy. Lots of New Yorkers were going there for the holiday. I finally arrived at Orono. I stopped at a gas station to use the pay phone. I forgot to look for Joseph Redwing. I finally found the address, asked some directions and took off.

His street was a tree-lined street with large homes on both sides. Some were red brick; a couple was made of stone and a few wooden ones. His was wooden with large round columns across the front. The driveway was cement and had lamp posts every few feet. I parked, walked up the wide front steps, and rang the doorbell. It clanged. No one answered. I pulled the cord again. I heard footsteps.

A middle-aged woman with graying hair slowly opened the door partway.

"Dr. Redwing doesn't receive students at his home. Make an appointment at his office on campus."

She started to close the door.

"Wait. I am not one of his students. I am Cheveyo, his son."

I don't know why I didn't say, Tony.

A Chevy truck pulled in. Aranck stepped out of the truck. He rushed up the steps, grabbed me, and swung me around and around.

"I see you have met Mrs. Nisgam. She is my housekeeper. Go in. I'll get your luggage."

"I have just one suitcase. Just staying for Thanksgiving if that's okay with you."

We both went back to my car, grabbed the suitcase from the trunk.

The first thing that struck me as I entered the house was the spiral staircase. It seemed to be suspended in midair. Aranck had Mrs. Nisgam show me to a room. At the top of the stairs, we turned left and walked down a long corridor that had dark wood paneling on the walls

Once in my room, she stopped and looked at me.

"Pay attention to what I tell you. If you want to use the fireplace, be sure the damper is open, turn this valve. Use one of these long matches to light the fire. This lever regulates the size of the flames. Your bathroom is through the second door. The first door is to a closet. Hang your clothes in there. Oh yes, I nearly forgot. Come."

We went into the bathroom. There she showed me how to turn on the heater. Just before she left, she turned and said, "He rises early in the morning. If you want breakfast be down by six. I have a question for you young man."

"Fire away," I said.

"Are you really Professor Redwing's son?"

"Aranck, as I call him, is my biological father. And Mrs. Nisgam, I have a question for you."

"Oh."

"I want the name of a quality restaurant, so I can make reservations for Thanksgiving dinner."

"I don't know if the professor wants to go out. He always stays home. I try to fix something nice for him before I leave."

"You don't live here?"

"Heavens no. I have my own family. You do have his eyes."

"Yes as well as those of my grandfather, Mundoo. Does he live near here?"

"You don't know where your grandfather lives? That's one for the books."

"What's one for the books Mrs. Nisgam?" Aranck said as entered the bedroom.

"That your son doesn't know where his grandfather lives," Mrs. Nisgam said, her face had turned red.

"Yes, it is. Yes indeed, Mrs. Nisgam. Now excuse us, I have something to discuss with my son."

Once she was gone, Aranck turned to me. The expression on his face was less than cordial.

"Why didn't you let me know you were coming? I am not prepared to have a guest."

His tone took me aback.

"I wanted to surprise you. I certainly didn't mean to intrude," I said.

I certainly didn't want to be where I was not wanted.

"I'll have something for you to eat in a few minutes. Come down when you are unpacked."

He turned, opened the door and left. I picked up my suitcase, and quietly crept down the stairs and let myself out through the front door. I got in my car and left. I can't believe this. I thought he liked me and was glad I was his son. *Maybe people here don't know about me and I'm an embarrassment,* I thought.

By the time I got to the main street tears were blinding me. I pulled over and stopped. Sobs wracked my body as I banged my head on the steering wheel. I hit the horn, and its noise startled me. I stopped at the local hotel. They were booked solid. They suggested a rooming house over on a side street. That was booked. I decided to drive to Bangor. It was now late afternoon, and my stomach was complaining. I pulled into a diner. I ordered a hamburger and fries. I tried two motels and they were also booked. Well, you've camped out a night before. No big deal. At least, you have a roof over your head by staying in the car, I thought as I finished my coffee.

I left the diner and looked for a park. I found one, pulled in, and found a place to stop. I walked around for a bit trying to understand Aranck's behavior. I spotted a park bench and sat down. As winter darkness closed in and I headed back to my car. Started the motor and turned on the radio. Frank Sinatra was singing. Once the car warmed, I turned on the heater, making sure I had a window cracked. I turned off the motor, pulled my coat up around me and tried to go to sleep.

Someone tapping on my car window woke me. I could see the lights of an automobile shining on my car. It was a policeman. I rolled down my window.

"Guess you can't read. There no overnight parking here," the officer said.

"Yes, sir. I've tried several places to rent a room for the night from Orono to here. I just thought it better if I got off the road for a while. Sorry."

175

He shined his flashlight in my face and then in the back of the car.

"Your driver's license and registration. One at a time," the officer said.

I handed him my driver's license and reached over to the glove compartment for the registration. His radio squawked. He walked back to his vehicle to answer the call. He came back and I handed him my registration. He copied down some information, and as he was doing that another patrol car drove up, and two policemen got out of the car.

"What kind of trouble are you in, son?"

"Sir? I am not in any trouble that I know of. Well, besides parking here to get some sleep," I said.

"You're quite a long way from home. What are you doing here?" another officer said.

"I came to Orono to visit my father, and he didn't want me. So I left."

"Who's your father and why didn't he want you?" the first officer asked.

"He's Professor Joseph Redwing and he teaches at the college. I wish I knew why he didn't want me."

"Aren't you Anthony Wells?"

"Yes."

"How is it you claim Doc Redwing is your father?" the first officer said.

"Wells is the name of my stepfather. Redwing is my biological father."

I was getting tired of the ten and twenty questions but didn't want to get into a real hassle with the cops.

"You follow us to the police station. And don't try to make a run for it. One of us will be in front of you and the other two cars will be behind you. You understand?" the first officers said.

"Am I under arrest? Surely, parking in a no parking area is not that serious offence."

"Just do as we tell you."

I followed them to the police station. Once there, two of the officers escorted me into the building. One told me to sit as he pointed at a chair. Two drunks slouched over in chairs snored loudly. I could smell them. I sat there for an eternity. No one paid any attention to me. I needed to relieve myself.

"You got a toilet I can use?" I said to the officer behind the desk.

"First door to your right."

I realized the door didn't lock. I finished my business, washed my hands, and went back to the waiting room. Aranck was there.

"Why did you run off? Where were you going?"

"I had the very distinct impression you didn't want me. In fact, you were annoyed that I showed up. I don't stay where I'm not wanted. How would you feel if two people in your life rejected you; first George and now you?"

"Who's George?" the officer at the desk asked.

"My stepfather."

"I can't change what was. Only you can do that."

"And just how am I supposed to do that? I am a bastard child," I said, fighting my growing anger.

"You can live in the past or move on. Cheveyo, I do want you. Have I not spent every summer with you since you were seven years old? God, how I wanted to tell you I was really your father. I didn't want to ruin what was left of your mother's marriage. I am leaving in a few hours for England. I am the main speaker at an international conference on indigenous peoples. Had you let me know you wanted to come and visit I would have told you I wouldn't be home."

"You could have told me that when I arrived, but you didn't," I said.

"True. What's done is done. Come back home with me."

"Am I free to go?" I asked the officer at the desk.

"Yes."

"May I have my driver's license and car registration back?"

"Here you go. Drive safely."

I got in my car, rolled down the window and said, "Have a good flight."

I started the car, pulled out and headed south. *Maybe*, I thought; *the college here in Maine is not the place for me after all.*

I hadn't gone far when a truck pulled around me and forced me to stop. It was Aranck. He got out of the truck and walked back to my car. I rolled down the window.

"You are to come back to the house with me. You are to stay there until I return from London. No arguments. Do exactly as you are told. Mrs. Nisgam will come every day and cook your meals. You got it?"

"And if I choose not to. I can go stay with Mundoo."

"Don't force the issue. You may be powerful, but there are some things you don't know yet. Had you let me know you were coming I could have postponed the trip until next spring."

"Big deal." I wasn't about to give in.

"My father, your grandfather, never showed me any affection. It wasn't that he wasn't proud of me; he just didn't have any love to give. I was shocked that he agreed to come to your ceremony. He lives in a neighboring town but I only see him on his birthday. I am not sure he would receive you. Come home, Cheveyo."

The tears wanted to start. *God what a cry baby*, I thought. All I could do was nod my head. *College in Main looks pretty good*, I thought. *But going home sounds even better.*

When we arrived back in Orono and walked into the house, the telephone was ringing. Aranck went into a side room and answered. The conversation was quite lengthy. Aranck's responses were generally 'uh huh'. I went upstairs to my room, and following Mrs. Nisgam's instructions, I lit the gas fireplace and then did the same to the stove in the

178

bathroom. It was then that I realized I didn't see a tub or shower. I walked over to some wooden doors and pulled them open. There was a huge tub, sitting on four legs with lion claws for feet. It was big enough for me to stretch my six-foot body all the way out.

I heard knocking on my bedroom door. It was Aranck.

"The trip to London is off. I just cancelled my flight," Aranck said.

"Why? What happened?"

"It seems that three of the panel members are ill and have cancelled out. One from South America and one from Africa, and one from Australia. He is already in London and is in a hospital. I have a question for you."

"Fire away," I said.

"Did you make these people sick?" Just a hint of a smile formed on his lips.

"No. First of all, I didn't know anything about a panel or who was on it. Second, and more important, it would be wrong for me to send bad medicine to innocent people."

Aranck grabbed me in a bear hug.

"Good. You want something to eat? Speaking of food, what do you want for Thanksgiving?"

"Yes, to your first question. I want to take you out for Thanksgiving. Mrs. Nisgam suggested the hotel. I can call them in the morning and make reservations. What time do you want to go?"

"You sure you want to do that? That'll cost you a pretty penny. At least twenty-five big ones."

"I brought a thousand big ones with me."

"Good god, Cheveyo. You shouldn't be walking around with that kind of money on you."

"I only have half of it on my person. The other half is stashed in the car."

"Go and get it. We'll put in my safe."

I couldn't resist sliding down the banister of the spiral staircase. I hit the floor with a large thud. I jumped down the front steps two at a time, unlocked the trunk of my car, grabbed the money, and hurried back in.

A shout from Aranck led me to the kitchen. A large ham and cheese sandwich and hot coffee were sitting on the table.

"You know what I miss about the Baskatong?" I said.

"Julie?" Aranck's laughter filled the room.

"Well that too, but the wild vegetables. Speaking of Julie, I went to Ithaca to see her. What a bust that was."

"Why so?" Aranck said, getting up from the table and opening the refrigerator. "Forgot a dill pickle."

"She's got a boyfriend."

"And that bothered you?'

"No. What got me was she introduced me as a high school student whose parents were friends with her parents. Talk about a put down. Talk about uncouth."

"That surprises me. The rudeness, I mean.

I polished off the last of my sandwich and washed it down with the coffee. I got up and placed my dishes in the sink.

Don't bother with the dishes. Mrs. Nisgam will take care of them in the morning. I usually have a snack in the evening and leave the dishes for her. Would you like to invite Mundoo for Thanksgiving?"

"Great. Where is Chepi? We can invite her, too."

"She is with Mundoo. We'll call them in the morning."

"She is not married?"

"Her husband is dead. A moose killed him. It happened not far from where she puts up her wigwam. She says she likes to be near his spirit."

***

Mrs. Nisgam had breakfast ready promptly at six AM. Because the house was warm, I arrived in my shorts. She wasn't happy to see me in my underwear.

"We come to table dressed," she said.

180

"Sorry, I didn't want to keep you waiting," I said.

Aranck sat there with a smirk on his face. I looked at him with a 'what's so funny' expression on my face. He immediately looked down at his plate of French toast.

I had just taken my first fork-full of my food when the phone rang. Mrs. Nisgam answered. The telephone attached to the wall had a cord long enough to reach Aranck seated at the table. She handed him the phone. She made sure it crossed my plate forcing me to lift it up. I guess it was her way of showing her displeasure over my lack of clothing.

Whoever was on the other end was very excited and talking very loudly. I couldn't understand because the person was speaking in a Native tongue. He handed the phone back to Mrs. Nisgam.

"Mundoo is very ill and Chepi wants me to come. When I told her you were here she insisted I bring you. She wants you to do a healing on your grandfather."

"Of course. I'll do whatever I can. Damn! I didn't bring my medicine bag."

"Medicine bag? You're awfully young to be a doctor," Mrs. Nisgam said.

"I am a shaman."

Her eyes got large and her lower jaw dropped. She looked at Aranck.

"It's true. Cheveyo is a shaman and the most powerful I have ever known. Even my father, Mundoo agrees. Finish your breakfast, Cheveyo. I will get some things together to take with us. And you better put some clothes on. It's cold out."

I woofed down the remainder of my breakfast and then ran up the stairs, dashed into my room, pulled on my clothes. I grabbed my coat and ran back downstairs. Aranck and I nearly collided.

"Want to take my car?" I asked.

"No. We better take the truck. It looks like snow and I have snow treads on. Got chains in the back. We get snow around this time and it generally stays. We'll be going to

Old Town. It's not far from here. Is that the warmest coat you have with you?"

"Yes. I didn't bring anything heavier."

"We'll stop at a store in Old Town and get you a winter coat. It's over a street from where Mundoo lives."

I got an anorak, a fur-lined hooded coat. Aranck insisted I also get some boots. These were also fur-lined. I had to admit the coat felt great and I did like the boots. We made one more stop. It was at a butcher shop. Aranck bought a large roast of beef.

"To make soup," he said.

Five minutes later we were at Mundoo's. It was a small white bungalow with green trim and a screened in porch. Chepi met us at the door.

She hurried through an explanation of what was going on with Mundoo as she showed us to his bedroom. Only the top of his head showed. He was apparently asleep. I noticed his skin color was a gray with a greenish cast. He opened his eyes and pulled a hand out from beneath the pile of covers.

I took his hand and give it a gentle squeeze. I pulled back four layers of blankets.

"Grandfather, I want to do a healing for you. Is that okay with you?"

I heard him whisper, "Yes."

My hands began to move over his body. They did not tremble nor did they turn red. I didn't understand. I placed a hand on each side of his head. I read his thoughts and that was a new experience for me. I replaced the covers, and gently touched him on his cheek, and left the room.

Aranck was in the kitchen with Chepi preparing the beef.

"I can do nothing. I read his thoughts and he wants to die."

"Oh no," Chepi said.

"You couldn't do anything?" Aranck asked.

"That's right."

182

"Do you know why he doesn't want to live?" Aranck asked.

"He said he had nothing to live for. To me, that means he's bored. He doesn't have a purpose. Guess what, I just thought of one. It's going to take some work but I think it is possible."

"I don't understand, Cheveyo, what are you talking about?"

"I would like to learn our language. If I am to be their shaman I need to have some knowledge of language, especially for the elders. What do you think? Will it work? I could buy a book and he could help me."

"Our language is primarily an oral language. There has been some effort to record it," Aranck said.

"Okay, let's get some recording equipment and get him to talk, explaining the words. Wouldn't that serve history and benefit the young people?"

"You may be right. It's worth a try."

"How old is Mundoo?" I asked.

"He is 75.

"Excuse me. I will go back and ask him to help," I said.

As I entered Mundoo's bedroom I said, "Grandfather sit up and talk to me. I need to know something."

He lifted his head. I propped him up with two pillows. His eyes were barely open.

"I asked my father to teach me our language, but he says he doesn't know enough. I then asked him to get me a book and I would study it. I believe if I am to be an effective healer for our people I should know something of the language. He told there me there wasn't a book available and that our language was an oral tradition language. Will you teach me?"

"Your father can teach you whant you need to know."

"He said he's too busy at the college. He's got a big conference in London coming up. I thought I would move here if you would help me but if you don't want to I will go back to live with my mother and George."

I looked as disappointed as I could. Then with a big 'ha', I said, "We could record the words, grandfather. That way everyone could learn the language. Naw, never mind. You're probably too old to do that. It was just a thought."

"I'm not dead yet. And don't get smart with your grandfather. Show some respect for my age."

Got him, I thought. *Yes, got him.*

Chepi and Aranck are making you some beef soup. We stopped at the butcher's and got fresh beef for you. I'll go see if it's ready.

In the kitchen, I related my news. Aranck seemed doubtful.

"Did he say he would do it?"

"Well, not in so many words. He said he wasn't dead yet."

"Time will tell."

When the soup was ready Chepi took a bowl to Mundoo. A scream shattered the quiet of the house. Aranck and I rushed to the bedroom. Chepi was lying across Mundoo sobbing. Aranck gently pulled her away, bent down, and checked his father. Tears slide down his cheeks. I walked over to the side of the bed and placed my right hand over Mundoo's heart.

My hand began to vibrate and I felt the heat build. The vibration intensified. I cried out in agonizing pain.

A voice filled the room: "He is mine."

"No! He is mine," I yelled.

"That's what you think," hissed the voice.

A bolt of lightning flashed in the room. I put up my right hand and shoved it forward. The lightning returned to its origin. Again there was another bolt, larger and more fierce this time.

"Come show yourself," I screamed. "Only cowards stay hidden."

The room filled with a terrible sickening odor and the most grotesque head appeared in a swirling mass of dark vapor. I doubled up my fist, opened it, closed it, and threw the ball of fire into the gaping mouth of the monstrous face. I immediately raised both arms, pointing my hands at the head. The sizzle of lightning filled the room. A steady stream of lightning flew from my hands. The face dissolved.

Neither Chepi or Aranck moved. Neither spoke.

Mundoo groaned and then said, "What is that awful smell in here? Somebody fart?"

Aranck roaring with laughter helped me to my feet. All the time he was laughing he was patting me. Chepi was at her father's bedside.

"Cheveyo, didn't you promise me a bowl of beef stew?"

"Yes, grandfather, I'll bring it right in."

Aranck went with me.

"Son, are you okay. Not even in the old stories has such a thing been told. A word of caution. You have now become known to the dark spirits, and they will seek revenge."

"I am fine. Just a bit shook up. Don't worry, I am well-guarded. It was my guardian spirit that battled that thing from the underworld."

Being called his son made up for everything. If he only knew how I used to long for George to call me that. Shit, he had never introduced me as his son until the Hendersons came to the Baskatong. I remember he decided to take me bowling with him. The men on his team said they didn't know he had a kid my age. Maybe the hurts have gone on too long to get over them. I wonder if I can really move on.

"Your grandfather is waiting for his stew, Cheveyo," Chepi said as she walked into the kitchen.

I waited for Mundoo to eat.

"I could use a glass of whiskey. Chepi knows where it's kept," Mundoo said. "The stew was good. Did you make it?"

"No, grandfather. Aranck did. Do you remember our conversation about teaching me your language?"

"Yes, I remember and I will do it. Chepi will be a great help. Some words I have forgotten."

"Great. I'll bring you the whiskey."

Chepi poured the required amount of whiskey into a glass and took it to Mundoo.

I asked Aranck about getting a tape recorder. He said he thought he could arrange to have the college set up professional recording equipment at Mundoo's house. That way he would not have to travel to the college. I was excited.

"I have to make arrangements to move here. Can I stay with you?"

"You have to finish school," Aranck said.

"I have enough credits to graduate. I don't have to be there for graduation. If the school won't agree to that, I'll transfer to a school here. No big deal. I think I read in the college catalogue about an early admissions program. I think I qualify with a straight A average."

"That you do, but I am not sure I can arrange for a scholarship for you this quick."

"I don't need a scholarship. I can pay the tuition. I have a question."

"Which is?"

"Will my presence here embarrass you? I know Dr. Henderson understands you are my father, but what about everyone else?"

"You are not an embarrassment, understand it, and know it. Are you sure George will pay your tuition?"

"I guess you forgot I have a million-dollar trust fund set up by my grandfather."

"Yes, I forgot. You will need to make some telephone calls. Get permission from George and your mother. Have your school records forwarded to Admissions in care of the college. You can live with me. You'll need to get a driver's license and register your car here and you'll need a parking permit and a complete physical. Do you think your mother can send your other clothes and items you want or is it necessary for you to go back and do that?"

"Whew! My head's spinning. First things first. Thanksgiving is the day after tomorrow. I need to make reservations someplace."

"Hmm. It's a bit late, but there might be one place. It's the inn where your parents stayed when they were here, where your mother and I met and you were conceived. Not sure how you feel about that. I think they maintain a suite there. Want to give it a try? It's in Bangor."

"What's it called?"

"Wells Inn."

"With a name like that, we'll have to give it a try. I drove by that one. It had a sign with a no vacancy lighted. Odd, they stayed at a place with the same name." *I wonder if there is a connection to George*, I thought.

Using Mundoo's telephone book, I found the number and called the Inn. At first, they said they were booked. When I challenged that, by telling the receptionist the George Wells suite had not been given over to anyone and that I was Antony Wells I was transferred to the manager. After a bit of hemming and hawing by the manger, I had reservations with room service for the four of us.

After that, I called home and talked to my mother. She wasn't sure she liked the idea of my leaving school and entering the college so far away. When I told her I would be staying at Aranck's she said she'd talk it over with George.

"Mom, what's George's connection to the Wells Inn in Bangor?"

There was a long pause.

"Why do you ask that?"

"Because I am having my Thanksgiving dinner there with Chepi, Mundoo, and Aranck. I understand you have a suite there."

"Your father owns the Inn. Are you staying there?"

"Not staying there, just going there for dinner. It's the only place around that I could get a reservation."

"Oh, I see."

"How long has he owned it and how's come none of us know about it?" I said.

"It belonged to George's great-grandfather and has been passed down. It never was a big-money maker, and I guess he never saw fit to mention it. Actually, that's where your father, ah— George, and I met. "

"No kidding."

"Yes. My parents and I vacationed there, and George was the desk clerk. He was so handsome."

Her voice trailed off.

"You still there?" I said.

"Yes. Just a short trip down memory lane. Sorry, dear."

"Do my brothers know?"

"No, I don't think so."

"By the way, have you or George told them about my trust fund?"

"Goodness no. They would have a fit and put up a big fuss. Your grandfather was a very stubborn man in many ways. At times, you remind me of him. Do you want me to send the rest of your clothes and things?"

"Great, if you don't mind. I need you to call the school and see about my graduating early and to have my records sent to the college."

"I can stop by there. I need an address. When will you come home?"

"I am home, mother."

Immediately, I wished I had not said that.

"I am here at least for the semester. If you go to the Baskatong let me know, and I will meet you there. I'll call you on Thanksgiving. And mom thanks."

CHAPTER TWENTY-ONE

We, Mundoo, Chepi, Aranck and I, went to The Wells Inn for Thanksgiving. They really went all out for us. They served a whole turkey and all the traditional trimmings. Pumpkin pie with ice cream topped the meal. Mundoo had an after-dinner brandy.

I spotted a phone, picked up the receiver, and a voice asked how she could direct my call. I gave her my parents' number. It rang several times. Finally, a voice said, "Hello."

It was my half-brother, John.

"Hey, John. Happy Thanksgiving. How are you, Beverly and Bradley?" I said.

"You want to talk to mom?"

"Sure and George, too."

"George? What the hell kind of talk is that? Calling your father by his first name."

"John, just shove it where the sun doesn't shine. If you can't speak to me civilly, don't bother. Now put mom on the phone."

I was really pissed. One of these days he's going to pick himself up off the floor, I thought.

"Hello, dear, happy Thanksgiving. How are you?

"I'm fine. Gee, what's with John? He about took my head off."

"Don't pay him any mind. How was your dinner?

I went through the kind of details I knew she would want to know. I talked to George and he sounded the best I'd heard him sound in a long time. I did not detect he had been drinking. I didn't mention where I was. I was sure mom had or would tell him.

"Listen," I said, "If you and mom plan to go up to the Baskatong this spring let me know. I can either meet you there, or I can come home and drive you."

"We probably will go. I'll let you know about driving us or meeting us. Take care of yourself, you hear."

"Sure will and you do the same, okay?"

I excused myself and went downstairs to the main lobby. The manager came out to speak to me. I told him the food was excellent as was the service. I paid our bill. It came to a tad over a hundred dollars. I also let him know I had talked to George. I asked him to send out the two waiters who took care of us. I gave each waiter a ten-dollar bill.

Aranck took us on a drive-through tour of the college campus. It surprised me that so many students were walking around. Aranck explained many students lived too far away and were from foreign countries to go home for the short holiday.

"Speaking of holidays, are you staying here for Christmas?" Aranck asked.

"Well yes, unless you would rather not have me," I said.

"Of course you are wanted and welcome. I just want to know what your intentions are."

He slowed the truck as a young woman waved. He rolled down his window.

"I thought you were travelling for the holiday?" Aranck said.

"Couldn't get a flight booked." You should have called me. You could have joined my son and me for dinner. Have you eaten?"

"The college had one of its cafeteria's open for those students who didn't travel. I ate there. Did you say your son?"

"Yes, this is Cheveyo. He will be attending the college next semester."

I liked her warm open smile. I liked the way she looked. We said hello. And Aranck then drove on.

"Is she one of your students?" I said.

"She is my student assistant. She helps with paper work and research. It's part of her scholarship."

"Neat. She married or engaged?"

"Don't get any ideas. You are here to study."

A loud humph came from the back seat. Mundoo was not asleep.

The college was closed until Monday. My grades wouldn't arrive there for a couple of more days or maybe longer. I felt good about the way my life was going even though I was not sure what I wanted to study or what career I wanted to follow. We dropped Mundoo and Chepi off at their house and then headed back to Orono.

We heard the phone ringing as we pulled into the garage. *A phone in the garage, how cool is that?* I thought. That was wild. I'd never heard of that. Most thought it was unusual that my parents had a telephone in their bedroom.

Aranck jumped out of the truck and grabbed the receiver. He turned and looked at me

"It's for you. George wants to talk to you."

"Hi, what's up?" I thought I could hear crying in the background. I strained to hear.

"Beverley chocked to death on a hunk of turkey. The ambulance just left with her body. Your mother is hysterical and John's in a stupor."

"My god! I am so sorry. How is Bradley? What a terrible thing for him to see."

"He's crying. I'll let you know about the funeral. Your mother says that if you are starting classes you are not to come. I agree."

"The classes are not an issue. Of course, I will come. I'll leave tomorrow."

"There's something else. Your mother said you had dinner at Wells Inn."

"Yes, we did. Does that upset you?"

"No. Did they treat you okay?"

"Yes. Great food. I can see why you and mom liked going there."

191

"You liked the place, then?"

"Yeah. It was great."

"It's yours."

"What?"

"The Inn is yours. I'll have the deed to the property and the other necessary paperwork ready when you get here. The manager will get notification of the change. It doesn't make a huge amount of money but it will be enough to pay for your education. That's your inheritance. Don't expect anything more. You understand."

"Yes, sir. Are you sure you want to do that? I know nothing about that business," I said.

"I am sure."

"Are you okay? I mean physically?" I said.

"Yes. Yes, I am fine, thank you. "

"That's great. I'll call you tomorrow just before I leave. It will be early morning. Take care. And George. . ."

"Yes.

Thanks. I'll take good care of the Inn. That's a promise."

I was in such a state I failed to tell Aranck I now owned the Wells Inn. Once we were in the house, he began calling the airlines to see if he could get me a flight out of Bangor. Luck was with him. I had an 8 AM flight.

I didn't sleep much. Ate very little for breakfast. I'd only been up in a plane once and that was Aranck's. I didn't want to get sick. I called George and told him I was flying back and asked if he could pick me up. He agreed.

As I paid for my ticket Aranck wanted the keys to my car so he could have snow treads put on and to get the car into the other garage stall. I said I'd call him when I got home. This home business is a real mess. I guess I should say to my mother's and or to my father's. The flight was uneventful and George was at the airport waiting for me. He looked good. I noticed he had gained a little weight. He was actually friendly.

"Tell me, Tony, are you still a virgin?" George said.

The question floored me.

"Sir?"

"Have you slept with a woman?" I don't see that's such a complicated question.

"Yes, I have. Several in fact."

I was sure my face must have been fire engine red. At least it felt that way.

"You take care of yourself?"

"Yes, sir. My coach gave me rubbers and told me how to use them. He gave them to all the guys on the team."

"I remember how it was with your mother. She totally did me in. You know what I mean. I don't know if I can explain this or not. It's not that I don't love your mother. I do. She is the only woman I have ever loved. Those others, all of them, are well, just getting laid. I never told these other women I loved them or that I would ever leave Charlotte."

I tried to get his rationale. I slept around. Guess the difference is he's married and I'm not. I've heard some other adults say something like sowing his wild oats when they talked about a young guy.

"What that tells me is that my mother didn't satisfy you."

"No. She does satisfy me. It's the challenge of conquest. Not all that different than the challenge in your sports. You know to subdue and conquer."

"I'd never thought of it that way. All I ever thought about was getting my rocks off," I said.

My total honesty surprised me. The way I said what I did was even wilder. I am not sure where all of this is going, but it sure is different.

"I know I've not been a good father to you. And I could blame my extramarital affairs on the fact I always suspected you were not my kid, but I don't want to do that. I'm sorry, Tony. You're a really great guy. I hope you won't judge me too harshly."

He offered me his hand to shake.

I shook his hand, giving it a tight squeeze.

When he pulled into his office parking space, I turned and faced him.

"How would you feel if mom was sleeping a number of men in town?"

After a long couple of minutes, George replied.

"I'd be really pissed. I get your point. We need to hurry along. My attorney is waiting for us. We have some papers to sign. I want to get this done before the funeral. You'll have time to change into a suit. There'll be a reception in the church after the burial."

We signed the necessary papers and a notary stamped them. I am now a business man. I am not sure what that all means but I'm sure I'll find out. My mother began to cry when I walked in. I gave her a hug, ran upstairs, changed into a suit, stopped by the bathroom, and brushed my teeth. John was not there; Bradley, however, was. I asked him if he wanted to talk about what happened. He shook his head, grabbed me around my neck, and held on.

"I'm afraid to eat. I don't want to have happen to me what happened to mom," Bradley whispered in my ear.

"It was an accident. Your mom hadn't cut the meat into a small enough piece. She was having a good time, talking and laughing and got distracted."

"You're sure it was an accident?" His eyes filled with tears.

"Yes," I said as I sat him down and placed both my hands on the sides of his head.

I let the energy flow from my hands. He smiled at me.

"What the hell are you doing, you creep. Get your hands away from my son." John yelled as he lunged at me.

Instinctively, I put my right hand up. John landed on his backside. I leaned down and said, "You really know how to set an example for your son, don't you? Talk about being a creep. Look at yourself, John. "

George, who had walked in on this, grabbed up Bradley. "If the two of you cannot behave in my house, then leave. Is that understood?"

"Yes sir," I said, extending my hand to help John up. As he grasped my hand, I sent him a little shock wave as a message. His eyes filled with terror. As soon as I released his hand, he said, "Sure, dad. Whatever you say."

The funeral service was the traditional Mass and a few brief comments at the grave side. I made myself scarce during the reception at the church. Afterwards, back at the house, I packed up some more of my stuff, called a buddy, and had him drive me to the airport. My goodbyes were short. I gave my mother and extra hug.

"If you need me, call and I will be here. You understand?" I said.

CHAPTER TWENTY-TWO

I was glad to be on my way home. Aranck picked me up at the airport in Bangor. I asked him to stop by the Wells Inn. I met with the manager and told him I would be coming by regularly. Aranck was surprised when I told him I now owned the Wells Inn.

"That was generous of George. How do you feel about him?"

Man, I thought, *these questions out of the blue are getting to be a habit.*

"We had a most unusual man to man talk about his sexual wanderings and about my own. He tried to explain his sex exploits in terms of sports. He said it was the challenge of conquest. How do I feel about him? I have mixed feelings."

"And how do you feel about your own sexual exploits?"

"First, I'm not married. Second, there is no love involved and no promise of love."

"And you feel that it's all right to have unlimited sexual partners."

"Sure. Is something wrong with that?"

"No, I guess not."

"What about your own sex life? I know you had a woman one of the times I called you."

"We'll talk about that later," Aranck said as he stopped the truck, got out, and pulled open the garage door.

When he piled back into the truck, I said, "Am I a problem for you in that area? If I am I can stay at the Inn."

"That's not an issue. I do think I have to put some restrictions on you."

"Restrictions?"

"No girls in your bedroom. None staying over for the night. And Cheveyo, I mean that. Think about the

196

consequences if you knocked one up and the word got out it was at my house. You could be put in a foster home, I could be fired."

"I get it. Here's my promise to you. No chicks at your house. I can go to the Wells Inn."

Mrs. Nisgam met us at the door from the garage to the kitchen. That ended that conversation much to my relief. *At least, he knows I have no intentions of living like a priest*, I thought.

After glomming down the lunch Mrs. Nisgam had ready for us, I hit the sack for some much-needed sleep.

Aranck woke me. It was 10 AM the following morning.

"You've missed breakfast. Mrs. Nisgam has gone shopping. Come down and I'll fix you something to eat."

I remembered how to turn the heat on in the bathroom. I waited a few minutes for it to warm. I also lit the fire in the fireplace in my room. I took my clothes into the bathroom to warm. After a quick shower, I hurriedly dressed and ran down the stairs to the kitchen. Aranck had ham and eggs, and salt-rising bread toasted golden brown. Three cups of coffee later, I finally began to feel more human.

"When does the Admissions' Office open at the college?" I asked.

"They are open. You want me to go with you?"

"No. I can find my way. I need to pick up the application, check to see if they got my high school grades, and pick up a catalog of course offering. Maybe when I get back we can go over to grandfather's house. Have you been able to talk to anyone at the college about setting up a recording system?"

"The Admissions' Office is the third brick building on your left as you enter the campus. We can go see Mundoo. The college tells me they are not able to set up a recording studio at Mundoo's. The noise level from the street is too loud."

"Crap. What about the radio and television studio in Bangor. Maybe they can help us out. We could have grandfather and Chepi stay at the Wells Inn. In that way, they wouldn't have to be on the road."

"It certainly wouldn't hurt to call them. I can do that for you while you are on campus. Have you had much experience in driving in heavy snow?"

"Not really. Why do you ask that?"

"We got well over a foot of snow last night and more is predicted for this afternoon. I did get the snow treads put on your car."

"Hmm. Maybe I had better walk. Thanks for the snow treads. How much do I owe you?"

"Nothing. I also had the car winterized. It's set for 40 below."

"What's your schedule? When do your classes begin?" I said.

"I had my first class this morning at 8. I have another at 4."

It hit me then. I will not be going to college this semester. It's too late to register. I won't go in the spring or summer. I'll be at the Baskatong.

"Why didn't you tell me it would be too late to attend classes this semester?"

"We have not begun a new semester. We go until next month. Have a month off and then begin again in the middle of January. I thought you knew that." Aranck said.

I caught the smirk on his face.

"What? What's so funny?"

"Nothing. There is a lesson here. Think about it and learn from it. Mrs. Nisgam is returning. I need to go and help her."

Hmm. Guess I should have gone to the college orientation meeting at my high school. Okay, off to the campus and let's find out, I thought as I ran back upstairs, grabbed my coat and a scarf. I stopped, located my boots, pulled them on, and ran back downstairs.

"Here are the keys to the truck. You hadn't better walk. It's ten below zero. Use the faculty parking that's close to the Admissions' Building. Remember, I have a class at 4 PM.

The offer of Aranck's truck nearly blew me away.

"Thanks. I won't be gone long."

I headed toward the door, stopped, and turned around. I grabbed Aranck and gave him a bear hug.

"See ya," I said and headed into the garage.

The garage door was stuck, and it took a little doing to get it open. I slowly eased the Chevy out into the street. I honked the horn and headed toward campus. I found the office, parked and went inside. The woman behind the counter, a Mrs. Wagoner, was very helpful. I picked up an application and a course catalog. I asked Mrs. Wagoner if she would check to see if my records had arrived from my high school. They had not. I thanked her for her time and left. I guess I better call my mother, I thought as I cranked up the truck.

Once I was back home, I went to my room and began to look at the course catalog. I wasn't interested in agriculture, nor teaching and nothing in science held any interest for me. The College of Arts & Social Sciences held my attention. Philosophy and psychology felt like a better fit for me. I would not take any classes from Aranck. Too much pressure. Once I got the application filled out, I went back down stairs. I didn't see Aranck in any of the rooms and went to the kitchen. Only Mrs. Nisgam was there preparing for our evening meal. I looked up at the clock. It's 3:30. *Of course, he's gone to teach his class,* I thought.

I decided to call my mother. I went to a phone in the hallway, dialed the number, and waited. No answer. I called George's office. When she answered I heard a click on the line. An image slowly formed. I could see Mrs. Nisgam listening on the kitchen phone. I blinked and the image went away.

"Hi mom," I said. "How are you?

"Fine, dear. And you?"

"Great. Very cold here. Did you have a chance to have the high school send my records to the College?"

"Yes. I asked Mr. Atwood, your principal to have that done. I did that the day you asked me. I wonder if it's been lost in the mail. I will call the school as soon as we hang up. I'll call you right back."

I heard the second click. Within ten minutes, the phone rang. I immediately answered it. Again, I heard the click.

"Hello dear, Mr. Atwood said the records had been mailed. They went out the day-after Thanksgiving. He asked about you. Said your team misses you. I miss you. Are you happy living with your father?"

"I miss you, too, mom. Yes, I am happy here. Aranck is very good to me. His housekeeper, Mrs. Nisgam takes good care of the both of us. She's a great cook."

I heard a distinct 'oh' and it was not my mother.

"I am glad. You mind your manners and stay well," my mother said.

"Say hi to George for me. And Mom, thanks for checking about my records. I call you again, soon."

She hung up. I tapped the phone. I waited. And I again heard the decided click. I wonder how many conversations she listens in when Aranck is on the phone. Maybe he had her listen in on my phone calls. No, that's not like him. *One way to find out. Ask*, I thought.

When Aranck came home, he announced Tom and Mary Henderson would be coming for dinner. That meant hors d'oeuvres and cocktails. Mrs. Nisgam was not at all happy.

"It's nearly time for me to leave. I don't have time to make extra. You should have called," Mrs. Nisgam said.

Aranck looked at her.

"I was talking to my mother. And then she called back. The school has sent my records," I said.

"I didn't try to call. I'll take over Mrs. Nisgam. You can go home now," Aranck said.

I looked at him. His stern voice had finality about it. Mrs. Nisgam stopped whatever she was doing, went to a coat closet, put on her coat and a hat and left.

"What can I do to help?" I asked.

"Let's see what she has going. I told her this morning I wanted beef stroganoff. To answer your question, no Julie is not coming. Tom said she didn't come home for the holidays. Went off with her boyfriend to meet his parents. Sounds serious."

"Good for her. Wonder if it's the same guy I met. Aranck, are you aware of Mrs. Nisgam listening in on your phone conversations?"

"No, should I be?"

"Well, she listened into both of my conversations with my mother. I heard her pick up the phone and hang up both times. On top of that, I had a vision, and I saw her doing that as I talked with my mother."

"Thank you for telling me. We'll deal with her tomorrow. Right now, I have two guests coming and have got to get cracking."

"I know how to make those little wieners in a roll. You got any hot dogs? "

Within thirty minutes, I had a plate full of hors d'oeuvres. I whipped up a catsup and horseradish sauce for dipping. I was grateful my mother let me help her sometimes.

"I'm impressed," Aranck said coming in from the dining room.

"I noted a small diner not far from here. I'll catch some supper there," I said.

"Why? You are included. Tom's got the film and photos of your ceremony. Don't you want to see them?"

"I sure do," I said, smiling. "Thanks for including me."

"You are my son and you will always be included. And don't forget it."

The Hendersons arrived right on schedule. They devoured the snacks with their martinis. Dinner went well with light conversation. I noted there was no mention of Julie. I decided to ask.

"So how is Julie? Last time I saw her she had a new boyfriend and seemed really happy."

"She's fine. Just fine," Tom Henderson said.

"No that's not true. We at least owe Tony an explanation after all he did for her," Mary said.

"I suppose you're right," Tom said. "Julie has had a nervous breakdown, and she's in a private hospital. She doesn't even recognize us," Tom said.

"Good god, Tom. I'm sorry to hear this. When did this happen?" Aranck said, breaking into the conversation.

"We are not sure. The college called us. We flew there, and she didn't even know who we were. The doctors said she had a complete nervous breakdown."

"Where is she?" I asked

"We'd rather not say. It wouldn't do any good to go and see her," Tom said. "She's in a private hospital."

I looked at him, held his attention for a moment. I reached over and put my hand on his shoulder. He smiled and said, "Thank you, Tony."

I got the information I needed. Man, that's a new one on me. Reading someone. It's one thing Aranck and me talking to one other in our heads, but this is off the wall.

A movie projector and screen was set up in the library. The film was excellent. Dr. Henderson caught my little display. He did not capture the man who tried to kill me.

"That copy is for you, Tony. And here are the still photographs."

"Thank you. May I help pay for the cost of development?"

"Oh, my no, Tony. Not after all you have done for Julie," Mary Henderson said.

They left shortly after that.

It was then I spoke to Aranck.

"I know where Julie is. She's in a hospital in Boston and I want to go there. And I want to leave tomorrow. Will you go with me?"

"Ah, I thought you did a reading on Tom. Do you have any idea what is wrong with Julie?"

"No, but I will find out."

"You want to try something?"

"What do you have in mind?"

"Come with me. It's time you were introduced to my secret room," Aranck said motioning for me to follow.

We went to the library and he pushed a shelf on the bookcase next to the large white mantled fireplace. The fireplace slowly turned until there was an opening large enough for a man to walk in.

"Come," Aranck said.

I followed him down a narrow set of steps. I found myself in another world. The room was filled with hundreds of Indian shamanic stuff. I couldn't think of any other word for it. I heard the door above close.

"Stay put until I get some light in here. I forgot to bring my flashlight."

"There's a small lamp just to your left. I don't think it's electric. A match book is just at the base," I said.

"How do you know that?"

"I can see in the dark. It's an eerie green," I said.

"How long have you been able to do that?"

"Since I was in the deep woods at the Baskatong. What are we going to do?"

"We are going to try to visualize Julie. Maybe you can determine what happened?"

He lit a small plate of herbs. I detected sage, and sweet grass and something else I couldn't identify. He pulled a small drum down from its hook on the wall. He sat down on the floor and I followed. He began to slowly beat the drum, gradually increasing the tempo.

I heard him say visualize the address and the room number where Julie is located. My eyelids felt heavy.

Everything in the room spun around me in slow motion. Just like when the film in a movie theatre goes off track. I was moving fast. I stopped in front of a large brick building. I floated there for a moment and then went directly to the fifth floor. I was in a hospital's psychiatric ward. I began looking for room 21. I found it and entered.

She was lying on her bed, strapped down. I went over to her, touched her on the forehead. Images from her brain flashed before me. One continued to repeat itself. A party, a young man brought her a drink, and as he handed it to her, he dropped a powdery substance in the glass. He encouraged her to drink up. She did. In a few minutes, she stood up and then fell forward, hitting her head on a table. The images faded, and I left.

I heard a sharp snap and opened my eyes. Aranck was sitting in front of me. My throat was on fire.

"Here, drink this," Aranck said.

Whatever it was, it had a mildly sweet flavor.

"Can you tell me what you saw?"

"Yes. They have Julie strapped down. I entered her mind, and I kept getting one image over and over."

I explained what the image was.

"Drugged. Bastard. Did you recognize the man?"

"No. He was not the man I had met."

"Did you get any image of what happened next?"

"Yes, she fell forward and hit her head on a table. I saw her being carried away on a stretcher."

"Good job, son. We'll go to Boston tomorrow. Pack your bag. I need to make some phone calls," Aranck said.

"Are you calling the Hendersons?"

"No. I'm a bit uneasy about them. Not a word about this to them or to anyone. Can you do one more thing for me?"

"Sure, what do you want?"

"Try to visualize the man who gave her the drug."

I sat very still, began slow deep breathing. Aranck beat the drum. I had the image. When I came back, I asked for a piece of paper and pencil. I immediately drew the man's face. When I was finished, I handed it to Aranck.

"Perfect. You are really something else, Cheveyo. Let's go and see Julie."

We left this inner room and when we were back in the library; Aranck showed me how to open the door.

"Never bring anyone in there. You may go in there as often as you like. Tell no one about it, not even grandfather or Chepi. You understand?"

"Yes. You got my word."

The night was too long. I got up and went downstairs. I went into the kitchen and fixed a pot of coffee. I was so preoccupied with my own thoughts; I didn't hear Mrs. Nisgam come in.

"What in the world are you doing in my kitchen?"

"Excuse me. Your kitchen, Mrs. Nisgam? I thought this house belonged to my father."

"Well, I'm the housekeeper. And why are you up at this hour?"

"Why were you listening to my telephone calls to my mother?" I said, ignoring her question.

Mrs. Nisgam stopped at the refrigerator, turned and looked at me.

"I have no idea what you are talking about, young man."

"Oh yes, you do. You know I am a shaman, and it isn't a good idea to lie to me. How long have you been listening to my father's conversations?"

"I don't have to listen to this nonsense, and with you pretending you can do things others can't."

"You will if you continue to work for me," Aranck said as he walked into the kitchen.

"I do declare; he's got you wrapped around his little finger. You being a professor and all."

"That's quite enough! I will send you your check with a month's severance. I, no we, won't need your services anymore. I'll see you out."

205

I thought Mrs. Nisgam was going to shit her pants. She put her coat and hat on and slammed the door as she left.

"I've been suspicious of her for a couple of months. It seems she's been charging me more for groceries than she's been buying. You want something to eat?" Aranck said as he poured himself a cup of coffee.

I downed a couple of slices of toast with a cup of coffee.

"Aranck," I said, "Did you think to get the extra keys from Mrs. Nisgam? She could get in and do some serious damage."

"Got them. You ready?"

I waited for him to back the truck out of the garage, and then I closed and locked the door. We headed to Bangor. There we boarded his plane, waited for clearance, and took off for Boston.

"How are we going to get Julie? We can't just waltz in there and carry her out," I said.

"We are not. I decided at the last minute to call Tom and Mary. They have called the hospital and told them to release Julie to us. We will bring her home with us.

"Why did you change your mind about the Hendersons?"

"I've known Tom for twenty years. It's out of his character to lie. I figured they might have had a good reason for not saying where she was. Having that young man who slipped her the drug get wind of where she is might not be a good idea. I have a question for you."

"Fire away."

"Can you refrain from having sex with her?"

Man, this sure is my time for questions, I thought as I took a deep breath and slowly let it out through my mouth.

"Yes. We ended that back at the Baskatong. We are friends. She said she didn't want to go back to college a virgin. I accommodated her need."

"And not your own?"

"Sure. I always have a need," I laughed and punched him in the shoulder.

We landed at a small private airport and hopped into a waiting car. Within thirty minutes, we were at the hospital and on our way up to the fifth floor. The floor nurse demanded to know what we were doing there.

"We've come to pick up Julie Henderson and take her home," Aranck said. "You should have been given a release order by her parents and physician."

"I haven't been told any such thing. You better get off this floor and now or I will call security. Only immediate family is allowed here."

I raised my right hand, drew a clockwise circle in front of the nurse. She smiled.

"Henderson's room is this way. I'll help you get her ready," the nurse said.

Julie was sitting in a wheelchair, strapped in and staring at nothing. Her eyes never blinked as we walked in. The nurse pulled out a suitcase, packed Julie clothes, and then put a winter coat on her and a blanket.

We wheeled her down the hall to the elevator. Aranck thanked the nurse. As the door closed I snapped my fingers and released her from my control.

The car was waiting at the front entrance for us. I picked Julie up and gently sat her down in the back seat. I got in with her. Aranck got up front with the driver. We sped off to the airport, got Julie on board the plane, strapped her in, and took off. Two hours later we landed at Bangor. Once we got her settled in the front seat between Aranck and me, we headed home.

Inside, we carried Julie to a bedroom on the second floor next to mine.

"I would like to begin a healing right away," I said.

"Of course. Anything I can do to help?" Aranck asked.

"Yes. We need to do a cleansing. Is it okay to burn sage in here?"

"Of course. I suggest cleansing her feet and hands. I'll bring up some herbs and oils."

"The phone is going to ring. You better get ready to answer it," I said.

The phone rang. Aranck walked down the hall to a small table in front of a window. He wasn't gone long.

"Tom and Mary are on their way over. They ask to be present during the healing. I agreed. Hope you don't mind."

"They have to remain absolutely silent, and they are not to touch Julie once she has been cleansed. I want you here to help me. I am not sure what will happen. I will ask my spirit guide and protector to join us."

"And I will ask mine. Do you have any sense of being able to help her?"

"No, I don't. There's the doorbell. The Hendersons have arrived."

The came in, sat down on the floor. Aranck lit the sage and slowly walked around the room. He smudged Julie and the Hendersons and then me. He removed Julie's shoes and knee socks. He poured something from a medium-sized bottle into the palm of his hand and rubbed it on her feet. He did the same to her hands.

He sat down opposite of me, placed a small drum between his legs and began a slow rhythmic beat. I sensed a very long night ahead of us. Sitting cross-legged on the floor I began to deep breathe in sync with the drum beat.

"Utpadyate. Utpadyate," I said.

A rush of air entered the dimly lighted room. I heard the tinkle of bells and then the voice.

"What is it you want my Cheveyo? How may I help you? I do not sense you are in danger."

"I need your help in healing my friend Julie Henderson. She has been drugged and has suffered a head injury."

"Place your left hand on the back of her head and your right on the front of her head. Hold them there until she reaches up to remove them."

208

"Thank you for your help. I appreciate it."

I got up from the floor, walked over to Julie. I sat down on the edge of the bed, placed my left hand on the back of her head and the right on the front, and applied a gentle pressure. I felt the heat on my hands build. My hands were burning up and blood began to drip from them. I struggled to hold them in place. I wanted to scream. The pain grew so intense I screamed so loud it cracked the mirror on the dresser. Julie reached up and removed my hands.

My head was spinning.

"Cheveyo, my god, your hands are a bloody mess," Julie said as she pulled herself up

"Why is it so dark in here? Is there someone else in the room? Goodness, my parents will be frosted finding you on my bed."

Aranck turned on another lamp. He brought wet towels from the bathroom and wrapped my hands in them. Once he had the blood cleared he gently rubbed each hand with a sweet-smelling ointment. While he was doing this, Julie realized her parents were in the room.

"Mom. Daddy. What?"

"We'll talk about it later," Mary said. "Right now you need to rest. Aranck has made a nice broth for you. Do you feel like having some?"

I got up from the bed so Mrs. Henderson could spoon feed Julie some of the broth. Professor Henderson opened his mouth to speak. I put my finger to my lips. He understood. The pain in my hands nagged me. Aranck noticed my continued discomfort. He left the room, went down stairs, and soon returned with a bucket filled with ice water. He indicated I should soak my hands. The water turned red. The room began to spin. Everything became a blur.

I woke up on the floor with Julie leaning over me. She was crying. Still sniffing she kissed me, and as she did she let her one hand caress me between my legs.

"I know just what you need," she whispered.

"Your parents are in the room," I said.

"I don't care. I want you. I need you. I love you. There I've finally said it. I've loved you Tony Wells since the day I first laid eyes on you."

I was dumbstruck. I pulled her to me and kissed her. When I let her go I said, "What is the guy's name you were with at the last party you attended before you fell and hit your head?"

I choose not to mention she had a drink or maybe more.

"Bill. Bill Navaro. Why? How did you know I was at a party and fell and hit my head?"

"I am a shaman, remember," I said rolling out from beneath her.

I helped her up. "Back to bed and stay there. I'll bring up some solid food. Mrs. Henderson did you bring some clothes for Julie? She will be staying here for a few days."

"Oh my goodness, no. In my excitement, I forgot. Tom can go home and bring some and bring some for us. Oh, is that alright, Joe that we stay?"

"Of course. I'll show you a room. Tom, can you see yourself out?"

I went downstairs with Aranck and Professor Henderson. Once the professor was gone, I asked Aranck to let me go into his hidden room.

"I want to try a visualization of this Bill Navaro," I said.

"Why do you want to do that?"

"I want to teach him a lesson, and I think I can do that with a visualization. If not, I am going to Ithaca and beat the shit out of him."

"Great, just great. You took an oath, remember. Have you forgotten the way of our people?"

"I would not go to Ithaca as a shaman."

"You just can't separate yourself from who you and what you are. Besides you have another more serious issue," Aranck said.

210

"What?"

"Julie. Not only did I hear her so did her parents. Her confession of love is serious. How do you really feel about her?"

"I admit I got the hots for her. Love? That scares me. And you know why. What do you suggest I do? I don't want to hurt her."

"If you are not in love with her, then you need to tell her, and you should not have sex with her. Remember my restrictions. "

"Yes, I remember your restrictions. Are you okay with my going into the sanctorum?"

"Of course. It's yours to use. Remember ..."

"Yes, I remember the restrictions."

I entered the chamber below the library fireplace. I found the small dish, placed sage and a small amount of rosemary on it and then lit it. I smudged the smoke over me and then sat down cross-legged. I began taking in deep breaths, holding them, and slowly exhaling them between my slightly parted teeth. I did this for a good fifteen minutes. Images began to appear, vague swirling images. Gradually, they cleared.

Conversation became audible, and I tuned in. Bill Navaro was talking to three other guys, real beatniks.

"So, Bill what happened to that babe you were with?"

"Yeah, we thought you two were a number," a second guy said.

"She flipped out. Her parents took her away," Bill said.

There was laughter.

"You helped her along with that just so you could get into her pants."

"Gee, how'd I know she'd go bonkers on a couple of pixies," Bill said.

"How many nuggets did you slip her?"

"I think four, not quite sure."

With a 'see ya' they split up. I watched Bill Navaro and followed him. He was walking along a bridge. I gave him a hard shove. He slammed into the stone wall of the bridge. He shook his head. I tripped him, and he went down on all fours. Dazed, he got up. Staggered out into the road. A car screeched to a halt just missing hitting him. He pushed back on the hood of the car, waddled over to the sidewalk. I gave him a swift kick in the butt, and he fell into the stone wall again.

A police car with two officers inside drove up. Bill stumbled into the side of their car. The officers got out of their cruiser, grabbed Bill, handcuffed him, and drove away. I added one final touch. I pushed against his stomach, and he vomited all over the two cops seated in the front.

I heard them cussing up a storm. Man, they were pissed.

Sometimes, I thought, a little revenge is okay. I stood up, shook my body, and left the room. I made sure the fireplace had returned to its locked position. I went upstairs, tapped at Aranck's door. He opened it.

"May I come in?"

"Sure," Aranck said.

"I know what that Bill Navaro did to Julie. He gave her four pixies whatever that is. He did it, so he could fuck her, the bastard."

"Pixies are the name for amphetamines, a drug to pep you up, to help you perform better. I hear some of the college kids are using these. I would guess this Bill over-dosed her. It's a wonder it didn't kill her."

"Didn't the docs test her for drugs?"

"I don't know. We'll have to ask the Hendersons."

"So, are you going to tell me what you did to this Navaro or not?"

"I helped him walk down the street. After a couple of trips, a little staggering, and falling into a cop's car, they hauled his sorry ass off in handcuffs. I didn't seriously hurt him. He vomited all over the cops. Man, were they ever pissed. I'm going to hit the sack. See you in the morning. Okay, dad?"

212

"Sure," Aranck said, giving me a hug.

"Dad, one more thing. I'd like to make an offering to the spirits tomorrow. Would you help me with that?"

"Glad to. Good night."

***

Around three AM, I slipped into Julie's room. I could see her father asleep on the floor and her mother in a chair. I tip-toed by them and sat down on the edge of Julie's bed. She stirred, and I placed a finger on her lips. She opened her eyes but couldn't see me. I leaned down, kissed her, and whispered "I want you, but I made a promise to Aranck, I would not have sex with you or any woman in his house. I can't break that promise. Can you wait?"

She wrapped her arms around my neck, kissed me.

"Yes, if you can."

"I can. Your mother is waking up."

I released her and said just a bit louder, "How are you feeling, Julie? Any sign of a headache or sick on your stomach?"

Before she could answer Mrs. Henderson had a light on.

"What are you doing in here?"

That woke the professor.

"I think you better get out and now."

"I came to see how Julie is. Frankly, both of you could show a little appreciation. If there's a next time, I may not be so inclined to come to her aid. And one more thing, I live here. This is my home and she as well as you are guests here."

"Well, I—,"

"Really mom and daddy. This is ridiculous. Tony and I have already had sex together. And we will again. Just get over it."

"You will not speak that way in front of us. We should have left you in Boston."

213

"Oh, Tom, what a horrible thing to say. You can't mean that."

"Mary, my god, you mean you approve of this—this adultery."

Mary reached over, took Tom by the hand, and looked up at him.

"Don't tell you have forgotten our first time, and we weren't married or engaged. I passed out." She gave a little laugh.

"Oh, for god's sake, Mary."

"You have grown old, haven't you? Come, pick up your stuff. We're going home. Julie, if you need anything, call me, you hear."

"I have a question for you Professor Henderson. Why didn't you have Julie tested for a drug overdose? Why were you so quick to put her in a psychic hospital?" I said.

"Drug overdose? What are you talking about? The doctor in Ithaca suggested she be put in a psychiatric hospital. We put her in the best in the country."

"Julie was slipped an overdose of amphetamine by a guy named Bill Navaro."

"My god! Julie did—,"

"No she did not willingly take them nor does she use drugs," I said.

"I didn't ask you," Tom Henderson said.

"Better calm down, Tom," Aranck said as he entered the bedroom. "I've known you for twenty years, and this is not the Tom Henderson I know."

"How the hell would you feel if you found your daughter in bed with a man?"

"I wasn't in bed with Julie. I was sitting on the edge of the bed," I said.

This whole thing was getting to me. I ground my teeth and clinched my hand into a fist. Aranck put his hand on my shoulder. I don't know if it was to calm me down or to show family unity. Anyway, I got a solid grip on my emotions and calmed down.

"Professor Henderson have you considered that Julie remained in an unconscious state longer than necessary because of your own actions? As far as I understand, and I gladly admit my understandings of things are limited, but it seems to me, you have made two very bad mistakes with your daughter. You nor she can afford a third. I am not asking that you be all kissy-face with me, or that you even like me but I am asking you not to be so judgmental."

I watched the professor's face as it turned beat red. His steel-gray eyes darted first to his wife, then to Aranck, to Julie and then to me.

"Tony is right, Tom. Give the guy a break," Aranck said. "He has, through the help from the spirit world, cured her, and he also saved her life from the wolverine."

"You don't have to throw that up in my face all the time," Tom said.

"Two-way street, Tom," Aranck replied.

Julie sat up, swung her legs around to stand up, and began to fall. I jumped by Mrs. Henderson and caught Julie before she hit the floor.

"Talk to me. What are you feeling?" I said.

"Dizzy," Julie said as I put her back in bed. I placed my right hand on her throat. I had no idea why. I looked up at Aranck and said, "Julie needs food. She's been underfed."

"I can help, Joe. Tell me what you want me to do," Mary Henderson said.

"Great. Come on Tom, you can help, too," Aranck said.

I waited for them to clear out, and then I sat back down on Julie's bed. She was absolutely beautiful, and I felt the urge building. I had to force myself to refocus.

"Julie I want to have sex with you, but I don't know what I feel is love. I would never forgive myself if we got married and then found I was not in love with you. That's a cruelty I don't want to put you through. Do you understand?"

"Yes, I do. I want you to know something. I love it when you screw me. It is totally wonderful. I've not let anyone else have me. Maybe that's why that jerk drugged me. I do know another thing, Tony."

"And that is?"

"I don't want you to stop screwing me. Can we live together without getting married? Sometimes I think my parents should not have married."

I leaned forward, kissed her. She held the kiss, pushing against me.

"I promised Aranck I would not bring women here to have sex with them. I can't break that promise. Remember." I said.

"Ask him, Tony. Ask him."

I didn't get a change to reply, the troops arrived with a platter of grilled chicken, mashed potatoes, carrots, and fresh fruit.

I got off the bed, so a tray could be set up.

"Mary and Tom suppose we leave the two of them alone for a while," Aranck said.

The three of them left. I pulled up a chair and watched Julie eat. When she finished, I got up, picked up the tray and headed out the door. I stopped in the hallway, stuck my head back into the room, and said, "I will."

Downstairs, I found Aranck in the library. I wasn't quite sure where the Hendersons were.

"Can we talk?"

"Of course. Shut the door."

"Julie wants to bed down with me, and she's asked me to ask you to let me out of my promise to you," I said.

"And."

"I explained to her that I did want her, but I didn't know if I was in love with her and that it would be a mistake to get married and then find out I didn't love her. Man, this is so hard. I don't know what to do."

"Is she returning to the college?"

"I don't know."

"Cheveyo, I believe promises are sacred. They are a form of an oath. They are not to be made lightly, to be

216

ignored, or to be changed on a whim. If they are, there is no value in them."

"Yeah, I guess you're right. Man, it's just so damn hard. Why does life have to be so complicated?"

"I don't have an answer for that. I do know that we throw up roadblocks, create unnecessary problems. I also know that if we lived in a perfect world, we'd be bored to death. We need problems to be happy. I know that sounds like a contradiction, but it's true."

"Switching gears here, I have my application filled out. Would you look it over? I've got a letter written to my English teacher and to my coach asking them for a recommendation. I left them upstairs. You feel like doing that now? It's time for breakfast. I can cook up a good breakfast while you check them out."

"You got a deal."

I whipped up a batch of French toast with poached eggs. I also made Julie an herbal drink. Once we had finished breakfast, I asked Mrs. Henderson if she would take the drink up to Julie and to make sure she drank all of it.

"Thanks for a great breakfast, Tony. I apologize for my very bad behavior. As an adult, I should have known better," Professor Henderson said.

I caught the dig and so did Aranck. I let it slide.

"Cheveyo, I've gone over those papers for you. If you have time, meet me in the library, and we'll talk about them," Aranck said.

We left Tom Henderson to do the dishes.

Aranck pointed out a couple of things for me to change. It was then I dropped a bombshell on him.

"I want to change my name to Redwing. How do I do that?"

"You have to have an attorney and go to court. You have to have a good reason for changing your birth certificate name. Why do you want to do that?"

"Simple, you are my father."

217

"That I am, but you may want to consider how this will affect your mother. George gave you the Wells Inn rather than to his own seed. He had a reason. Most likely he felt you would keep it going and someday turn over to one of your own sons."

"You don't want me to take your name?"

"That's not it. I would be very proud to have you take my name. I just think it's a good idea to give some serious thought to doing that. After all, you know yourself as Tony Wells. One other thing, we will need to go before the tribal council and petition."

"Am I not their shaman?"

"Yes."

"Then why the petition?"

Tradition."

"Okay, I will think about it. Are you sure you have no objections?"

"None whatsoever."

"Dad, I will keep my promise."

CHAPTER TWENTY-THREE

Julie was not particularly happy about my decision to honor Aranck's restrictions. I told her about The Wells Inn, and that we could go there, have a nice dinner and spend the night. That seemed to appease her. There was another reason I turned down having sex with her. Her physical and emotional being concerned me. I had no idea if traces of the drug were in her system, or how long it would last. The Hendersons had stayed over. I decided to confront them about Julie's real condition.

"Dr. Henderson, I asked you once before if the doctors tested Julie for drugs, and you didn't give me an answer. Did they and did they tell you anything the lingering effects?"

"I'm not sure I care to discuss the details of my daughter's medical records with you," Henderson said. He actually had the balls to sneer at me.

"Okay, have it your way. If she has a relapse you are responsible and this time she may very well have to be put away permanently."

"You would like that wouldn't you?" Henderson said.

"What are you talking about? Have you lost your mind? Good god."

"She told she was pregnant."

"Not by me," I said.

"What? She said the two of you had sex."

"Yes, that was at the Baskatong months ago. Holy shit! Did you force her to have, what you call it? "

"Abortion," Aranck said as he walked into the room. "Did you force her to have an abortion, Tom? Is that what happened in Boston? "

"I did not. I am moving my daughter out of here, and you can't stop me. Mary, go and get her ready. Enough is enough."

"I am not going anywhere. I am of legal age, and you can't force me to do anything. I am staying here. I am not returning to Ithaca. I am going to enter the college here."

"We've spent a fortune on you, and this is the way you thank us."

"Tony, have you told her of your decision?"

"Yes and she accepts that," I said, reaching over and putting my arm around Julie's shoulder.

"What decision?"

"Not to have sex in this house," I said. "I promised Aranck I would not bring any women here to sleep with. And I have not broken that promise. I'll help you out with your stuff when Mrs. Henderson has it packed."

And this time he got the message. Julie went back upstairs. I heard her yelling at her mother. Aranck shook his head. I wasn't sure if it was in disgust or disbelief. I feel he may be sorry for letting me move in. Sure hope not. True to my word, I helped the Hendersons out to their car. The wind was blowing, making the cold seem even colder. It fits with their dispositions. I watched them drive down our road until they were out of sight. I saw Julie peering out an upstairs window. I went back in and told Aranck I wanted to take my application over to the Admissions' Office. He decided to go over to the campus and check in and offered to drop me off. Julie decided she would not go out.

At Admissions, Mrs. Wagoner was on duty. I gave her my applications. She recognized me and said my records had arrived and letters of recommendation.

"Mrs. Wagoner when will I know if I am accepted. I can't wait to tell my dad."

"Goodness, you've listed Professor Redwing as your father. I think you mean your faculty advisor."

"No, he is my father.

"I didn't know the professor had a son."

"I've been living with my mother and step-father in Pennsylvania. I now live here."

"Oh," Mrs. Wagoner said smiling.

I could tell she was delighted with a piece of juicy gossip. Aranck had checked the applications, and if he had any objections to my listing him as my father, he certainly hadn't raised an issue about it. I thanked Mrs. Wagoner and went outside to wait for Aranck. He was already in the parking lot.

"How did it go?" Aranck asked.

"Great, I think. Mrs. Wagoner was shocked to learn you are my father. I am sure she's on the phone telling everyone she can think of. You are okay with that?"

"Sure. You in a big hurry to go home?"

"No. What have you got in mind?"

"How about going to a movie and then stop off at the diner afterwards."

"I'm for that. Can't remember when I was to a movie. What's showing?"

"Singing in the Rain."

"Let's go for it. Oops. What about Julie?"

"I forgot about her," Aranck said.

I heard the disappointment in his voice. Actually, I felt the same way. *Chalk one up for not being involved*, I thought.

We had barely parked the truck in the garage when the door from the kitchen flew open. It was Julie.

"Come quick. Chepi is on the telephone. She says Mundoo has collapsed."

Aranck picked up the garage phone. I heard Chepi's excited voice.

"We'll be right there. Have you called for an ambulance?" Aranck said.

Evidently, she had not; by the way Aranck was shaking his head.

"Come, Cheveyo," Aranck said as he headed back into the garage.

"Wait. I'm coming, too," Julie said.

221

I waited for Aranck to back the truck out and then closed and locked the garage. Julie sat between us. As we left town and headed north we found the road had no sand on it. Aranck didn't slow down. A couple of times we went into a spin, but he brought the truck back under control. A car coming at us had its bright lights on and blinded us. We went off the road and ended up in a field. As hard as he tried, Aranck could not get the truck to move. I got out and tried to push as he rocked the truck back and forth. The truck just sunk deeper and deeper. I tried shoveling around the rear tires. That didn't work. I spotted a tarp in the truck bed. I dragged that out and tried shoving it under the tires. That didn't work.

"You two stay in the truck. I am going to hike the rest of the way. Start the truck and run it for fifteen minutes every half-hour or so to keep warm. Be sure to crack a window," Aranck said.

"No, you don't. The three of us go. Julie, do you think you can make it?" I said.

"Yes. Let's get going."

"Grab that flashlight in the clove compartment. I think there are a couple of flares in the box in the back," Aranck said as he climbed out of the truck.

He walked around to the back, climbed up into the truck bed, and popped a large chest.

"Got two. We will light one and carry it as a torch. When it burns out we'll light the other. It will take us quite a while to get there. We've got a good four miles to go."

The wind whipped the snow into swirls, stinging our faces and making it difficult to see. I was amazed at Julie's stamina. Aranck and I had Julie between us. She slipped, and as she struggled to stay upright, she bumped Aranck, and he went down. I heard the snap. My stomach did a flip-flop.

"Arm or leg?" I said.

"Leg. By the feel, it's the tibia, and it broke through the skin. Better grab that flare," Aranck said.

"I am so sorry, Doc," Julie said as she began to cry.

"Not your fault. Cheveyo, check to see how much blood I am losing. You ever set a broken leg? "

"Not on a human. Practiced on a beat-up dummy in health class. By the looks, you are bleeding pretty heavy. I need to stop that before I try to do anything with your leg."

I wish I had my Indian jacket. I would have had some rawhide strips. Shoelaces? No, I need those to keep my boots on. Belt. My belt that will work. Yes! I thought.

I whipped off my belt. Bent down to Aranck.

"Julie, hold the flare," I said.

I remembered I had a pocket knife with me. I opened it and carefully cut a slit up Aranck's paint leg. I could see the bone sticking out. I guessed about two inches. By the way, the blood was pumping out I felt an artery had been punctured or severed. I slipped one end of the belt under his leg, pulled it through the buckle, and pulled. I continued to pull until I was sure it was tight. I watched the blood. It slowed.

"Julie set the flare close by. Make sure it stays upright. Then grab this end of the belt and keep it really tight. I will tell you when to let up a bit."

I tried to look around for something to give Aranck to hold on to, but I didn't see anything useful. I wasn't sure if I was feeling beads of sweat or snow on my face. It's one thing doing something to a dummy, but it's a whole different ball game doing it to a person.

" Aranck, this is going to hurt like hell. I need to put my foot under your arm pit in order to pull your leg," I said.

"Put me in a trance," Aranck said.

"Oh man, why didn't I think of that? And I'm supposed to be a shaman."

I began to hum. I increased the pitch but not the volume. Next, I ran two fingers down his eye lids. He was under. I sat down, took my hat with the ear muffs, and placed that under Aranck's arm pit. I removed my boot and placed my foot in his arm pit. I pulled hard on the broken leg. Nothing. I yanked hard with all my strength. Aranck screamed. I looked, and the bone had gone back under the skin. I heard a low snap and assumed it went back into place.

"Loosen the belt just a little," I said to Julie.

I watched to see the amount of blood. *It is coagulating. Good sign*, I thought.

Okay, we need to make a splint. I don't see a thing here that can be used."

"I can go back to the truck and see if there is something there," Julie said.

"Absolutely not! Too dangerous."

"Leather. I can use the tops of his leather boots. It will take some doing to cut through, but I think it can be done."

I untied Aranck's boots, and part way down I slowly see-sawed the knife to cut through. I cut as fast as I could. Finally, I had the tops from both booths. I placed one underneath the break and one on top. I cut the shoe laces, tied the pieces together, and wrapped those around the leather. I pulled them as tight as I could, tied them off. I pulled out my shirt from my pants, cut three strips. The cold and wind stung my flesh. I wrapped those around the splint and tied those off.

"I am going to try a healing. I don't know if it works out here in this freezing weather. I placed both hands around the broken bone. I felt the heat build in my hands. So did Aranck. He groaned. I kept my hands in place. As the heat had built, so it lessened. That was new. I removed them and put my gloves back on.

I bent over Aranck and blew on his face. He opened his eyes, blinked.

"So, what's the damage?" Aranck said.

"The bleeding has stopped, and your leg has been set. Get up, but don't any weight on that leg. Use me as a crutch," I said.

With Julie's help, we got him up. I bent down, picked up my hat, stuck in back on my head, and pulled the flaps down.

"Julie, I want you to hold Aranck up for a couple of seconds. Can you do that?" I asked.

"Yes. Don't worry, I can do that."

Once she had him secure, I bent down under his abdomen and lifted up. Wrap your arms around my shoulders, Aranck."

"My god, you can't be serious. Carrying me on your back."

"I am not leaving you. Wrap your legs around me. I think you can bend the broken one at the knee. You ready, Julie? Let's go."

She took hold of my arm.

There were no stars out to help me navigate. I could see a faint glow in the distance. I assumed that was Old Town where Mundoo lived. Anyway, I headed that direction. The road would have been invisible except for the guardrails. I used them to guide me along. I wondered why my so-called night vision hadn't kicked in. *The flare, dummy,* I thought. *Can't put that out. Someone may come along and run us down.*

An hour into the walk, Aranck shouted, "Put me down. You need to rest. Both of you."

Gently, I eased him down. Julie immediately went to Aranck to help him balance on one leg and to move both legs a bit; one at a time.

I rotated my shoulders, stretched my arms, and did a couple of squats. We repositioned ourselves and began walking. I should say trudging. I think I felt the vibrations before I saw the lights. Within a couple of minutes, a vehicle with roof lights and high beams on came at us. Julie began waving her flare. I held my breath because I wasn't sure it was going to slow down or plow us under. There was no place for us to go. Fortunately, it slowed and stopped. It was an old truck with a plow on the front.

"You Aranck?" the driver shouted.

"No, he's the one on my back."

"What's the matter with him?"

"Broken leg. Help me get him aboard."

Once we had Aranck in the truck, I told the driver to put Julie next. There really wasn't room for me.

"I'm not leaving without you," Julie yelled over the roar of the truck's motor.

"I'm getting in the back. I'll be fine. Driver what is your name and how did you know to come out and look for us?"

"The name's Rex. Chepi called me and said her brother needed help and I was to look for him."

"Do you know how Mundoo is?" Aranck asked.

"She said he lingers. She thinks he's staying alive until someone she called Cheveyo arrives."

"I am Cheveyo," I said.

"I guess we better get going," Rex said.

With a few short backups and turns, Rex had the plow turned around and headed back to Old Town. I was surprised at the number of people at Mundoo's house. They brought oil drums and built fires in them to keep warm. I saw several bottles of whiskey and coffee mugs. When I jumped down from the back of the truck they began to chant, "Puoinaq" over and over.

As I helped Aranck out of the truck, I asked him what they were chanting.

"They are calling you 'healer', and that you are," Aranck said.

Seeing that he was injured two of the men who were waiting stepped forward and helped him into the house. They immediately went back outside. Julie and I went in. Chepi was delighted to see Julie. She gave us both a hug. I knew where Grandfather's room was and went there. Aranck hobbled along behind me.

"Grandfather," I said as I entered the room. I went to him, took both of his hands into mine. My hands began to heat.

"I have been waiting for you. Thank you for coming. I do not want you to bring me back this time. I am ready to join my ancestors. You understand, Cheveyo?"

"Yes, grandfather, I understand"

"Aranck, take care of your sister. You are all she has left. My will is in the nightstand drawer."

My hands turned cold. Grandfather closed his eyes and sighed. He was gone. Aranck reached over to a table, picked up a drum and began drumming. He sang and slowly meshed his baritone with the beat of the drum. Drumming and voices from outside joined him. The thing that happened next nearly blew me away. Chepi and Julie entered the room. Chepi knew the drumming meant her father was gone.

The single light on the nightstand blew out. There was a swoosh of air, and a sweet smell filled the bedroom. It was not rose or lilac. More like a lavender. The room took on a greenish glow. An oblong shape swirled up from Mundoo and floated around the room. It changed into Mundoo. His face was peaceful. As it floated to each of us, it gave a little nod and left.

"What was that?" Julie whispered.

"You just had the privilege of seeing a soul leave its body," Aranck said.

I saw his tears and put my arms around him. I didn't say anything. There was no need.

Aranck opened the drawer of the nightstand and removed a long white envelope. He read the letter and the will. He cleared his throat.

"In keeping with my father's wishes, I will now read his will out loud."

We listened.

Grandfather left the house to Chepi. He left a bank account to Aranck. He had opened a bank passbook and showed it to me. The passbook listed a little over twenty thousand dollars in the account. I was really surprised because Grandfather left me his regalia, pipes, and drums. I remembered the beautifully feathered headpiece he wore at my acceptance ceremony at the Baskatong. Aranck read the details for Mundoo's burial and ceremonies. Aranck, using the telephone on the nightstand, made a phone call to the local funeral parlor.

Chepi called a doctor to come and look at Aranck's leg. He cleaned the wound, and removed my splint, remarking it was a good one and put on a new one. The doc brought a pair of crutches with him. Fortunately, they were the right size.

Chepi laid out several layers of blankets for Julie and me to sleep on. Aranck had the other bedroom. The rest of the night was short lived. I was grateful Julie didn't start anything. Maybe, I thought, she has really accepted the restrictions. She sure is something else.

Breakfast was scant. I reminded myself to speak to Aranck about that. It was strange that Mundoo didn't at least leave her some money. I noticed there wasn't a whole lot of food in the cupboards or in the refrigerator.

Rex arrived at the front door. He came with his tractor to go and pull Aranck's truck out of the field. I went with him to drive the truck back. The roads had been plowed and sanded, but the going was still slick. Once we got to the truck, Rex turned the tractor around. He had a wench on its back end. He hooked that to the underside of the truck and slowly pulled the truck out of the rut. Then he hauled the truck out onto the road. As soon as he had the wench unhooked, I jumped into the cab, started the truck, and headed to Old Town. I wasn't in a big hurry. Going slow gave me the chance to do some serious thinking.

Maybe I should move out of Aranck's house and get an apartment. Julie could live with me. Who'd say we weren't married? The Wells Inn would be great except for the daily trip to the college. I think there's still something else about the hospitalization in Boston. Something isn't quite right. I hit a rut, and the truck bounced. That brought me back to the business at hand, getting back to Chepi and Aranck.

By the time I got back, grandfather Mundoo's body had been removed. Aranck was busy going through Mundoo's papers, notes, books, and photos.

"Dad, can we talk?" I said sticking my head into the room.

"Sure. Come in. You can help me with some of this stuff. What's on your mind?"

"Chepi has very little food in the house. I feel we should go to the store and stock her pantry."

"Good idea. I can put this aside, and we can walk down to the grocery. I think there's a sled around back that we can pull."

"I don't think you will be walking with that leg," I said.

"Forgot all about it. You can go. I'll give you some money."

"I got money. Speaking of money, what does Chepi have?"

"Actually very little. I thought I would give her half of Mundoo's bank account. What do you think?"

"That's great. Do you plan on hiring another housekeeper?"

"I guess so. I haven't given it much thought."

"Why not bring Chepi to live with us," I said.

"I will ask her. Good idea, Cheveyo."

"Do you mind if I take the truck? I'll take Julie with me."

"You still have the keys. Be careful."

Julie was busy helping Chepi. I motioned for her to step into the hallway. I explained what I was going to do. She was game to go. Aranck hobbled out to the kitchen where Julie and I were creating a grocery list.

"Before you buy a whole lot, better wait a bit until I ask Chepi if she will come and live with us," Aranck said.

"That would be wonderful," Julie said. "She's an angel."

"You should be using your crutches," I said.

"Too much stuff to maneuver around. By the way, you mind doing another healing on my leg when you two get back?"

"No problem," I said.

Within a few minutes, Aranck returned. At least, this time he was using one crutch.

"Chepi has declined my offer. She says she belongs here. I have to respect her desire. I've arranged to have the bank account put in her name. Take her into town with you and stop at the bank. Make sure she signs the card to get her name on that account. And while you are at it, put your name on the account. Use your legal name. I've called the bank. They are expecting you."

"Sure. No problem," I said.

Aranck must have read the disappointment in my voice. He added, as an afterthought, that it might be a good idea to bring Chepi back before Julie, and I did the shopping. He said she needed to get ready to go to the funeral parlor.

Signing the cards at the bank took only a few minutes. Chepi wanted to stop at a shop and order flowers. After that stop, she wanted to go to her church. It never occurred to me that she and grandfather belonged to a Christian church. Julie and I waited in the truck for her. On the way back I asked Chepi why she didn't want to come and live with Aranck and me.

"You have found your home, have you not?" Chepi said.

"True."

"Well, I have mine. Do you understand, Cheveyo? "

"I think I do, Chepi."

I waited for her to get in the house before heading back to town to shop. On the way in, Julie snuggled against me, and I put my arm around her, placing my hand on the back of her neck, just below her hair line and gently rubbed the images came fast and furious. I slowed the truck. I felt sick to my stomach. *That bastard*, I thought. I eased to a stop in front of the A& P store. Julie sighed as I shut off the motor. Once inside, we soon filled the shopping cart. I spotted the wooden barrel filled with dill pickles. I filled a small box and double checked to make sure its lid was secure. That's all Aranck would need. Dill pickle smell throughout his truck. I didn't buy a large amount of meat because the freezer compartment at the top of Chepi's refrigerator was small. I did buy a ham and a beef roast. The butcher ground up a couple of pounds of beef for burgers. The bill came to forty dollars. I paid with two twenties. I gave the cashier a five and asked for change for the pay phone I had spotted outside the store.

After we got the stuff loaded, I asked Julie to wait for me in the truck. I wanted to make a phone call. I pulled out the business card for Stephen J. Watkins. He was the attorney; I had drawn up my will. He answered the telephone immediately. I told him to destroy the letter in which I asked the police to investigate George in the event of my unnatural death. Then I asked him to hire a private investigator. I explained what I wanted. He said that would be expensive, at least fifty a day plus expenses.

"I want the best there is. I really want to know what happened. I need proof. I'm in Maine at my Grandfather's. I will mail you a check to cover five days. When you get the list of itemized expenses, I'll send you a check for those as well."

He agreed. I gave him Aranck's phone number. Julie was asleep when I walked over to the truck.

"Hey," I said, leaning over and giving her a kiss. She wrapped her arms around my neck and held the kiss.

The smell of her was intoxicating. I was fully aroused. The pressure against my pants hurt. I removed myself.

"Tonight," I said and cranked up the truck.

We unloaded the truck. Julie was distant and didn't have much to say. People came to the door to extend their sympathy. The phone was a constant ring. Aranck and Chepi went to the funeral home. They took grandfather's

231

clothes with them. He was to be buried in his Indian clothes. Tomorrow would be the wake. I wasn't sure exactly what that was. While they were gone, Julie continued to pout. That's what I decided it was, a damn pout. When Aranck and Chepi returned, he announced we were going back to Orono. That meant Julie and I wouldn't be getting it on. Julie was in a big pout all the way home.

"Do I have to go to this wake thing tomorrow? And the funeral?" Julie said.

"No, it is not necessary for you to go," Aranck said.

"Oh, good. Tony, you can stay with me," Julie said.

"I am going to my grandfather's wake and to his funeral. Perhaps you would like to go home or maybe stay with a girlfriend."

"Maybe I'll just call up an old boyfriend. How'd that suit you?"

"It's your choice. But if you are going out it would be a good idea if you left before we did so Aranck can lock up."

"Boy, I sure know where I stand. I thought you loved me," Julie screamed.

"I have never told you that I loved you. I have explained all of this to you once, and I thought you understood. Obviously, I was wrong. I'll help you pack and then call your parents to come and get you," I said.

I was really getting pissed. This yo-yo behavior is just too much. The ringing of the telephone interrupted us.

Aranck answered. I heard him say just a minute.

The call was for me. It was Stephen Watkins. I listened to what he had to say without comment. When he was finished, I asked if he had absolute proof. He did. It seems Bill Navaro had not cashed the check from Julie's father and was willing to give a deposition.

"What about the other issue?" I said.

"You were right. It cost an extra hundred but we got what you need."

I thanked Attorney Watkins and then went to find Aranck.

"Aranck, I need to talk to you and privately," I said.

We went into the library, and he shut the door. I quickly explained what I was doing. I told him about the images I had picked up from Julie of her rape by her father.

"What should I do? Confront Julie or go after her father? What's so sad about all this is that her mother knew this was going on. Her father forced her to have an abortion."

"Confronting Julie may bring a total denial. Without her cooperation, you really haven't got legal grounds beyond the Navaro person," Aranck said.

"But Navaro has the check signed by Julie's father, Dr. Henderson," I said.

"Henderson can come up with any number of reasons why he gave Navaro the check. It's he said versus he said. What does your lawyer say?"

"He didn't. Sure explains a lot about Dr. Henderson's behavior at the Baskatong, doesn't it," I said.

"Yes, and as I look back it explains some other things."

My attorney said an Indian woman saved something from the abortion and it can be used to do some kind of test to establish its father. He said that would nail Henderson to the wall."

A knock at the library door stopped our conversation.

"You two going to stay in there forever?" Julie said.

I opened the door and said, "Come in."

"Have you decided to throw me back to the wolves?" Julie said.

"You mean to your father," I asked as I walked over to her. I placed my finger on her nose, leaned into her and whispered in her ear. Aranck knew what I did.

"You think it's a good idea, Cheveyo?"

"I don't know. Let's see what happens."

I asked Julie to sit down at a table. I joined her. Aranck sat in a leather chair. He laid his one crutch across his lap.

I asked Julie to tell us about playing house with her father. That was the place I first saw him raping her in her mind's images. She revealed the whole sordid and ugly mess.

"When I told mommy how daddy hurt me between my legs she told me never to mention it again."

Julie cried. That got me. I put my hand on her head, drew a line down her nose, leaned forward, and whispered in her ear. Next time, I would just have to say the word, and she would be under. I snapped my fingers. She shook her head, looked around, and said, "What are we doing in here?"

"If you go to Mundoo's funeral, would you like to say a few words?" I asked.

"I really don't know him, Tony. What could I say? I think my father knew him. Maybe he would want to say something," Julie replied.

"Okay. Dad and I have our suits ready, and a few personals packed. How about you? Have you made arrangements to go home or stay with a friend or are you going to go with us?"

"I have a nice dress and a long winter coat. I think I have a pair of heels with me."

"How about gloves and boots? Maybe you shouldn't wear heals with all this snow.

"I have boots that fit over my high heels. I'll be right back."

While she was gone, I asked Aranck what he thought the next move should be. I sure didn't know. What he said rocked me back on my heels.

"What lesson have you learned in regard to young Navaro?"

"I don't understand," I said.

"Did you find out about all the circumstances of his involvement in Julie's situation before you took action?"

"I don't think that's fair. I knew he slipped a drug into her drink, and that was all that was necessary."

"Wrong. For starters, had you checked all the information you would have realized earlier Tom's involvement and could have saved Julie . . ."

"Saved me from what?" Julie asked.

"From having to go back and get gloves and boots," Aranck said, easing himself up on his crutch.

The drive back to Old Town was pleasant. I drove; Julie sat between Aranck and me. She played her fingers up and down my right leg, teasing me. Be patient, I thought. Pulling the truck into the driveway, I counted a good dozen people still milling around in the front yard. They waved. We nodded.

Chepi was waiting for us.

"Aranck," she said, "You should wear traditional. You are still a shaman as was your father. I think Cheveyo should also wear traditional and as the new shaman, he is responsible for the soaug [8]. I would like to have a Feast of the Dead. [9]"

"Chepi, you know we can't strip the flesh from Mundoo's body," Aranck said.

"Of course not. We can have the dance, food, songs, and games though. Mundoo would like that," Chepi replied. "Another thing, let the preacher go first. Once he's done, you can come forward and Cheveyo you will come last."

"Chepi, I didn't bring my Native clothes, and I don't think Dad did either," I said.

"Your father has a set of clothes here. I have fixed one of your grandfather's outfits for you. You are to wear the headdress he gave you and the wolverine necklace. Many here know its story."

"But Chepi I don't know what I am supposed to do," I said.

I was sure those standing outside heard my groan. It didn't phase Chepi one bit.

"Come. You need to get dressed so I can make any adjustments," Chepi said.

We went into a back room. I looked at the piles of open boxes containing animal skins, cloth, beads, feathers, and sea shells. A sewing machine sat under the single bulb hanging from the ceiling. It was the kind with pedals. On a hanger hung a beautiful beaded white leather vest. Beneath it, a pair of white leather moccasins.

"Here," Chepi said as she handed me a pair of white leather pants. "Try these on."

I hated it when she demanded I take my clothes off. I didn't have any underwear on because Mrs. Nisgam had not done the laundry. That is something I am going to do when we get home, learn how to run the washing machine.

I stripped down.

"My, my. You have grown. You get any bigger a woman won't be able to hold all of that," she giggled.

"Chepi behave," I said as I jumped into the pants.

They were very tight and showed a large bulge in the front, and I didn't have a hard on.

"Chepi I can't wear these into a church," said.

She just giggled.

"Behave yourself old girl. You act like you are in heat."

That sobered her. Then I wondered if she had been hitting the bottle. I didn't smell any booze as she made an adjustment. She stuck me with a pin.

I yelped. *I bet she deliberately did that*, I thought.

I tried on the vest. It was a perfect fit. I wondered if she expected me to wear that and no shirt. She did.

"I'll freeze out there with no shirt," I said.

"Wear your coat. When it's time for you, take your coat off. Here, try this arm band."

I tried one on each arm. They rattled. She gave me one for each ankle. I sure wasn't going to put those on while the preacher was doing his thing that's for sure.

I started to remove the clothes.

"Don't. We have to leave within the hour. We go to the funeral parlor and from there to the church, and then to the

236

cemetery. While we are gone some of the local women will set up the hall for the reception."

I knew one thing and that I wasn't going to let Julie see me in this outfit. She'd climb all over me. The whole bit about not wanting to return to college as a virgin stuck in my craw. I wonder how many other lies she told me. I don't want to harm her, and with my first semester of college coming up things have to change.

"You are wool-gathering, Cheveyo. Tell me your thoughts. Your face says you are troubled," Chepi said.

"It's Julie. I don't want her to see me in these overly tight pants. You know what I mean? Would you go into the living room and bring me my top coat? "

"She is in love with you, Cheveyo. Do you love her?"

"That's just it. I don't know. There is no question that I want to get into bed with her. Is that love? Chepi, is that love?"

"In the beginning, it's heat. Then it develops into something stronger, more enduring. That's love."

She left and soon returned with my top coat. I put it on, slipped the bracelets into my inner coat pocket, and went into the living room. I carried my headdress in my hand. I went into grandfather's bedroom to look for a drum. The one that had hung on the wall was gone.

"Are you okay, Cheveyo?" Aranck said.

"Yes. I was looking for the drum you had used. I would like you to use it to drum me into the church."

"I'll get it. I was taking it home."

"You can add this headdress to the collection once the ceremonies are over."

"Thank you. I appreciate that."

The four of us squeezed into the truck and headed to the funeral parlor. We went inside, and in a private room, we viewed the remains of Mundoo. He looked like he was taking a nap. The plain wooden casket surprised me. A wooden box was more like it. I noticed tears in Aranck's eyes as well as in Chepi's. I tried to picture how I would feel

237

if George or my mother died. Once the family approved of the way Mundoo looked, the funeral director closed his casket. We were ushered out the door to a waiting black Cadillac limousine. Eight men whom I did not know were loaded into two other cars. Other cars lined up behind the limousine

The hearse slowly moved out and headed down Main Street. We followed. I noticed some people who were on the sidewalk stopped and waved. Some of the men took off their hats. We snaked our way around two sides streets and pulled up in front of a white wooden building with a sign that read God's Church

CHAPTER TWENTY-FOUR

The driver of the hearse opened the back end, and another man pulled out a set of wheels to put the casket on. The eight men lined up along the sides and ends of the casket, picked it up and headed into the church. Two other men held the doors open. Aranck, Chepi, and Julie and I followed. An usher met us and escorted us to seats in the front pew. Nothing like being right up front, I thought.

A choir sang Amazing Grace, and then the preacher read several verses from the Bible. He spoke of Mundoo's life and what a good man he was. The choir sang Onward Christian Soldiers. Aranck spoke of his father with a tenderness that I had not witnessed before. He spoke of Mundoo's work as a healer. I slipped out of my seat and went to the back of the church. There I dropped my overcoat, put on the arm and ankle bands, headdress. I waited.

"And now once again, I am honored to introduce my son, Cheveyo and our new shaman."

The tong-tong drums beat. I knew the drummer was not Aranck. Those assembled turned to the back of the church. I started down the aisle, dancing from side to side, and sometimes bending low. I heard the gasps and ooh and ahs come from those present. I did a low half-circle as I ended up in front of Julie. I watched her stare at my crotch. I raised up my arms, and from somewhere came "Yeha-Noha." Aranck picked it up and then Chepi. Around the room, it went. And back to me. I clinched my right hand into a fist, pushed it up toward the ceiling, opened it and a flame appeared. I drew a large circle with my right hand, and a ring of fire followed it. I lowered my arm, closed my hand and slowly opened it. No flame this time.

239

"For you Mundoo who now resides with the Great Sprit. Our wishes for your happiness have been sent on the flames."

I walked back up the aisle, removed the arm and ankle bands, and the headdress, and picked up my topcoat. I slide into an empty seat and waited. Seconds passed into minutes and the way I felt those passed into hours. Finally, I realized the pallbearers were passing by me. Aranck, Chepi, and Julie stopped at my pew. I got up, joined them, and left the church. We climbed into the limo and waited for the hearse to leave.

"That was some performance," Aranck said. "Who were your drummers?"

"I don't know. I didn't see anyone drumming," I said. "Are you displeased?"

"No! Absolutely not."

"And you Chepi, are you displeased?"

"It was beautiful, Cheveyo. Your grandfather would have been thrilled."

"He was," I replied.

"I thought you were totally sexy," Julie said. "I bet there wasn't a woman in there that didn't have wet panties."

"You would," I said, leaning over, and kissing her.

Grave side sobered her. It sobered all of us. There was a finality, one that couldn't be taken back.

CHAPTER TWENTY-FIVE

Aranck decided to spend the night at Chepi's. That meant Julie and I had to stay, and I wasn't sure what we were going to do all evening. Sitting around would be a bore. I hit on the idea of Julie, and I helping Aranck sort the papers and photos left behind by Mundoo. At least that would be something to do. Chepi beat me to it.

"Aranck, why don't you have Julie and Cheveyo help you with all that stuff in Mundoo's bedroom. Have them pull out those boxes and bring them here so we can see what's in them."

"It needs to be done. You two want to help?"

"Yes," I immediately agreed. "Before we get started, why don't I do another healing on that leg of yours?"

I moved over to the chair in which Aranck was sitting. I pulled a foot stool around for him to put his leg on. I got down on my knees. I raised my arms high over my head, drew a clockwise circle, and slowly brought my hands to just above the break in Aranck's leg.

"That's different. It feels like little electrical shocks," Aranck said.

"Different for me, too. I am not sure what will happen next. "

My hands hovered near each side of his leg.

"Lift your leg up by bending your knee. Keep your foot flat on the stool," I said.

As soon as his leg was up, my hands cupped the wounded area. The heat built rapidly, and my hands turned bright red. They didn't bleed this time. After three minutes the heat lessened, and my hands cooled.

"You can walk tomorrow without the crutch or cane. When you start out, go slow, testing your comfort level. If you feel pain, stop immediately," I said.

Aranck removed his leg from the stool, reached over for his crutch and slowly got up from his chair. He headed to Mundoo's bedroom. Julie and I followed. We soon had half-dozen boxes in the living room, several small bags, and a locked file box. Aranck found the key in the drawer of the nightstand. Chepi came in with an arm full of fresh bedding.

"Can't have you two sleeping in dirty sheets," she said, looking at me.

I stole a quick glance at Aranck. He didn't seem concerned. I gave Julie a little nudge. She pursed her lips into a round 'O' and raised an eyebrow. I wasn't sure which of us was in greater need, but I did know that Mundoo's bed was going to get one hell of a workout tonight.

Finally, Chepi said it was time to go to bed. Aranck agreed. She asked Julie and me to set the dining room table for breakfast. On our way down the hall to the dining room, I gave Julie's butt a squeeze. I doubt if the table had ever been set so fast.

We hollered good night and headed to our bedroom. Within seconds we had our clothes off and jumped into bed. The bed was warm.

"Chepi," I said, "warmed the bed."

I pulled Julie to me and moved my hands over her firm breasts. Her silk skin excited me as I tenderly kissed each breast. Rolling my tongue over her nipples hardened them into firm nubs. Her perfume tantalized my nose as I tongued my way back up along her neck; lingering long enough to nibble on her ear lobe. Clutching her long black hair around my fingers, I pulled her closer, teased her lips to part, and played a game of tag with her tongue.

She was breathing hard and wiggled her body along my leg.

Softly, she whispered, "Yes, yes Tony. Take me," as she wrapped her arms around my neck.

With each new downward push, she shoved up to meet me. She began to whisper in my ear. At first, I wasn't sure what she was saying. Then, like an exploding stick of dynamite, it hit me.

"Daddy, please. Please, daddy. I promise to be a good girl."

My stomach did a flip-flop. I rose up, removed myself from her, and sat on the edge of the bed. *Oh shit! I wonder if it will always be like this.*

She lay there, softly moaning. She got very quiet. She sat up.

"Tony, what's wrong? Why are you up? Get back in bed. I need you."

I didn't answer. After pulling my clothes on, I left. Come morning, Chepi found me in the kitchen huddled next to the wood burner cook stove. I answered her question by telling her I was sick on my stomach.

"Must have been something I ate at the reception. I thought I was going to puke my guts out," I said.

Chepi whipped up a batch of biscuits. By the time those baked, she had a platter of scrambled eggs keeping warm in the warming oven. Aranck joined us and to answer his quizzical look I said Julie was sleeping in.

"We need to go home, Chepi. I have to prepare for next semesters' classes, file Mundoo's last will, and testament, and find a new housekeeper," Aranck said.

"What about Julie?" Chepi asked.

"What about me?" Julie said as she walked into the kitchen. She stopped by my chair, leaned down, and kissed me on the cheek.

My lack of response didn't escape Aranck's attention. His presence seemed overly strong and it was then I realized he was attempting to mind-talk. Clearing my mind, I began to concentrate on the sentence. I'll explain later. He understood.

"I was asking Aranck why he didn't hire you as his housekeeper," Chepi said.

"Love it. That way I can save on college housing and meals."

"Not so fast. You will need to study. It's a big house and it's a full-time job. I'll find someone," Aranck said.

Julie's lower lip went into a pout. She played in her food, barely eating a half of a biscuit.

"I'll go get my things together. Tony do you want me to pack your clothes?" Julie said.

"I'm all packed. As soon as you are ready we can leave.

We said our goodbyes and thanked Chepi for her hospitality. On the way out the door, I turned and said, "See you at the Baskatong, Chepi?"

"Probably not. I think I've made my last trip."

I felt she was right. It won't be the same there without her, I thought.

We headed back to Orono. I insisted I drive; wanting to make sure Aranck's leg had ample time to really heal. As I turned on to our street I saw Tom Henderson's car parked in our driveway. I pulled in and stopped. He had parked so I could not drive into the garage. My car was on the side we were now facing.

Aranck eased himself out of the truck with Julie following. I exited and walked around the back of the truck.

"I've come to get my daughter. I have a court order declaring her incompetent," Henderson blurted. "Turn her over to me."

CHAPTER TWENTY-SIX

A cop's car drove up and blocked our driveway. *Henderson is a son-of-a-bitch*, I thought as I watched two policemen get out of their car.

I felt Julie grab my hand and squeeze it. I slipped my arm around her waist. Even through her heavy coat, I could feel her quivering.

"Please come with us Miss," Officer Hale said as he stepped toward Julie.

I saw the handcuffs.

"I am not going with you. I am an adult and I have my rights," Julie said.

"I'm sorry miss, but I have a court order here to pick you up. Were you not confined in a private hospital in Boston? Says here that you escaped with the help of two men," Officer Hale said.

He looked directly at me and then at Aranck.

"Let's go inside. We are returning from my father's funeral and it's been a long couple of days," Aranck said.

"Say aren't you a professor at the college? Officer Williams said. "Sir. I was in your class a few years ago."

"Yes, I am Professor Redwing. Let me see, yes, Jude Williams, is it not? This is my son Tony and his . . ."

"Girlfriend," I said. "She's shivering. May we go in?"

"Mundoo, the shaman? My grandfather and him were great friends. The stories they used to tell," Officer Hale said. "Sure, let's go in. Better than standing out here in the cold."

Tom Henderson stomped his feet as he trudged behind us through the garage and into the kitchen.

"Officer, do your duty. You can charge these two with obstructing the law or something," Henderson said.

"Officer Hale, may I see that court order?" Aranck said.

Hale handed over the paper he still held in his hand.

"Hmm, I see Judge Langley signed this order. Excuse me a minute. Tony, why don't you have Julie help you put on a pot of coffee and warm up some of those biscuits Chepi sent back with us."

"Have a seat. Coffee will be ready in a jiffy," I said.

The officers sat down at the kitchen table. Julie opened the bag of biscuits, put them on a plate, and put them in the oven on warm. Henderson refused to sit down; instead he opted to pace the floor.

"Of for heaven's sake, daddy, sit down. Where's mom? Why isn't she with you?" Julie said.

Before he answered, Aranck came back into the kitchen and said, "Officer Hale, Judge Langley wishes to speak to you. You can use the phone right here."

Hale's eyes widened. He opened his mouth to speak, changed his mind, and picked up the receiver.

"Yes, sir. Yes, I understand. Anything else, sir?" Hale said.

Officer Hale hung up the receiver and turned to Officer Williams and said, "We are done here. The judge has rescinded his order."

"He can't do that. A court order is a court order," Henderson yelled. "It's your doing, Joe. You won't get away with this."

Henderson lunged at Aranck.

I put my right hand up, drew a circle and then shoved my hand toward Henderson. He slammed into the kitchen cabinet. I clinched my fist and slowly opened it. Fire appeared. I was ready to throw it at him when Aranck put his hand on my shoulder. I closed my hand and then opened it. The flame was gone. I looked at Julie. She had her hand over her mouth. I went over to her, quietly spoke to her.

"Officers, I think you better get ready to take notes. Julie has something she wants to tell you," I said.

"Julie, keep your mouth shut," Henderson said.

When Julie had finished, the officers sat dumbfounded. Henderson slumped back on the floor. Finally, Officer Hale got up, walked over to Henderson, read him his rights, and put handcuffs on him.

"You better go and check on Mrs. Henderson. He's slapped her around in the past. Who knows what has gone on now," I said.

"Tell me, son, how did you knock him down like that and where'd that fire come from?"

"Glad to explain," I said. "Why don't I do that on the way out?"

On the way back through the garage, I stopped, as I shook hands with each, I looked directly at their eyes, held them for a moment, and then said, "No fire."

I picked up the conversation. "I took Judo in high school. I just used his own body force to cause him to fall down."

"Oh," Jude Williams said.

"I did add a little extra shove," I said.

I waited until they drove off and then went back into the house. Julie was sobbing. Aranck had a box of Kleenex in his hand.

"It's over, Julie. No more bad dreams," I said.

"Oh, Tony. I think I should go home and see about my mother," Julie said.

"You want me to drive you there?"

"No. I have keys to daddy's, I mean to my father's car. I can drive that. I'll call you in a couple of days. Got a lot to do and to sort out," Julie said, kissing me.

I wiped a remaining tear from her cheek and kissed her.

I walked her out to the car, pulled her to me and kissed her. She clung to me for a few seconds and gave me a forced smile as she got behind the wheel. She tooted the horn and waved. I felt a sudden shudder and went back inside. Aranck was sorting the mail.

"Cheveyo, this one is for you."

247

It was from the college. I ripped open the envelope, sucked in my breath. I let out a big sigh when I read the word 'congratulations'.

"I'm accepted," I shouted, grabbing Aranck and dancing him around the room.

"Have you selected your courses?" Aranck said.

"I have. Not sure when I have to sign up for them. Ah, here it is," I said re-reading the letter. "Registration for classes begins January 15th. I want to take psychology, philosophy and a course called Ancient Cultures. You think I should sign up for a couple more?"

"You will have to take English, history, and some math course. That's a heavy load for the first time out, Cheveyo. Maybe you ought to drop one of the other courses."

"I took six courses every semester during my three years in high school, played two sports, and still maintained an "A" average."

"It's okay by me if you want to try but please remember the college is different from high school. You can always drop a course if things get too rough and then go back and take it at a later date. College brats get free tuition and as my son, you qualify."

"No kidding. I was going to ask you to go into town with me to a bank so I can have money transferred here from my trust fund."

"We can do that tomorrow if you want. What do you want to do for Christmas?"

I hadn't even given a thought to Christmas or to presents. I remembered Chepi's biscuits and took them out of the oven.

"Perfect. I'm starved," I said.

As we drank our coffee and chowed down the biscuits. Aranck had found some honey for that extra added touch. During our snack, I said we needed to do some Christmas shopping and a trip to Bangor was in order.

"We can stay at the Wells Inn. Can you take the time?"

"Absolutely. You want to go tomorrow?"

"You're on."

I felt better. The whole episode with Julie's father was upsetting but Julie calling me daddy while we were having sex got to me and has stayed with me. I knew we would never have sex again. I also knew I was not in love with her. What got me was how to say goodbye without hurting her. She's had enough of that to last many lifetimes.

Aranck's hobbling across the tile floor snapped me out of my wool-gathering.

"What are we going to do about a housekeeper?" I said.

"There's an agency I will call. Might as well do that now."

"No young chicks to tempt me, okay?" I said laughing. "By the way, let me do another healing on that leg of yours. Roll up your pant leg. I can do that while you are on the telephone."

A small red mark was all that remained of the place where the tibia pierced the skin of his leg. I completed the healing by the time he had set up an interview with a potential housekeeper.

"A Mrs. Clark will come by tomorrow at 8:00 AM. We can both meet her. We don't have to make a decision until we've checked her credentials. Do you want to leave for Bangor right after that?" Aranck said.

"Perfect. May I use the telephone to call the Wells Inn and make reservations?"

"Of course. You don't have to ask permission to use the telephone. Maybe you'd like one in your room. You can have a private line of your own."

"That will be great. Thanks."

"I'll call the telephone company and have them install another line and telephone. Do you think you can occupy yourself for a couple of hours? I need to do some writing. I like to have fresh and new lectures at the beginning of each term."

"No problem. I'd like to spend some time in the sanctuary if you don't mind."

"Help yourself."

"Crap. I forgot. I'll be right back."

"What?"

"I left the box of Mundoo's regalia in the truck."

I hoped leaving the box out there with Mundoo's headdress didn't ruin it. I grabbed the box and ran back into the house and quickly opened the box. Taking great care, I slowly removed the headdress and let it fall full length. I gently shook it. There was no damage. I put it on my head, picked up the box and headed for the sanctorum.

Inside, I placed the headdress as well as the pipes, beads, the wolverine necklace on a long table. Aranck could arrange them in whatever way he wanted. One of the items Chepi gave me was a beautiful round highly polished stone with strange markings. I don't know why, but I decided to keep it.

I sat down, cross-legged, closed my eyes and began to breathe deeply and slowly exhaling. Gradually, I began to relax. At some point, I became aware I was fingering the round stone. I thought I heard a voice. I opened my eyes to see if Aranck had come in. He had not. I began the deep breathing all over again.

"Who is it that calls me?"

"I am Cheveyo. May I ask who you are?"

"I am that I am. Why did you call me?"

"I was not aware that I had. I was trying to meditate. Where are you?"

"Everywhere. You rubbed the green stone. How did you come by that?"

"My grandfather, Mundoo, left it for me."

"Ah, yes. Mundoo."

"What are you and why did Grandfather call upon you?"

"I am a Mi'Kmuesu and the great Mundoo asked for my help in healing. I note you are a puoinaq, the successor to Mundoo and Aranck. You have a question that bothers you, do you not?"

"Yes. I've been having sex with a beautiful young woman, but I do not feel I love her. Will I know love?"

Laughter filled the room. It was then I saw the shadow along the far wall, undulating. Slowly, the image cleared. Standing before me was a man more handsome than any movie star. His smile was warm and his glowing eyes bathed me.

"Yes, you will know love. Don't seek it. It will find you. Young men look for immediate gratification. Don't confuse the two. One may precede the other."

"Which?" I said.

More laughter.

"You have already experienced that. And you will again."

All was quiet except for my breathing.

I got up. Pushed the button and exited. I made sure I heard the click of the door as the fireplace closed.

Aranck was in the kitchen cooking. Whatever it was, it triggered my hunger pangs.

I did the dishes after dinner. Aranck went back to the library. I went to bed.

Six AM came and I got up, showered, and went down stairs. Aranck was already up and in the kitchen cooking breakfast. The sweet smell of hot waffles filled the air.

"Tony, go out on the front porch and get the morning paper while I finish the waffles."

I went out to the front porch, grabbed the rolled-up paper and hustled my butt back inside.

As I went to the kitchen I opened the paper. I stopped dead in my tracks. The headlines announced the arrest of Dr. Tom Henderson for the rape of his daughter. There in glaring detail were Julie's accusations. The article also provided information about the attempt at chemical inducement of a miscarriage and a forced abortion.

"My god, dad, it's all here. Nearly every word. Those god damned cops spilled their guts to the press."

I was yelling as I threw the paper down on the kitchen table.

"Oh my god. I am sure there will be a full academic hearing. They even gave our address where the arrest took place."

"I am so sorry. I didn't mean to bring all this shit down on you or on Julie."

"Don't blame yourself, Tony. It would have come out sometime. Who would have ever suspected such a thing? All the times he and Mary were in my home, I never had a clue."

We finished breakfast just as the front doorbell buzzed.

Mrs. Clark arrived.

Aranck showed her throughout the house except for his secret room. He explained what her duties would be. She was to have Sunday and Monday off. She would have an allowance to run the house and to buy groceries.

Deciding to hit the issue head on, Aranck said, "Mrs. Clark have you seen this morning's paper?"

"Yes, Professor. That poor girl. What a wonderful thing you and your son did. Stopping that horrid man."

"My son and I wanted to make sure that this unfortunate incident would not cause you issues. We'll check your recommendations and get back to you in a couple of days. Thank you for coming."

I saw her out.

"She seems okay to me. What do you think?" I said.

"Seems is the correct word. I still want to check out her recommendations."

***

We stopped at a local back, opened an account in my name. The bank manager nearly fell over himself when he called my back in Pennsylvania.

"You're quite young to be a major stock holder in a bank," the manager said, peering over his glasses. "They said you were on the board of directors."

I just looked at him. His tone annoyed me.

"Yes. My grandfather owned the bank. I also own the Wells Inn at Bangor. There will be monthly deposits coming from there. Is there anything else you need to have?"

"No, no, of course. Excellent. If you need anything, anything at all, just call me direct."

I thanked him for his time and Aranck and I left.

"What a pompous ass," I said as we piled into the truck.

The trip to Bangor went quickly. The roads were well plowed and sanded. The Wells Inn was ready for us. We left the truck parked and walked to the stores. Christmas was definitely in the air as people were scurrying in and out of stores with their arms full of packages. I was at a loss as to what to buy Aranck. In one window, I spotted a lady's purse with matching gloves and scarf. Perfect for my mother, I thought. That bill came to fifty bucks. I had them mail it.

I remembered many people gave George a bottle of liquor, a carton of cigarettes, or a tie. None of those items appealed to me. And there were Bradley and John. Bradley would get a game, and John would get the tie.

"Aranck," I said as we walked along a busy street. "Is there a good sports store here?"

"Sports' store? Hmm. Yes. It's a bit of a walk. Maybe we should go back to the Inn and get the truck."

"Your leg bothering you?" I asked.

"No, but anything you might buy in there could be cumbersome to carry back."

We returned to the Inn, got the truck, and drove to Dicks Fine Sports. I read about a new fiberglass fishing rod. The store had one. I played with it a bit, and I had Aranck try it

"I'll take it. Do you have a case for it? I'd like it mailed. Here's the address."

"Uh, yes I have a case. It's very expensive. Frankly, do you have that kind of money?"

"Well, how much is it?"

"It's one hundred dollars. And you'll have to pay for the shipping."

I laid two one hundred-dollar bills on the counter. The man's lower jaw dropped.

"I need to get something for Julie and something for you. What would you like," I said?

"You don't have to get me anything. Just having you here with me is gift enough. Young women like perfume. The gift shop at the Inn carries imported French perfumes. You can look there. I'm ready for lunch. How about you?"

I liked both ideas. We drove back to the Inn. We had our lunch brought up to our suite. The clam chowder was fantastic. Aranck said he needed a nap. I went downstairs to the gift shop and bought a bottle of perfume and had it gift wrapped. I asked the clerk if she knew of an office supply store nearby.

There was one about a block away. I found exactly what I wanted for Aranck—a new portable typewriter—a Smith-Corona. It even came with a case that locked. They put it in a box and taped it shut. When I got back to the Inn, Aranck was up and was taking a shower. Pleased with myself for the gift selection, I jitter bugged across the living room. After his shower, we went to see Dancing In the Rain. The movie theatre was packed. We had our dinner sent up to our suite. After finishing a seafood platter, I called Julie.

Her voice was flat.

"When can I see you?" I said.

"You can't," Julie said.

"What do you mean I can't?"

"Our family lawyer says it's not a good idea."

"And you accept that?"

254

"I have to."

"Did you get registered at the college?"

"No. How can I go after all this? Did you see the paper?"

"Yes. Those to cops should be fired."

"A lot of good that will do. I can't talk to you anymore. Please don't call and do not come over here. It will just make things worse—worse for both of us. Promise me, Tony. Promise me."

"Okay, have it your way. I won't come by and I won't call. Take care of yourself. If you need anything let me know."

I heard the click and then I hung up.

"Not a good conversation, I take it," Aranck said.

"You got that right. She doesn't want to see me anymore."

"Give her time, son. She's got one hell of a mess on her hands. I suspect her mother, Mary isn't much help."

"Yeah, you're right. See you in the morning. I'm hitting the sack."

Sleep wouldn't come. I got up, put my clothes on, and let myself out of the suite. It was 3:00 AM. I unlocked the front door of the inn as quietly as I could. A night clerk dosed at the check-in desk. For some reason, the cold early-morning air felt good. The whole area had an eerie quiet about it. Almost too quiet. That was short lived. Somewhere, in the distance, I heard a dog barking. I began to walk into the shopping area. Neon signs flickered creating a runny-water-color image on the snow. I walked about three blocks. A police cruiser pulled up, flooded me with a spotlight. The cop on the passenger side rolled down the window.

"So, what's your excuse this time?"

It was the same policeman who had challenged me for being parked overnight in a park.

"Nice to see you again, officer. I'm staying at the Wells Inn and couldn't sleep. So I came out to walk."

"Hmm. Yeah, I remember, you said there was no room at the Inn. That right?"

"Yes."

"So you have a room there now?"

"I own the place. My father George Wells gave it to me. It's been in the family for a good many years."

"You don't say. Well, suppose you get in and we'll just go there and find out."

I got in. No use arguing with them. At the Wells Inn, the poor night clerk was nearly beside himself when the two officers pounded on the front door.

"Oh, Mr. Wells, I didn't know you were out," the night clerk said.

"Mr. Wells?" one of the officers said.

"Yes, sir. He is the owner. Sorry, Mr. Wells, is there a problem?"

"None. These officers were just giving me a lift. I left my key in my suite."

Aranck, dressed in his pajamas and robe, walked in.

"Tony, is there a problem? I woke up and found you gone. Are you okay?"

"Fine. Sorry, I worried you."

The two police officers shook their heads, shrugged their shoulders and left.

"Worried," Aranck said.

"Confused more likely. My god, raping your own daughter. I just don't get it."

"What about you and Julie?"

"I can't see her anymore. We are really into it and she starts calling me daddy. I can't handle that."

"So, you're saying you are not in love with her?"

"Yeah, I am. And as I said before I don't want to hurt her or add more grief to what she already has."

"I suspect she knows you aren't in love with her. Telling you not to call or stop by is her way of saying goodbye."

"You're probably right. You know, you've never said why you're not married or why you don't have a lady friend. What's your story?"

"When I was young, like you, I had several lovers. Career got in the way. I had a long-term relationship with a former faculty member. Then I found out you existed and I spent all my time trying to find you, getting to know you."

"What happened to your faculty friend?"

"She died. She had an aneurism in the brain."

"Gross. Totally gross. How long ago was that?"

"Ten years ago. It happened while I was at the Baskatong."

I walked over to him, gave him a hug. The desk clerk coughed.

"Okay, dad, let's go home. I got my Christmas shopping done."

Within fifteen minutes we had my stuff loaded in the truck, paid for our meals, left a nice tip, and headed back home.

CHAPTER TWENTY-SEVEN

Instead of driving directly home, Aranck did a detour to the Blane Airport. He stopped at the gate, waited a minute or two and a man with Dave written on his coveralls let us in. Turned out he was Dave Blane, the owner.

"Hey, Doc. How are things? Read in the paper you had quite a thing going on at your place."

"Unfortunately," Aranck said.

"Damn shame. A pretty young girl like that. Anyway, what can I do for you?"

"This is my son, Tony. His Native name is Cheveyo. I want him to have flying lessons."

My heart went into high gear. I couldn't believe my ears. *Wow! Flying lessons*, I thought.

"No problem," Dave said. "When do you want to start him?"

"Whenever you have time. Sooner the better. Use my plane."

"How about Saturday. Say around 10. One hour lessons."

"Great. I'll be here," I said.

"Merry Christmas, son," Aranck said.

I was ecstatic. I danced my way over to the truck.

"Yes!" I shouted. "Thanks, dad, how did you know I wanted to learn to fly?"

"Intuition," he said, cuffing me aside of the head.

The closer we got to our house I felt anxious. My nerves were tingling. I closed my eyes and tried to do a visualization. Nothing happened. When we pulled into the drive way, I said, "Let's just sit a minute or two."

"Sure. Something is wrong. You know what it is?"

"Not sure. I need to listen to the house so we can't talk for a couple of minutes."

I wasn't sure where that came from. I listened. I heard the refrigerator humming.

"Nothing unusual," I said.

I got my Christmas package for Aranck out of the back of the truck, picked up our suitcases, and followed Aranck into the house. As usual, we went through the garage into the kitchen. As I sat down the suitcases the telephone rang. Aranck answered it on the second ring.

"Yes, sir. Oh, no!" Aranck said.

He picked up a sheet of paper, wrote the word 'president' on it. I nodded that I understood. I picked up the suitcases and started to go into the hallway to go upstairs. Aranck motioned for me to stay. I sat down at the kitchen table and waited.

Aranck was pale. His lips quivered. He plopped into an empty chair.

"Very bad news, son. Julie Henderson is dead."

"What? How?"

"She slit her wrists in a tub of hot water. But that's not all. Tom was released on bail and when he walked in Mary shot and killed him and then killed herself. Apparently, there is a letter."

I felt the waves of nausea come up into my throat.

The telephone rang. Aranck answered it.

"Certainly not. We will not be giving any interviews. No, you may not speak to my son. We are deeply shocked and saddened by all of this. Tom, Mary, and Julie will be missed."

The doorbell. I'll get," I said.

I looked through the door's side window. Police. Two of them. I opened the door.

"Officer Williams," I said.

"Tony. May we come in?"

I escorted them to the library. Aranck had come from the kitchen.

"Hello, Jude. Officer Hale."

259

"We are sorry to come by at a time like this, Doc, but we have to ask some questions. Do you mind answering them?"

Aranck said he didn't mind. After the ten and twenty questions. I decided I had a few of my own to ask.

"I understand there was a letter left. To whom was it addressed?"

"You."

"And where is it?"

"It's at the station, part of the evidence in an on-going investigation."

"Do you know what was in the letter?"

"Yes," Officer Williams said.

"And are the two of you going to give it to the paper as you did Julie's statements made in this house accusing her father of rape?'

"What. . . we . . . never..."

I cut him off.

"Don't even try to lie to me. You are responsible for all three of these deaths. When my attorney gets through with the two of you, you both will wish to god you had never become policemen. No get out and don't come back."

"This way," Aranck said.

"That son-of-a-bitch, that filthy bastard," I yelled.

"Which one, Tony? And calm down."

"Officer Hale. His wife works for the paper. He showed her his notes."

"Let me make a telephone call. Stay put."

I heard him ask for the district attorney. Then he called someone else.

"I called the State Attorney General. He's one of my former students. He'll personally look into the whole matter. You are right, Tony. Hale is responsible for these deaths."

"Three more funerals," I said

Sure it got me that Julie had committed suicide and her parents were dead but no amount of persuasion would get me to participate in any ceremony at their combined funerals. Turned out they didn't belong to any local church. A non-denominational church stepped up to the plate and offered to provide a service. I slipped in and sat in a back row. There were no caskets. Aranck said the Hendersons had been cremated, and their remains dumped at sea.

***

A couple of dozen College faculty members were there, including the President. He asked if there were those in attendance who wanted to say a few words. Some students and former students spoke of Dr. Henderson's mentoring. Two women spoke of Mary's social work. Aranck spoke of Tom Henderson' devotion to his students, their friendship. No one else seemed to be in the mood to speak. I stood up, cleared my throat.

People turned to look back at me. I took my time looking at them.

"I am Tony Wells. Julie Henderson was my lover. I failed her. I want you to know why I failed her. You see, she told me she loved me. But I---I could not tell her what she most wanted to hear. I didn't know why I could not. My aunt Chepi and my father, Doc Redwing could not give me an answer. As I sat here, I realized why I could not say, Julie, I love you. You see I was raised in a family where I was not wanted. One can't give what one doesn't know.

I paused, struggling to hold back tears, I said, "Someday, Julie. Someday, I will."

END NOTES

[1] Created in 1927 when the Canadian government built Mercier Dam. It's an area of over 150 miles and is located 180 miles northwest of Montreal. In the 1940s we called the area where our cabin was located, the Little Baskatong which joined the Big Baskatong via a small waterway.

[2] The powers of shamans, claimed to derive from the spiritual and animal worlds, has been said to include the ability to fly through the air, go down through the earth, remain under water for a chosen period of time, and to transform into an animal.

[3] Sanskrit. Means come forth.

[4] A spiritual being who can take human form and who can appear and disappear at will. He can give supernatural powers to humans.

[5] Means 'wishes for happiness' is from a 1994 song by Sacred Spirit, a German musical project. Appears in the album *Chants and Dances of the Native Americans*.

[6] Algonquin. Means Great Spirit.

[7] For a more detailed listing of rules of protocol see Nova Scotia Past and Present: A Resource Guide. Nova Scotia Department of Education and Culture.

[8] A memorial service of two parts: the passing of the pipe and surrounding the deceased with family and friends for prayer.

[9] A communal burial. Last done in 1695. See Henderson, Helen. *Holiday Symbols and Customs: Feast of the Dead, Fourth Edition*. Detroit. Omnigraphics, Inc. 2002.

ALSO BY NORMAN W. WILSON, PhD

<u>Textbooks:</u>
Butterflies and All That Jazz with Drs. James G Massey and
James A Powell
Windows & Images: An Introduction to the Humanities
with Drs. James G Massey and James A Powell
The Humanities: Contemporary Images
How to Make Moral and Ethical Decisions: A Guide

<u>Nonfiction:</u>
Shamanism What It's All About
So You Think You Want to Be A Buddhist?
Promethean Necessity & Its Implications for Humanity
DUH! The American Education Disaster
The Sayings of Esaugetuh: The Master of Breath
The Shaman's Journey Through Poetry with Gavriel
Navarro
Healing-The Shaman's Way
Activating Your Spirit Guides
Shamanic Manifesting

<u>Fiction:</u>
The Shaman's Quest
The Shaman's Transformation
The Shaman's War
The Shaman's Genesis
The Shaman's Revelations